KILLER RABBITS

Dedicated to Jesse for your love and support

Killer Rabbits

PHILLIP GAVIN BARRINGTON

Barrington Guides

CONTENTS

THE DAY AFTER THE END OF THE WORLD

TWO DAYS AFTER THE END OF THE WORLD

THREE DAYS AFTER THE END OF THE WORLD

ENDINGS & BEGINNINGS

ISBN-13: 979-8-9896236-3-1

Cover design by: Phillip Gavin Barrington
Printed in the United States of America

First Printing, 2024

Prologue: A long time ago...

Thousands of years ago, in what is now the country of Nigeria, there was a young farmer named Josiah of the Nupe people. He had a small farm, a good wife, and two young daughters. He made a modest living and lived a basic, content and happy life. Josiah, along with the rest of the Nupe people, revered Soko the Creator above all other gods.

However, man himself could not communicate directly with Soko. Instead, it was known that Soko used animals to communicate and the animals did not always tell Soko what the living tell them, so it can, and often did, lead to issues.

One day, a day not unlike any other, Josiah was working the fields. It was a warm day, and beads of sweat pooled on his forehead. He wiped his brow with his bare arm and saw the sweat glistening in the bright sun. He gazed out over his farm and thought he saw something move. He rubbed his eyes, and looked harder. Josiah saw a creature with long ears, black eyes, fur and a puffy yet stump of a tail. He had never seen one of these creatures before yet he could plainly see it was eating his crops. He moved closer to the creature and shooed it away. It scampered off and Josiah went back to his work.

That evening Josiah went to see his uncle, who was also a farmer. Josiah explained to his uncle the creature he had seen. His uncle was much older than Josiah and had seen many things in his life. He told Josiah that the creature he saw was called a rabbit. 'They are bad for farming. They are also tricksters, those rabbits, so don't even converse with one, no matter what the promise or tell you.' Josiah thanked his uncle and returned to his farm.

The next morning Josiah surveyed his farm and saw five rabbits. "The previous day there had been one rabbit, today there were five," Josiah lamented to his wife, "I had better go get rid of them."

Josiah, armed with a rake, attempted to rid his farm of the rabbits when one of the rabbits approached him. "Get away from here you!" Josiah said to it.

"Now is that anyway to talk to an honored guest?" the rabbit responded.

Josiah was startled by the rabbit's words; however it was not uncommon for Soko to speak through animals. Still he did not want the rabbits to eat his crops. Thus he responded, "I have not invited you here. You are no guest of mine, and surely not an honored one at that."

"Alas that is true, you did not invite me," the rabbit said then nibbled on grass before continuing, "but do not be so ready to be rid of me, at least not yet."

"What is your business then creature?"

"Creature is a crude term. I am a rabbit and my name is Kuwo. I speak for Soko."

Josiah was a bit surprised to hear the rabbit invoke Soko's name, but not shocked. Josiah remembered what his uncle had said about not speaking with the rabbits, but this one mentioned Soko by name. 'That must mean something. I should listen,' Josiah thought before disregarding his uncle's warning.

"I see you are intrigued. Let me tell you what I offer."

Josiah nodded.

"I know you have two daughters. Very beautiful. But I know you want more children, sons, and your wife has been unable to conceive since your last child. That is very unfortunate. I could speak to Soko on your behalf, convince him to allow you to have more children."

"That would be very good, however I doubt you would do this for nothing. So I ask what would you want from me?"

"You are a wise man Josiah; let no man or beast tell you different. What I want is simple; to be allowed along with my family to live on your land."

"I don't know. I have been told rabbits are tricksters and are bad for farming."

"Someone is spreading lies about us then. We only want to nibble on grass all day and lie out in the sun. Nothing more."

"How many are in your family?"

"Only five, see them there. That is all."

Josiah did want a larger family. His wife had undergone the fertility ritual but that had yielded no more children. He needed sons to work his farm, to carry on his line. Josiah had an idea. "How many sons can you promise me?"

"That is a good question, Josiah. I knew you were a smart man. I can promise you three sons. Is that enough?"

"And will they be healthy? Will they grow into men?"

"Yes, I can promise you they will grow to be healthy men and live to an old age."

Josiah needed more sons, and did not have the funds to take on a second wife. This would be the only way to enlarge his family. And all he had to do was allow five rabbits to live on his land. 'How bad could five rabbits be?' he thought.

"Hmm. That is an interesting proposition. I wonder how you will get Soko to agree to this?"

"That is my business. I can assure you that if you agree all I have promised will occur. If I am lying have Soko strike me dead."

Josiah, having weighed his choice as well as noting Kuwo did not die, agreed to the rabbit's proposal.

"That is excellent news! Tonight, Josiah, bed your wife and in the morning, she will be pregnant with your first son. The other two will come after. They will live to ripe old ages, and I can assure you only my family will live on your land."

Josiah nodded and went inside to tell his wife the good news. Four years later Josiah had three healthy sons and a farm overrun with rabbits that had proceeded to make his land unsuitable for continued farming. So, Josiah went to see Kuwo again.

"Josiah, I have heard you just had your third son. Congratulations!" Kuwo said.

"Yes, I have. But they will have no farmland to inherit since all my land is infected by rabbits!"

"Be calm Josiah. I kept my end of the deal and you will as well."

"But I have no land to farm! How will I keep my family alive?"

"That is your problem, not mine. I gave you three sons. That was our deal, right?"

"Yes...but there are so many of you, they can't all possibly be from your family."

"They are. I have fathered many myself, and so has my brother and my sons have started their own families as well."

"You know what? What if I don't care anymore about our arrangement," Josiah grabbed Kuwo by the ears and whispered, "how about I kill you right now? Then the rest of your family. That will save my farm."

"No!" Kuwo thrashed but Josiah would not let go. "Wait, wait, I have another proposition for you."

"I've grown tired of your propositions Kuwo, I think I'll just kill you," Josiah said and went for the machete he wore on his hip.

"It's a solution to both our problems I promise. I gave you three sons, at least just listen!"

"Ok, fine," Josiah said and let go of Kuwo, "What is your offer this time?"

"There is a plague coming. I know this because Soko told me himself. It will kill all the people in your village as well as many across the land. But he told me that I could save those I felt were worthy."

"You lie! None of our priests have said anything about this. They would know better than a stupid rabbit."

"And how would they know? They are men, not animals. You know I can speak with Soko because he granted you your sons. Believe me now and it will save you later."

"Go on."

"Soko told me that if I bite a man in a certain place he will be spared. I promise you this is true. Once your family is spared you will have your choice of farms."

"Where do you bite?"

"On the hand. The soft skin between the thumb and forefinger. Anyone with a rabbit bite there will be spared, Soko told me this himself."

Josiah again contemplated what Kuwo the rabbit had offered. 'His first offer had not totally backfired on me; I do have three sons. If what Kuwo said was true then how could the second proposition be any worse? And what did he have to lose except a little pain from a rabbit bite?' he reasoned in his mind.

"Alright, I agree. You will bite me first. Then my family. If you hurt any of them too much I will kill you. Understood?"

"Yes, yes. This arrangement should work out for both of us. Give me your hand."

Josiah did and Kuwo bit his hand. Josiah grimaced. "See? It wasn't that bad," Kuwo said.

"You'd better be right." Josiah said.

Kuwo the rabbit was right. In the fall of that year a great plague swept through his small village, killing all but Josiah's family and relatives. Josiah and his family took another farm as their own and left their previous farm to the rabbits. It all worked out just as Kuwo had said. Josiah and Kuwo lived to an old age and eventually died. But Kuwo's family kept breeding, kept expanding and eventually took over all the farm land, even Josiah's family's new land. Josiah's ancestors eventually had to leave the village and move to another, far away from the rabbits.

However, all of Josiah's ancestors, and after a time all Nupe children, when they were six, had the rabbit bite on their hand, as a sign of life and prosperity.

THE TIME LEADING UP TO THE END OF THE WORLD

Part I

| 1 |

Four Weeks (before the End of the World)

This is Jonas Johnston with your Morning News on KRTV Channel Six. Today's first report comes from the world of rabbits. Yes, that adorable and rapidly breading woodland creature that your children may even have as a pet.

This morning, we will be talking about something unfortunate that is happening to our furry friends, specifically a new disease called RHDV. RHDV is an acronym for the Rabbit Hemorrhagic Disease Virus which, at last check, has killed two hundred million rabbits worldwide so far with the death toll rising by the minute.

Today we have Dr. Angela Van Broxton, noted veterinarian and scientist at the University of Auckland, New Zealand. "Good morning Dr. Van Broxton."

"Good morning, Jonas."

"What can you tell us about the origin of RHDV?"

"It began in April of this year. A supply of Angora rabbits was sent from Germany to China, which was not an uncommon occurrence, as the Germans have been selling rabbits for many years to the Chinese. However, unknown at the time, these particular rabbits showed the symptoms of a new disease, RHDV. The disease quickly spread throughout commercial rabbitries in Germany and China, and within weeks to the rest of Europe and Asia.

Within a month of the initial outbreak RHDV had spread to rabbit populations in New Zealand, Australia and Africa. By the end of May rabbits were infected in both North and South America. As of today, RHDV has achieved pandemic status among the world-wide rabbit population."

"What else can you tell us about RHDV?"

"It has been determined that the two main factors when dealing with RHDV are that it kills the host within 48 hours, and the host usually shows no outward signs of the disease except for some small lesions in the armpits and pubic regions. These lesions are hard to spot on rabbits due to their dense fur. Once infected internal hemorrhaging of major internal organs like the lungs and kidneys kills the host.

We have determined that RHDV is transmitted through direct contact with infected rabbits and through carriers such as insects, especially flies. By our estimation RHDV will kill around seventy-five percent of the rabbit population worldwide within the next month, and thus is especially dangerous."

"Seventy-five percent? That is quite a high number."

"Yes, it is Jonas. The rabbit population on earth today will be approximately one quarter less than it was just over two months ago. It will affect environments in ways we cannot determine as of yet. Also affected are owners of rabbits and commercial rabbitiries, as they have and will continue to experience massive loss for the foreseeable future."

"But don't rabbits breed quickly?"

"They do breed very quickly, however RHDV is killing faster than they can replace their lost numbers. It is quite frightening."

"How are government's worldwide responding?"

"Those countries where rabbits are widespread have been advised not to have contact with rabbits; not to kill, eat, or clean their hides until further testing can be completed by scientists. The Egyptian government has ordered the slaughter of all living rabbits countrywide in a rash decision. The US and the rest of NATO have restricted the importing of rabbits and many other countries outside of NATO have followed suit, including China, Australia, New Zealand and Japan."

"Do you have any advice for our viewers that own a pet rabbit?"

"Keep it indoors, that's the safest way to keep it from contracting the RDHV."

"Thank you for your information and for joining us this morning Dr. Van Broxton."

"It's been a pleasure Jonas, thank you."

| 2 |

Chapter Two

"Sometimes I wonder as I walk through the masses of people every day if they despise me as much as I despise them. Now individually, I like most people. And I think I'm a pretty nice person. But on a general people level, I could do without most people, if not all of them."

James' therapist, a middle-aged woman with dyed red hair and tiny reading glasses, asked, "And why do you think this is?"

"I don't know," he continued, "I guess the question is why do I despise humanity. Is it the single mind cohesiveness? The herding sheep mentality? The asshole-ness of most people, the "you don't know me" syndrome that dictates daily interactions in our country. Or do I despise them because I *am* one of them? I'm not sure."

"That's interesting."

"Furthermore, sometimes I think, hope even, for the world to end, for a nuclear war, for famine, for a meteor to hit the earth, or some disease that wipes out most of the population. As a teenager I really used to hope for this, along with the power to be invisible and the power to stop time. I figure ever kid does. But I always imagined I would live through this and have a chance to start over. But then in college I started reading post-apocalyptic books, and they started to change my view."

"How so?"

"Now I'm ok if I'm one of the ones that die."

"Really James? You would be willing to die along with everybody else? That's interesting."

"Yeah, it doesn't bother me. I'm not afraid of death. I mean, I don't want to die, but I'm not afraid of it."

"Hmm..." she said, jotted down a few notes, but remained silent. She wrote with her right hand. James was left-handed. As he aged, he began to take more notice of his fellow left-handed people. It was a right-handed person's world; everything was geared toward them. James couldn't stand doing math in school, not because he didn't like it, but because he would smear his paper every time he wrote in pencil. Scantron tests were no better. James felt a kinship with his fellow lefties.

"You know how the genre got started?" James asked her.

"What genre?"

"Post-Apocalyptic?"

"No, I'm not familiar."

"Probably because all you read are romance novels and books about vampires."

"That's not fair James."

"I know. I'm sorry. I didn't mean that," he said and smiled and she smiled back. Then he continued, "Anyway the post-apocalyptic genre was started in the early years of the cold war. It went along with fallout shelters and the general fear of the Russians. Those A-bombs really did a number on people's psyches, making everyone more paranoid about the end of the world. Like it really could happen. Now it's an even more popular genre with terrorism and all."

"That's interesting. I did not know that."

"Well sometimes I'm good for something."

"Don't be like that James. You know you have a lot to offer."

"I know, I know."

I want to get back to something you said a bit ago. About being ok with death."

"Ok, what do you want to know?"

"Most people are afraid of death. Do you hate them for that?"

"I don't hate anybody. My parents taught me hate is a strong word. But despise? I already told you I do."

"Ok, but let's not argue semantics. What I'm trying to get at is why? Why do you despise them?"

"Like I said, I really don't despise anybody individually, I just really dislike the collective humanity. Like when I'm at the store, or the mall, or stuck in traffic, the rudeness and lack of regard for others amazes me. And those are basic human daily interactions. It doesn't even take into account murderers, rapists, you know, the real dregs of humanity."

"It can be aggravating I understand. But they're not doing any-thing to you personally."

"That's true. But why would they treat other people like that?"

"Now you're contradicting yourself. You say you don't like other people because people do bad things to other people. But then why do you care?"

"I never said my outlook on life doesn't have holes. We all contradict ourselves. No one is infallible."

"But again, why do you care?"

"I don't know really, not for sure."

Looking up from her notepad his therapist asked, "So you said you're ok with dying as part of the collective death of humanity, but what about the people you do like, like your family and friends, are you ok with them dying as well?"

"Ok, ok, I know that if something like that occurs, my friends and family would most likely die..." James said and looked to the floor, avoiding her gaze.

"And..." she was looking right at him, her reading glasses slightly crooked on her face.

He took a deep breath and said, "And I guess would be ok with that too. I wouldn't be happy about it, who would? But if that's what happens, then that's what happens."

"What if you lived and they all died?"

"Don't know. Maybe that's what I'm hoping for." James' face turned a light red.

"It's ok, don't be embarrassed, it's what you feel James."

"I'm not embarrassed. It just isn't a thought I think most people would think."

"Maybe that's why you despise them."

"Maybe so..." James smiled a little smile.

"What are you thinking right now?"

"I'm thinking that yes, I would be ok with this, with everyone I know, including myself dying."

"Why does that make you smile?"

"Because the possibility exists."

| 3 |

Chapter Three

"Another tattoo Rubina?" her grandmother Mimi asked.

"What's wrong with tattoos Mimi?" Rubina said and gave Mimi a kiss on the cheek.

"Nothing, I guess I'm just old fashioned. When I was young only sailors had tattoos. I guess I'm glad it's not another piercing. I don't know if you can fit anymore in your ears. You know I do find your nose ring kind of cute though."

"Thanks Mimi. And look, I listened to you about the tattoos. None on my face, neck, or hands."

"Good sweetie. So let me see it."

Rubina took off her t-shirt so she was just in her bra. Mimi could see her nipple rings poking out through her bra, but didn't say anything. This new tattoo covered her upper right arm. "Minnie Mouse? Why's she dressed like a nun? And what's she holding? A sword, and Mickey's head? Rubina…"

"What, you don't like it?"

"I mean, it is beautiful colored. The colors are really bright, and the artwork is great. I can tell you drew it first, it has your style. But what does it mean?"

"I don't know, I just think Minnie gets crapped on by Mickey and the rest of them. She should feel strong as a woman, and if I were her and Mickey treated me like that that's what I would do. I've been working on the drawing for weeks; I think they did a real good job."

"It is something..." Mimi said.

"I knew you'd like it Mimi. Anyway, I got to go to work," Rubina said as she changed into her work uniform, a white polo shirt and khaki pants. Mimi tugged at her sleeves as she could still she part of the tattoo. "It's ok Mimi, at work they don't care," Rubina said.

"I know, but I do."

"So now you don't like it?"

"No I just, just don't want people to get the wrong impression of you."

"Don't worry about me Mimi, I don't care what people think."

"Ok sweetie. What time will you be home?"

"I get off at ten. If I won't be home I'll call you," Rubina said and gave her grandmother a kiss on the cheek. "Love you," she said on her way out the door.

"You too sweetheart," Mimi said.

Rubina had been living with Mimi for the last four years, ever since Rubina's parents died in a car accident when Rubina was sixteen. Mimi's daughter was Rubina's mother, and Mimi missed her own daughter terribly. Rubina was a good kid, and Mimi couldn't imagine how she dealt with her parents' death.

After high school Rubina didn't want to go to college, and Mimi didn't push her. When Rubina was eighteen she said, "How can I go to college? Who will look after you?"

"I'll be fine Ruby. You have your whole life ahead of you. I don't want you to feel like you missed out on something."

"I want to be by you. You're the only family I have left," Rubina had said.

Mimi didn't bring up college after that. When Rubina got her first tattoo (of a goldfish on her ankle) and her first upper ear-piercing Mimi didn't get mad, didn't judge. She just told her to keep tattoos off any place on her body that couldn't be covered up like clothing, just in case. Mimi knew that Rubina would appreciate the gesture one day, like when she went applying for a 'real' job.

Rubina lit up a cigarette once she got out of sight of Mimi's house. Mimi knew she smoked but something about it embarrassed Rubina, especially doing it in front of her grandmother. Mimi had been there for her when her parents died and she loved her so much but she hated disappointing her. On the other hand, she loved getting tattoos and piercings; they made her feel more unique, less like everybody else. Because most everybody else had their parents, at least one of them, alive, she thought. Mimi never judged her, and Rubina took a crappy job near her Mimi's house so she could be there for her, to protect her.

Rubina worked in the video department of a local grocery store called El Supermercado. It didn't pay much but she basically set her own hours and worked with a few people she could at least stand to be around for more than a couple hours without wanting to rip their voice boxes out. Rubina parked her car in the employee parking lot and walked up to the store. Her friend Mae saw her once she came in and said, "Hey girl you know you're already five minutes late?"

"I know, I know," Rubina said as she quickly walked toward the time clock.

"You get a new tattoo? I can see it under your sleeve."

"Be quiet Mae I don't want the boss to see it."

"Well, you should've worn a long sleeve shirt then," Mae said and giggled.

"But it's so nice today and I wanted to get some sun."

"It is hot today, and you are the palest white girl I know, so I get it."

"Shut up girl," Rubina said.

Rubina went to the time clock and swiped her card through the machine. 1:06. Late by just six minutes. The boss would probably say something, the anal-retentive prick. But it didn't bother her as she was still excited about her new tattoo.

Mae left her post at the video desk to go talk to Rubina. "Let's see," Mae said.

"Ok," Rubina said a rolled up her sleeve.

"You white girls and your Mickey Mouse, Minnie Mouse, Hello Kitty tats, you're funny," Mae said as she touched Rubina's arm.

"What? You got tattoos too. Stars and guys names and your name on the back of your neck. At least mine have some color."

"Mine have color too," Mae said laughing.

"Ha ha," Rubina said, "So do you like it?"

"Girl it is pretty badass."

"Thanks."

"Mae leave Rubina alone and get back to stocking the new movies," the manager came out of his office once he saw the two girls conversing for too long.

"Ok," Mae said and walked with her head down back over to the video desk, picking up a pile of movies on the way.

"So, you got a new tattoo Miss Rubina?"

He called everyone Miss or Mister and then their first name. It was annoying to her, but at least he didn't bring up the fact that she was late. Yet. "Umm..." Rubina stammered.

"I can see it under your sleeve."

"C'mon, it's not a big deal. It's barely noticeable."

"It is noticeable. I'll let it go today, but you need to wear long sleeves next time you come in."

"Gotcha. Well, I better go start, see you," Rubina said and quickly walked to the video department where Mae was giggling. Rubina gave her the finger.

"What'd boss man say?" Mae asked.

"Nothing, said I got to wear a long sleeve shirt next time."

"Told you. Still, it's a cool tattoo."

| 4 |

Three Weeks (before the End of the World)

This is Jonas Johnston with the Weekend News here on KRTV, Channel Six. This morning we will continue our popular series on "How the World May End." Nuclear War, Asteroids, and Black Holes have preceded today's episode, Epidemic diseases. Examples include the Bubonic Plague, Spanish Flu, Ebola, and more recently SARS and the Swine Flu. Our guest today is biologist Dr. Alberto Grasso from the University of Vermont who specializes in epidemic diseases.

"Dr Grasso welcome. Can you shed some light on epidemic diseases and how they work?"

"Certainly Jonas. First, epidemic diseases that attack humans do not originate in humans. For lack of a better term, they 'jump' from other hosts, especially species that live in close proximity to humans, like farm animals, and, in some countries, birds, monkeys, dogs, rabbits, and pigs for example.

A reason why epidemic and pandemic diseases like the Bubonic Plague, Spanish Flu, AIDS, Ebola, SARS, and Swine Flu originate from places like Africa, Asia and Mexico is because these are places where much of the general population still lives in close proximity with a multitude of animals. But for a disease to change hosts, and for it to infect humans, it takes a mutation."

"How likely are mutations Doctor?"

"More likely than one would think Jonas. Mutations occur all the time in nature, and they occurred with all the aforementioned epidemic and pandemic diseases."

"Are you familiar with RHDV, the Rabbit Hemorrhagic Disease Virus?"

"I am, yes."

"About a week ago we had Dr. Angela Van Broxton on the show to talk about RHDV. She provided some startling statistics about RHDV. My question for you is do you think RHDV could 'jump' from rabbits to humans?"

"It's possible, yes. Likely? No."

"Let's say it did. Do you think RHDV would kill as many humans as rabbits?"

"Honestly Jonas it would be impossible to say. There are too many variables that are in play."

"Ok, could it kill as many?"

"It's not probable, however anything is possible Jonas."

"Dr. Grasso, thank you for your time. It's been a pleasure."

"Thank you, Jonas."

"For those of you that have enjoyed our special 'How the World May End' series you'll want to watch as we have the fifth and final part airing tomorrow morning at nine. This one is aimed at our sci-fi fans. The topic will be zombies and how the undead could take over the world. After a quick commercial break we'll be back with the weather report for what's shaping up to be a beautiful spring day."

| 5 |

Chapter Five

"How are we today, James?"

Every session started with the same question. So open ended that it would fill their hour together and make it seem like no time passed at all. James sat in the same deep purple chair, made from material that was abrasive yet welcoming like short carpeting with light wood armrests that he liked to tap his finger nails on.

James had been seeing her for a year, which was pretty good, for him anyway. Most shrinks he couldn't stand but his parents wanted him to go. Ever since he saw his brother die. Hit by a train when James was ten. His brother was twelve, the family daredevil. Thought he could beat the train. James told every psychologist he had seen this story. Early on it defined him but with more recent shrinks he just told them at the first session out of habit. He answered her question, "He died fifteen years ago this week."

"Your brother?"

James nodded.

"I'm sorry James."

"Thanks. But it's not a big deal. I mean now I've lived more without him than with him. I think my parents have the bigger problem with it."

"Why do you think that is?"

"I don't know; he was their kid. They didn't have any more after me. I think two kids suited them."

"You don't miss him?"

"I didn't say that."

She paused and took off her glasses. She got a tissue and cleaned the lenses. "I know. I did."

James watched as she was meticulous with the glasses. 'She didn't like having to wear them,' James thought. He could see the little lines of disgust on her face when she looked at them. It made him smile. "I do miss him, I just don't know what else I can do. For my parents, I mean."

"I'm sure you do enough."

"But I can never do enough. I mean I know they're proud of me. I know that. But they would've been proud of him too. And now that I haven't accomplished anything I know I let them down."

"You're only twenty-five James."

"So? There are a lot of people who are successful well before twenty-five."

"And a great many more that were successful after, and well after, age twenty-five."

"Yeah, but-," James said. 'She's right,' he thought.

"Say what you're thinking James."

"I'm thinking maybe you're right. Maybe I've put too much pressure on myself. I mean at least I have a job and parents that love me, and at least I don't live at home like a lot of my friends."

"That's right. Focus on the positive."

"But it's so easy to look at the negative, you know? Like last week. Remember I was talking about the end of the world and all that?"

"Yes I do."

"I was watching TV today and saw a news report on killer diseases, you know like the black plague and SARS and stuff?"

She nodded.

"Anyway, this guy was talking about how right now there's a disease killing rabbits, and it might jump to humans, and then it might kill all humanity. I mean that's what I'm talking about."

"What are you talking about? I heard a lot of might's, what-ifs, possibilities."

"Yeah but-"

She continued, "But back to the point, what about the positive? What about your probable options? Those are the things that are tangible, that are real. Are you going to go to work tomorrow? Are you going to be happy about it? Are you going to ask that girl from down the hall out on a date? Those are tangible possibilities. Don't think about a killer disease, because that's not likely. Think about tangible possibilities for me for next week, ok?"

"Ok, I will," James said as he rose from the chair. He said good-bye and walked out of her office.

| 6 |

Two Weeks (before the End of the World)

This is Jonas Johnston on KRTV Channel Six with your Morning News. Our regular viewers may remember a report from two weeks ago about the Rabbit Hemorrhagic Disease Virus, or RHDV, that has been decimating worldwide rabbit populations. Now upwards of ninety percent of the worldwide rabbit population is infected, prompting major concern around the globe.

However, in a startling new development the virus is now not only infecting rabbits but human beings as well. If you've watched our series "How the World May End" you will recall we discussed this very possibility with today's guest, biologist Dr. Albert Grasso from the University of Vermont.

"Hello Doctor."

"Good morning, Jonas."

"We'll get right to the point Doctor. Today we have learned there are confirmed reports coming out of New Zealand and Australia of a new disease infecting humans."

"That's right Jonas. Remember when we spoke about mutations and that animal diseases can 'jump' from animals to humans?"

"Yes, I remember."

"Well, RHDV has proven to be no exception. A mutation has occurred in regards to RHDV and now we have HHDV, or Human Hemorrhagic Disease Virus."

"What does this mean Dr. Grasso?"

"Right now, we do not know for sure. It could be another Flu variant, and it could be on the level of SARS or the more recent Swine Flu, which while they inspired panic in many did not prove to be very deadly for the human population. As of now it is highly unlikely it will be more deadly than either of those two. We should have a greater grasp of the situation within the next 24 to 48 hours."

"You say this because CDC officials are currently en route to Australia to learn more about the disease, right?"

"That's right Jonas."

"CDC officials said at this time a vaccine is premature. Would you agree with their assessment?"

"Vaccines do not absolutely prevent one from getting a virus; they can help in prevention and thus are not infallible. As we have only the first case in humans a vaccine I would agree would be premature. Developing, testing and mass producing a vaccine would not be prudent or cost effective."

"Many in the news media have taken to calling HHDV the 'Rabbit Flu.' Would you agree with that name?"

"Well, it certainly speaks to the cause of the virus."

"Thank you for your time doctor and I hope you will be available once we know more about HHDV."

"Of course."

"In local news the police are currently seeking two men for questioning in regards to a double murder that occurred overnight in the 4000 block of Grand Avenue. We've been told that one of the victims is a police officer. The officer's name has not yet been released to the press however the police commissioner has issued a statement saying "We will find the individual or individuals that did this quickly and efficiently. Justice will be swift. God bless our fellow officer and his family; our thoughts and prayers are with you."

One of the men being sought by police for questioning is D'Maurice Armstrong, younger brother of Marcus 'Brother Theo' Armstrong, leader of one of the city's largest gangs, Brother Theo's Disciples. You may remember Brother Theo was indicted last year in a brutal homicide but was later acquitted. We will have more on these stories and others in our second hour. Now over to Dan with sports."

| **7** |

Chapter Seven

Nadia sauntered her way through the strip club, all swaying hips and fit, tanned legs taking long strides. She looked good and she knew it, looking at herself in the one of the club's many mirrors that lined the walls. She surveyed the room, looking for shoes. Expensive shoes, preferably leather or some other kind of animal skin, no sneakers; shoes were the best way she learned to determine how much a guy would spend.

Nadia saw a youngish guy with nice shoes, polished black leather. The guy was alone, smoking a cigarette. She saw a green bottled beer on his table, half-full. Nadia was wearing a pink corset and a pink thong with pink 3-inch heels. Her boobs overflowed, and she asked him, "mind if I sit down?"

"Nope," the man said and took a drag of his cigarette.

Nadia motioned for him to uncross his legs and she sat on his lap. Her tanned legs hung over his, her breasts inches from his face. "How are you doing tonight sweetie?" Nadia said.

"Fine, and you?"

"I'm great. My name's Roxy," she said and offered her hand, "what's yours?"

"Carl," he said, limply shaking her hand.

"Nice to meet you, Carl. Hey can I bum a cigarette?"

"Yeah sure," he said, took one out of the pack on the table and gave it to her.

"Got a light?"

He lit her cigarette as well and said, "You want me to smoke it for you too?"

"You're funny," she laughed.

"What do you do Carl?"

"Graphic design."

"Nice," she said as she watched Carl's eyes focus on her breasts. When she first began working as a stripper it would annoy her, every stray male eye on her larger than average breasts. But it didn't bother her, not anymore, because she knew her breasts made her more money.

"You do anything else, besides work here?" he asked.

"Nope."

"I bet you make some good money," he said and took a drink of beer.

"I do ok."

"Yeah, I bet you do ok," he said and shook his head.

They sat in silence for a few moments while Nadia checked her bright pink nails and looked through her tiny pink purse. They continued to smoke their cigarettes. Nadia expected what Carl was going to ask, as they all did eventually. How much could two people in this type of situation talk about? "So have you been working here long?"

Nadia answered, "On and off for about a year. Weekends mostly."

Nadia remembered the first time she dealt with the haze of cigarette smoke, the day-glo colors of the carpeting and the walls, and the low ceiling that made the club feel like a damp basement. The rough hands of laborers, the soft hands of businessmen, men's hands touching her soft body. They only touched her where she wanted them to, but still it affected her. In those early days it would often leave her feeling depressed. Depressed until she'd fan out all the money she made, look at all the clothes and shoes she now had, which made her smile.

"I dig your look," Carl said. "Are you Mexican?"

Nadia shook her head. "I'm Albanian and Italian."

"Oh, well that's cool. My grandmother is Italian."

Nadia didn't respond, just smoked her cigarette. She didn't like being mistaken for a Mexican, and around here it happened all too often. It wasn't that she was racist, she just didn't like it, and if asked about it she would tell the truth. The only real truth she ever told the customers.

Nadia eyes wandered around the strip club. A stripper named Star was on the main stage, but the two side stages were empty. A slower than usual Friday night. Two men were tossing crumpled singles at Star and she was rubbing her breasts on their faces. But there weren't many other people there. He noticed it too. "It's kind of slow tonight, eh?" Carl said.

"Yeah. I'm not making any money." Nadia made a pouty face.

"That sucks."

"It is only ten o'clock. I bet it picks up later."

"It usually does. "Just depends, you know?" Nadia said and ashed her cigarette in the cheap black ashtray, "You have cute dimples, you know that?"

"Thanks. You're pretty cute yourself."

"Oh Carl, you're too kind," Nadia said and took a final drag of her cigarette before putting it out. She turned to him and said, "Say, you want a dance?"

"Nah, I just got here. Maybe later."

"Ok then. I got to go onstage, take it easy Carl," Nadia said a kissed him on the cheek. As she got up he gave her rear a playful slap and Nadia turned and made a sultry face. With the lack of guys that evening she'd have to come back around if she wanted to make any money. He had nice shoes, after all.

| 8 |

One Week (before the End of the World)

Good day, this is the KRTV Channel Six Morning News. I'm Jonas Johnston. We have an update on the Rabbit Flu Epidemic currently affecting the South Pacific including Australia and New Zealand.

The CDC held a press conference today in regards to the Rabbit Flu. They first summed up what is already known; that Rabbit Flu has spread quickly throughout Australia and New Zealand with an estimated one million people showing signs of infection within one week since the first documented case. Doctors and scientists are most concerned with this extremely rapid pace.

They went on to say that CDC doctors are currently in Australia and New Zealand attaining as much information about the Rabbit Flu as possible. They also addressed the issue of a vaccine, stating that:

"A vaccine will be developed as it is necessary to prevent the spread of HHDV; however there are no reported cases outside of Australia and New Zealand and CDC officials are working with government officials from Australia and New Zealand to prevent the spread of this disease. Let us also mention there have been no fatalities in regards to the Rabbit Flu. We expect the Rabbit Flu to be no more lethal than recent animal flues, with very low fatality rates. There is no reason for alarm."

However, as a precautionary response the US government has restricted all imports and exports from countries of the South Pacific and the FAA has restricted all flights to and from countries of the South Pacific for the foreseeable future.

In local news the funeral for fallen police officer Frank Semple was held earlier today. In attendance were the police commissioner, the mayor and various other city dignitaries. One of the men sought in the death of Officer Semple, D'Maurice Armstrong, was apprehended early this morning and brought to police headquarters. It is thought that prosecutors will request he be held without bail and his arraignment is set for later this afternoon. We will have more on this story as well as the Rabbit Flu as it becomes available.

| 9 |

Chapter Nine

Brother Theo sat, alone, at his dark oak desk in his Italian leather chair and watched the news on a small flat screen television on his desk. Brother Theo's God-given name was Marcus Armstrong but he bore a striking resemblance to the Theo character from the Cosby Show, and since he came up when the show was big, everyone had been calling him Brother Theo, and eventually just Theo, for as long as he could remember.

Theo watched the news report that the police had his brother in custody. He loved his younger half-brother and couldn't believe how stupid he had been. 'Killing a cop D'Mo? What the fuck were you thinking?' Theo thought and shook his head. Theo had provided him a hide-out flat but D'Maurice still went out to a bar and that's where the cops got him. 'Stupid, stupid,' Theo thought.

His mother had gone to pieces when Theo himself had gone to prison more than ten years ago. Now it felt like a lifetime ago to Theo. He had served seven long years for being in possession of a gun used in a murder. He had committed the murder but had an alibi; it didn't matter to the jury. Thank God their mother had passed the year before, because D'Mo was her baby, and she wouldn't have been able to handle the predicament his younger half-brother was now in.

Since his release in three short years Theo had become the leader of one of the cities' largest street gangs named after himself, Brother Theo's Disciples. He had started building the gang in prison, and upon his release was already one of the city's largest gangs.

D'Maurice wouldn't give up his brother, Theo knew that, but there was nothing good about his brother being arrested for killing a cop. There just wasn't. Theo had called his lawyer and sent him to see D'Mo in jail. That was all he could do for his brother right now.

While he was in prison Theo had heard the story of Josiah, Kuwo and the rabbit bite, told to him by a man named Neshif. Theo remembered Neshif because he had these scars, three small cuts under each cheek, on his face. Neshif told Theo they were tribal scars. He thought the story was bullshit but after the news reports he felt it wouldn't hurt to find and keep a rabbit around, just in case.

Theo went over to a small wire pet cage sitting in the corner of his office. He took a baby carrot from a bag next to the cage and fed it to a California-colored plump rabbit, with a white coat with black paws, ears, nose and tail. Its name was Sally Jesse. Rabbits were in extremely short supply, what with the virus killing them by the millions. Sally Jesse was brought to him by an underling trying to advance his standing in the gang. It was the only living rabbit he knew of.

Theo opened the cage and took Sally Jesse in his arms. He caressed her fur and fed her another carrot. As she ate the carrot Theo positioned his hand near her mouth, waited until she finished the last bite of carrot, and let her nibble on the skin between his thumb and forefinger. Then he pinched her, hard, and she bit down on the skin. He uttered a guttural moan as she sunk her teeth in. Theo saw the blood and the tiny teeth mark on his hand and smiled.

He then returned her to the cage, gave her another carrot, and sat back down in his leather chair.

A bell ringed in his office and he changed the channel on his television to the closed-circuit camera he had on his front door. One of his more trusted disciples stood on the stoop of his building. He buzzed Clint in and heard his loud footfalls as he walked up the stairs to Theo's office.

"Hey boss," Clint said, closing the office door behind him, "What is going on with D'Mo?"

"He's been arrested, don't you watch the news?"

"That's what I mean, I heard about that. Anything I can do boss?"

"There is actually something you can help with, but it doesn't concern D'Mo. It's about this Rabbit Flu."

"Yeah, I've heard about that. Fucking up people in Australia or Tanzania or Tasmania or something."

"Oceania. And Tanzania's in Africa."

"My bad."

"Clint, I have an important job for you," Theo said, "You see that rabbit there?"

"Yeah."

"Her name is Sally Jesse. I want you to take Sally Jesse down to the Spot. Most of our men are there, right?"

Clint nodded.

"I want you to have Sally Jesse bite them in the hand, right here," Theo said and pointed to the loose skin between his thumb and forefinger on his right hand.

"You sure boss? Is that like going to protect us or something?"

"Clint, I'm taking precautions. You know what that means, right?"

"Yeah, yeah, you're being careful. I got you. I can do it for you boss, but I don't know how the guys are going to see it."

"You tell anyone that doesn't want to get bit he can come visit me and I'll take a lot larger bite than Sally Jesse will, you feel me?"

"Gotcha," Clint said, and was poking at Sally Jesse through the wire cage.

"Get her out of the cage, Clint," Theo said, "because you're going first."

| 10 |

Chapter Ten

James walked away from the train station toward his apartment. He stopped at the local gas station which he frequented quite often for potato chips and soda pop or beer and cigarettes depending on the time of day. Today he bought a bag of Doritos and a Strawberry soda, and paid the clerk, a young man of Pakistani decent with bright white teeth and a friendly smile. The clerk's nametag read "Baba."

He knew Baba insofar as James was often in the gas station and Laba recognized him whenever he entered, greeting him typically with a head nod or slight wave. The gas station was a family business as far as James could tell, and James assumed Baba was the younger brother of the owner, who didn't wear a nametag and was nowhere near as friendly. Baba handed James his change with a big smile and James wished him a good rest of the day.

James continued on toward his apartment and saw a balding man in paint splattered overalls painting the brick wall of a church burnt sienna. He assumed it was a church as a twenty foot tall wooden cross was partially hidden behind an oversized oak tree.

The cross also needed painting and James wondered if they painter would be getting to that next.

A cigarette hung casually from the painter's lips. James stopped and examined the painter's work, and the painter said to him, "What do you think?"

"Looks good."

"Thanks," the painter said and took a sip from a clear plastic straw connected to his gallon jug of unknown drink as he sat on the front steps leading up to the church.

"Hot day, eh?"

"Not too bad. I got my gallon of soda here."

"Nice."

The painter continued to alternate between drags off his cigarette and sips from his soda. "You a religious man?" the painter asked James.

"Not particularly."

"I was only asking because you've been standing here, in front of our church."

"Ah, so you go here. I was wondering if you were just the painter or if you attended," James said, "So is it a Baptist church, Lutheran, Mosque, Temple, what?"

"The New City Church of God. There's a City Church of God over on twenty-second street. Not the same."

"Good to know. So non-denominational I take it?"

"That's right."

James decided the church really didn't fit it among the surrounding businesses. A nail salon, a liquor store, a boarded-up computer repair shop, a tax business closed until January, and this church. There was also an old hanging sign with broken glass and broken bulbs that swung from above. "You guys getting this fixed?" James asked.

"Yep, once we get the funds. We're going get one of those electronic signs you can change the message using a computer. We're going to put Bible passages and other uplifting things on it."

James nodded and said, "Good idea."

"We're a small church now, but growing. We're an accepting group, and always looking for more members. I'm Danny," he said and extended his hand.

"James," he said, shaking Danny's hand, noting the stark difference between Danny's rough and coarse hands and his own soft ones.

"We've all had problems. Sister understands that, and has led us to better times like this new church. We used to meet at the Y."

"Sister?"

"Yeah, she's our pastor and spiritual leader. You'd like her. You should come. Sunday nights at 6pm is service."

"Yeah, ok. Good talking to you."

"Bring your friends," Danny said as James walked away. He flicked his finished cigarette butt into the street and returned to the burnt sienna paint bucket.

| 11 |

Chapter Eleven

Good morning, Jonas Johnston here with your Morning News on KRTV Channel Six. Two weeks ago, we first learned of a new disease called HHDV or the Rabbit Flu as it is now more commonly known. The first infected, known as Patient Zero, has died today from the Rabbit Flu at age thirty-three. Her name is Alison Burton, a commercial rabbit farmer from Guyra, Australia. The world mourns her loss as it waits and watches for what is to come.

Doctors and scientists from around the world are quickly researching and putting together reports for world leaders on how to deal with this growing pandemic. Coming to us live from Australia we have frequent guest Doctor Alberto Grasso from the University of Vermont. "Dr. Grasso, thanks for joining us."

"My pleasure Jonas."

"Dr. Grasso, what can you tell us about the rapidly approaching Rabbit Flu epidemic."

"From what we know it comes on like a normal flu, with a low-grade fever, the chills and coughing, as well as extreme fatigue and these initial symptoms occur within the first 24-48 hours after the initial infection. Next small brown lesions on the armpits and pubic regions, which bear a resemblance to moles, occur within 48-72 hours after initial infection. Extremely high fever and extreme fatigue along with more skin lesions that cover the whole body take place up until the death of the host."

"Is that what happened in Ms. Burton's case exclusively?"

"I wish I could say that. Unfortunately, Mrs. Burton's parents, husband, their three children as well as many of their neighbors and those in the surrounding areas are showing increased signs of the infection. They have been quarantined since Mrs. Burton was diagnosed however that has not stopped the spread of the disease. The major cause for alarm is that it is now apparent that Rabbit Flu is transmitted through the air and has also proven to be highly contagious."

"How contagious are we talking Dr. Grasso?"

"We have reports of infection in China, Japan, South Korea, India-"

"Excuse me Dr. Grasso I've just been told there are also reports of Rabbit Flu in Brazil, Peru, and Argentina."

"I've also heard that Jonas, but let me stress that those reports are unconfirmed. Something to keep in mind is that we only have one known death attributed to Rabbit Flu. That does not mean a killer disease, or the end of the humanity."

"But what about RHDV? The initial disease that infected rabbits. It had a very high fatality rate."

"Our immune system and how the virus affects our species may be very different from rabbits, so I would not say that Rabbit Flu will have the same fatality rate in humans. However, it could. Really Jonas what worries me most is Ms. Burton's age."

"Thirty-three?"

"Yes. While most flues have previously been deadly to children and the elderly, typically the middle-age population, from age eighteen to fifty, is typically less affected. However, HHDV has taken the life of a seemingly healthy thirty-three-year-old rabbit farmer. That is something I myself and I'm sure CDC doctors are taking very seriously."

"Can you tell us anything about a vaccine?"

"I have heard a vaccine is currently being developed as we speak. I am not personally working on this project, but I have spoken with colleagues that are hard at work on a vaccine. Whether it reaches us in time to be effective is the question."

"Do you think it will?"

"In all honesty, my personal opinion without any knowledge of what the CDC is currently developing, is that it will not. Vaccines need trials, immense testing, and unfortunately the rapid spread of the Rabbit Flu is not allowing for this. I also am awaiting word from the CDC."

"The CDC has announced a news conference tomorrow, so it appears we will learn more about a possible vaccine. One last thing doctor; it seems the internet has become the host to wide ranging home remedies to combat the Rabbit Flu, the most popular currently being the ancient African rabbit hand bite. Are you familiar with this doctor?"

"I am. All I can say is that having a rabbit bite your hand will save you from catching the Rabbit Flu just as much as covering yourself in Vaseline will Jonas."

"And let me guess, you wouldn't recommend that either."

"No, I wouldn't."

"Thank you for your time today Dr. Grasso and stay safe out there."

"I will. Thank you Jonas."

| 12 |

Chapter Twelve

"The price tag said \$2.99, and now you're telling me it's \$3.99? That's some crap miss, excuse my language. My kid is sick and he needs this medicine. The label said \$2.99 I swear."

'It's been deathly slow all day, and this lady is arguing over a dollar? When there's people starving in Africa and sick kids with cystic fibrosis and endangered pandas and global warming? Seriously,' Rubina thought.

She looked at this woman, this pathetic, middle-aged ugly woman, who she wanted to punch in the ear, and said nothing. She simply picked up the phone and said on the intercom, "price check register three, price check register three."

"If you want, I'll go get the label, or get another one."

Rubina didn't respond. She just stared at the large fluorescent lights above her. "Miss is someone coming?"

Rubina shrugged her shoulders and crossed her arms. They waited for the price check, not making eye contact. After two minutes of looking around, waiting for a price check that hadn't yet arrived, the woman spoke, "Can I show you the label Miss?"

"I'm sorry, I can't leave the register."

Rubina knew what this lady what doing. Or thought she did. People like this were either really cheap, really bored, or both. Rubina had to work her eight hours, so it didn't matter to her. At work she was never in any hurry.

An older couple came to her register and began putting their groceries on the conveyor belt. Here was the moment of truth for the woman. Rubina asked her, "Ma'am do you want me to ring up the cough medicine? If not I have to take the next customers."

"How much is it?"

Rubina scanned it, and the price read $3.99. "Ma'am?"

"Alright fine."

The woman paid, then Rubina rang up the older couple, and then she sighed. She didn't care about the dollar and it wasn't about principle. It was simply about passing the time the best way she could and if that meant taking joy in the frustration of another over one dollar then so be it. Her manager had watched the exchange from his cushy office but now she saw him walking toward her. "I guess you didn't hear me say price check?"

"Would you have wanted me to check?"

"Eventually."

"That's what I was waiting for. Do you know if Mae is off today?" he asked.

"You make the schedule, you should know."

"But I'm asking you," her boss sneezed into a white paper towel.

"Bless you," Rubina said, "She's not here, and I'm not her mother, so I would say yes, she's off today."

"I was just seeing if you knew. Actually, she called in sick. A lot of people have been doing that lately."

"I've been here every day this week."

"Good for you."

"Thanks," she said and rolled her eyes, "I'm here, on like, no sleep, while nobody else bothered to show up. I think I deserve a raise."

"Yeah right, you barely do any work as it is."

"But look at my assiduousness. That has to count for something, right?"

"If that means you're an ass then you're right."

"Ha ha."

"But seriously you haven't heard about the Rabbit Flu?"

"Yeah, I guess. "My grandmother said something about some disease killing rabbits and some customers have said something, but I don't really pay attention to what they say. But how do dead rabbits affect me, you know what I mean?"

"How do you remain so sheltered? It's all anyone on TV can talk about."

"I don't watch TV, at least not that much."

"What about the internet?"

"I don't go to news websites," Rubina said, "What's the big deal anyway?"

"What's the big deal you ask? Are you dense? Where is everybody? I have one checker, two cart pushers and one already went home sick, and you and me in the whole store. I've been stocking shelves by myself all day. You haven't noticed?"

"Uh…I guess not."

"No, you're not getting it. There's this new Flu, and it's called Rabbit Flu, or that's what the news is calling it."

"Catchy."

"It's infecting people in Australia, Europe, China, a whole bunch of countries. They're worried it might come here, to the US."

"Should I be worried?"

"You haven't noticed the people wearing those surgical masks?"

"I've seen a few, I figured they just raised the terror alert to orange or red or whatever color means super fear. This one lady was wearing one earlier, but I've seen her wear a construction helmet in here before. People are strange, so I didn't think much about it."

"I ordered a ton, but they're on backorder; pisses me off. Corp told me to lock up the doors tonight and not re-open until I hear from them. I've never gotten that call before so it's weird, you know?"

"Yeah, real weird. I'm sure it's nothing, people just get caught up in bullshit sometimes. The new fad disease, like that pig flu."

"Swine flu."

"Right," Rubina said, "But more to the point, can I leave, like right now?"

"Yes, you can leave."

"See you later then," Rubina said, clocked out and left the store.

| 13 |

Chapter Thirteen

At four in the morning Nadia made her final walk through the strip club to the locker room. She stood in front of her locker, counting the money she had made. One hundred fifty dollars. For six hours. "What a shit night," she mumbled to herself.

Before she left the asshole who ran the club came into the locker room. He was a rotund man who smelled of cigar and sweat and, in his case, he fit the stereotype of strip club boss to a T.

Most of the women were already dressed; Nadia had done a dance for a guy just before closing so she was still in her pink corset and thong. She sat on the bench in front of her locker taking off her heels, rubbing the lines the straps made in her skin. The manager clapped his hands loudly twice, and the few women stopped what they were doing and looked at him. "Ladies," he said, "as of now we're closed-"

"No shit, it's four," a stripper Nadia knew only by her stage name, Star, said.

"You're a smartass, you know that. More importantly, we're closed until further notice. Some of you may have heard about this

Rabbit Flu, and the cops are shutting all the clubs down to prevent the disease from spreading. I'm sure it's nothing, but-"

"Figures you'd make us work all night first though," Star said, "Bet you knew about this before we came in. Jackass."

Some of the women laughed, including Nadia. "Well shit yeah, got to make money somehow girl," the manager said, then "So I don't want to see any of you until we call you. Until we call you, got it?"

The women nodded and "yeah'd" their understanding. "Alright then get the fuck out of here."

***

Nadia knocked on the door to her boyfriend's apartment before she let herself in. "Pete, hey Pete you here?"

She heard a faint moan from the bedroom, then heard her name. She went into his bedroom, saw him under the covers. "You haven't been answering your phone. It's too dark in here," Nadia said and opened the curtains, "Are you hungry, thirsty? Do you want me to get you anything?"

"Nope, I'm fine," he said and sat up in bed.

"You don't look so good baby. Maybe I should take you to the hospital."

"Nah, I'm ok. I'll get better soon as this fever breaks."

Nadia cleaned up his room, picking up clothes. She went into the bathroom and brought back a damp cloth and put it on his head.

"I probably caught it from this guy I was sitting next to in that meeting. He was sneezing, coughing a lot. I shouldn't have shaken his hand."

"So that's why you weren't answering your phone?"

"C'mon Nadia, don't bug me. I was in Houston for that meeting. I just got back yesterday and I'm feeling like shit," he said and turned over on his side, away from her.

"I'm sorry baby, let me take care of you," she said climbed in bed with him. She rubbed her hands under his shirt. "Jeez you're cold."

"I know…I know. I'm freezing."

"Let me make you some chicken noodle soup. That'll make you feel better."

Nadia got up and went toward the kitchen, and said "You think maybe you got that Rabbit Flu they keep talking about?"

"It isn't in the US, least that's what the news said. Just regular, plain old flu. Let me sleep and I'll be fine in the morning."

Nadia came back into the bedroom and said "Ok baby I'm sorry. I don't want to upset you." She kissed him on the back of the head and continued, "The club's closed until further notice. I don't have anything to do at least until they re-open. I'll take care you honey, don't worry."

| 14 |

Four Days (before the End of the World)

This is Jonas Johnston with a breaking news report. We have learned that that the first case of Rabbit Flu in the United States has been confirmed in Houston, Texas. As such the governor of Texas has closed all schools and government offices until the potential outbreak can be contained. We are awaiting word from the President of the United States who has a press conference scheduled in about fifteen minutes, and we will bring you that live.

Our correspondents in Sydney, London, Rio de Janeiro and other major world cities are reporting infection numbers upwards of 90% of the earth's human population. While these numbers seem high that does not mean the rate of fatality will also be at the same percentage. To calm growing fear a press conference was held earlier today to address the Rabbit Flu in Atlanta at the Center for the Disease Control. Our Atlanta affiliate reporter Charlotte Daniels is currently outside the CDC. "Hello Charlotte. Can you tell us what the CDC said in this morning's press conference?"

"Certainly Jonas. CDC officials confirmed the first case of Rabbit Flu in the US. The man infected is Alonzo Gomez from Houston. He is a sixty-two-year-old salesman and had recently returned from Costa Rica where he was visiting relatives. We were told earlier today that he is in quarantine at the CDC facility here in Atlanta."

"Did they advise what to do if you may have come in contact with Mr. Gomez?"

"Officials said that they are operating under the impression that as currently only Mr. Gomez is infected. They said they will deal with other cases as they arise. They did advise staying in your home unless it is absolutely necessary to prevent spread of disease."

"Was there any mention of a vaccine for the Rabbit Flu?"

"Yes. The CDC said a vaccine is currently being developed and is in testing stages. They did not say when the vaccine would be ready for mass consumption. They advised the use of surgical masks and rubber gloves for all interactions to prevent the spread of the disease. They did urge calm in the face of this growing pandemic, and more information would be forthcoming."

"Did they mention anything in regards to the fatality rate of the Rabbit Flu?"

"They did not address that specifically but did say they feel the vaccine would be ready in a prompt manner."

"We also have heard about protestors outside the CDC. Can you tell us more about that Charlotte?"

"There are about fifty protestors here now, with signs and chanting, wanting to know what the government is doing, wanting a vaccine. No violence currently, however we have learned that National Guard troops will be dispatched to the CDC as a precautionary measure."

"Now let's take you live to the President's address."

"Good evening my fellow citizens. I know you have many questions and concerns in regards to the Rabbit Flu and I will address them as best I can. I have just gotten off the phone with the governor of Texas and he has confirmed the news that the Rabbit Flu has come to our country. I know this is cause for alarm however I urge all of you out there to remain calm and to keep a level head. The governor has decided to close all public agencies and here in Washington we will follow suit. All government offices will be closed to prevent the spread of the disease including Congress and the Supreme Court. I have also been in contact with officials at the CDC and they have assured me that taking these measures will help prevent the spread of the disease.

This is no time to panic or be fearful. The United States is much more ready to deal with the Rabbit Flu compared with many of the rest of the world's countries. We have our top doctors and scientists working on analyzing this flu and we expect them to come up with a solution that will benefit all of us. I will continue to work with my advisors and the CDC to bring you more information in order to keep each and every American safe and healthy. As such I will not be taking any questions. God bless you, your families, and God bless America."

| 15 |

Chapter Fifteen

Rubina parked her car behind her grandmother's ancient Buick. It was two-tone tan and brown, and rode like a boat, with each corner of the car its own entity. As a child Rubina would sometimes get seasick riding in it. Now, it hadn't been driven for years; Rubina doubted it worked, but her grandmother always wanted the option. Rubina couldn't blame her. She walked in the back door, and her grandmother was on her as soon as she came in. "Ruby I was so worried," her grandmother said and hugged her forcefully.

"I'm fine Mimi, why, what's up?"

"This Rabbit Flu. Haven't you heard?"

"Yeah, that's why I'm home early. Store's closed."

Rubina took off her windbreaker and put it on the back of the chair. "Are you hungry Ruby?"

"Nah I'm fine Mimi."

"You sure? You should eat something. You're too skinny."

"I'm good," Rubina said, then "Mimi are you alright?"

Her grandmother was old but healthy. Mimi didn't smoke and hadn't had a drink since well before Rubina was born. But still she worried since Rubina knew that diseases hit the elderly hard.

"I feel fine sweetie."

"Ok, but if you start feeling sick you need to let me know."

"I will, I promise. I made some veal cutlets and broccoli for dinner. Do you want me to warm you up some?"

Rubina knew not to resist. As long as she ate some Mimi would be happy. After eating a few bites she said, "Mimi that was really good but I need to go call Mae. She called in sick today."

Rubina stepped out the backdoor onto the stoop. She looked at the small garden her grandmother used to keep but not since the arthritis became too much for her. Ugly weeds and patches of grass littered the garden now. Rubina lit a cigarette and took out her cell phone. Mae picked up on the fifth ring. "What are you doing girl, letting it almost go to voicemail?" Rubina said.

"Nothing," Mae said and coughed loudly.

"You alright?"

"Yeah, yeah."

"Missed you at work today. Nobody showed up anyway. It was so boring."

"Yeah?"

"You know they closed the store 'until further notice?' So, you don't have to go in the rest of the week."

"That's cool," Mae said, coughing again.

"You're sick, aren't you?"

"Me? No, I just got this cough. I think I smoked too much this weekend."

"If you smoked normally it wouldn't mess you up as bad."

"Whatever. I've taken a ton of cough medicine so I'll probably be fine."

"Have you been watching this shit on the Rabbit Flu? It's all my grandmother can talk about. Same with the boss man at work."

"I've been watching it. But I don't have the Rabbit Flu."

"I didn't say you did, I was just worried, that's all."

"Thanks for the concern. Anyway, I'm going to go get some sleep."

"Feel better. You want me to come by, check on you tomorrow?"

"Call me."

"Ok, bye."

"Bye."

Rubina put her finished cigarette into the ceramic pot that had become home to an overflowing amount of cigarette butts. When her grandmother could make it outside, she would usually empty it, but she hadn't, and Rubina made a mental note she would forget the moment she walked in the door to dump the pot of cigarette butts.

| 16 |

Chapter Sixteen

James walked into his psychiatrist's office and noticed her nose red like she had been crying or sneezing a lot. "Are you alright?" he asked.

"What, this? Just a head cold I think."

"You sure? It could be the Rabbit Flu."

"Could be, but I'm not worried. Just congested, allergies probably, there's a lot of pollen. Didn't you have the Swine Flu last year?"

"How could I forget? Some asshole co-worker gave it to me. He got it from his daughter, then like a jerk he came into work and got me sick. That's why they give people sick days, am I wrong? He was a nice guy I guess, but what an ass for pulling that shit. I cursed his name while I was freezing under the covers."

"But you lived, right?"

"I'm here now, so yeah."

"I'll be fine. Don't worry. Why don't you sit down?"

He sat in the deep purple chair while she sat across from him. She adjusted herself in the way she liked to do, crossed her fat legs, which James imagined were all veiny and hairy, but he didn't know, she always wore pants, for which he was eternally grateful.

She started, "So what do you want to talk about James?"

"Nothing is coming to mind. What do you think?"

"Alright, what's a typical Friday night for you James?"

"You really want to know?"

"I asked, didn't I?"

"Ok then. I get home from work around six-thirty, then I smoke some weed. Then I eat some dinner, a frozen pizza or something. Then I'll smoke some more weed, maybe read or play video games. Around ten I'll hit up a bar nearby, the ones I go to are populated by hipster losers, these guys that spend so much time on their look only to make it seem like they didn't. Girls too. But I like checking out the girls; that look does it for me. I have a couple drinks, a few cigarettes, and then home to masturbate, then bed."

"Do you have any specific people you go to meet at these bars?"

"Nah, I mean I've made small talk with some of them at the bar, learned a few names, but nothing more than that. I'll usually talk to the bartender too. The one bar has this really cute bartender there. I'd ask her out, but I think she's married or something."

"Do you know for sure?"

"I don't. But what's the point?"

"The point in what?"

"In any of this? What you're asking."

"I want to know more about you James, that's all."

"Yeah, my really awesome life is eye opening I bet."

"Let me ask you a question."

"Ok."

"Do you think this girl, the bartender, is out of your league?"

"Probably, I mean she's really hot."

"So then, what's your plan? You're going to show up night after night-"

"I go to two bars."

"Ok, show up at one of two bars, night after night, have a few drinks, make some small talk, and then go home? Every night?"

"It seems to be working out so far."

"Seriously James. You need to make a choice."

"But isn't 'not making a choice' making a choice?"

"That's true, but it's a cop out and that doesn't make it ok or the best choice for you. You need to start thinking about what you want out of life. What's the overall point for you, for your life?"

"I don't know," he said, but he really wanted to scream it, "What's wrong with that? I'm not religious, so I don't want my spirituality spoon-fed to me, but I realize it's a big thing, just too big for me to deal with right now. And I'm ok with that."

"With what specifically?"

"With living. Just living, no more no less. I don't hurt anybody, I just keep to myself, work and come here. I don't see why I *need* a mate. A fuck buddy would be nice, but me and my hand are doing just fine so far."

She smiled. "James, I can't tell if you're being serious or joking."

"I'm serious. It's too much work, too much effort, to find a girl, keep a girl, or get a better job, or a job I might like more."

"But nothing worthwhile comes without effort. Life is hard, it takes effort. Don't let anyone tell you differently."

"But I think I'm content in my life."

"I don't think you are. Or else you wouldn't be here."

"Hmmph. Well maybe I don't need this either."

"Maybe you do, maybe you don't. Think about that for our next session."

"It's that time already? Wow the time just flies in here."

"That it does," she said and got up from her chair. She took a few tissues from a box on her desk and blew her nose loudly.

James went for the door and said on his way out, "I hope you feel better."

| 17 |

Three Days (before the End of the World)

Good morning this is Jonas Johnston with the latest news on the Rabbit Flu. Less than 24 hours after the first case of Rabbit Flu in the US we have reported cases of Rabbit Flu in every state as well as Mexico and Canada.

In an effort to keep Hawaii isolated from the Rabbit Flu all flights have been cancelled and no one is allowed to enter or leave the islands except authorized military and government personnel. The President is in route to Hawaii as of this moment. We have also learned that the President's oldest son has been infected with the Rabbit Flu and as such he is not accompanying the President to Hawaii.

We have reports of armed militias being formed with the intent of attaining a Rabbit Flu vaccine around the country and even in our own city. We have no world from the CDC or any other reputable news outlet that a vaccine exists or is available, however that is not stopping those currently outside hospitals, protesting and demanding one. As such city police in conjunction with the mayor's office have declared a 10pm curfew on all city and county residents. This will cover all businesses, bars and restaurants, and the curfew will continue, they said, until further word from the government.

Hospitals and clinics we are told cannot handle the overflow of patients and those who are exhibiting signs of the Rabbit Flu are advised to remain in their homes until further notice.

The Vice-President remains in Washington. Broadcasting on radio and television earlier today he urged calm and that citizens follow the law. He also said that non-peaceful protesting and rioting would not be tolerated, addressing the tension between protestors and police occurring at most hospitals. In response he announced the dispatch of National Guard troops to forty major US hospitals immediately, including our own South General and County hospitals here in the city.

He said those that attacked hospitals would be dealt with severely, however martial law would not be declared. "This is still America," the Vice President said. Finally, he repeated the advisory for citizens to stay in their homes unless it is absolutely necessary, even if they are not infected to prevent the spread of the virus.

Right now, we are going to bring you Dr. Albert Grasso coming to us from his home in Vermont. "Hello Dr. Grasso. What did you learn about the Rabbit Flu when you were in Australia Doctor?"

"It's, it's something…beautiful almost in its structure."

"That's…interesting. But what about practicality? Specifically, how is Rabbit Flu different from other epidemic and pandemic viruses we've seen in the last twenty or so years?"

"Ok take for example Ebola. Remember that disease from the mid-nineties? Ebola is a deadly virus but its problem with being a population destroyer is that its incubation time is extremely short. That's why whenever there was an Ebola outbreak, isolation of the infected usually prevents the disease from killing more than a few villages before it snuffs itself out.

Honestly, we do not have a comparable disease in history. Even the Bubonic Plague or the Spanish Flu pale in comparison to the Rabbit Flu."

"This is an unprecedented disease where humanity is concerned?"

"Unfortunately, yes."

"Is there anything else you can tell us about the Rabbit Flu?"

"The airborne status is what really sets it apart. Also, the four to six day incubation period has allowed HHDV to be carried and spread quickly, and that's why in under a week the whole world has been infected."

"Dr. Grasso, you've had extensive dealing with the Rabbit Flu, would you agree?"

"Yes, I have."

"And how many of your patients, how many have survived thus far?"

"Within the five-day period from initial infection to death we've only had one survive past the five days."

"Out of how many?"

"I'd say ten thousand that I've seen. Maybe more. In all honesty Jonas no doctor or scientist could have predicted how quickly RHDV would spread once it mutated and became HHDV. When it mutated and began infecting humans it didn't take 48 hours to kill, like it did in rabbits, instead it is taking four to six days.

Now that may not seem like a big difference in time but to a deadly disease it has made the difference between the deaths of few thousand people and billions. We don't know the exact percentages of how deadly this disease is, but I would say we're dealing with a disease that could possibly wipe out much of the human race."

"Um...I...don't know what to say."

"God help us all. I think those are the words you were looking for Jonas."

"Yes, yes thank you Dr. Grasso. Please take care of yourself."

"You as well Jonas."

| 18 |

Chapter Eighteen

Mimi wouldn't let Rubina leave the house. Mimi was providing constant updates on the Rabbit Flu, the militias, anything the news said. But Rubina was sleepwalking through, not paying attention, not wanting to pay attention.

Mimi was getting sicker by the moment; that much was true. Rubina made her soup she wouldn't eat, hot tea she wouldn't drink. Still Rubina made chicken noodle soup from a can and brought it to her grandmother. Rubina knocked on her bedroom door as she entered, "Mimi?"

"Yes dear?"

"I brought you some soup and some toast. You should try and eat some."

"But I'm not hungry."

"I say the same thing to you all the time, and what do you tell me? You need to try and eat something, for me."

"Ok," she said and sat up.

Rubina brought the bowl to her face, and Mimi took the spoon, had a couple sips. "That's enough Ruby, thank you."

"You're welcome, Mimi," Rubina said, then "Hey, the TV is off."

"Nothing new. No new information on the Rabbit Flu. I just can't watch anymore."

"They say TV rots your brain…" Rubina said but Mimi didn't get the joke.

"Come here Ruby," Mimi said and Rubina went to sit at the end of the bed.

"Ruby, you know how much I love you?"

"I know Mimi."

"I…I get the feeling like I'm nearing the end."

Rubina started to cry and went to hug her grandmother.

"It's ok Ruby, I've lived a good life. I don't want you to feel sorry for me."

"But Mimi…" Rubina said between sobs.

"I don't want you to worry. I'm going to a better place, I know it. But…but I'm worried about you Ruby." Mimi said.

"Why?" Rubina said.

"Because the world has changed, can't you feel it? You're not sick and I don't think you're going to get sick either. Call it a grandmother's intuition. We used to be scared something like this would happen. But we always thought it would be the Russians and nuclear war. Who would've thought it would be rabbits?" she coughed.

Rubina nodded. Mimi asked, "Can you get me some water Ruby?"

"Sure," and Rubina did so.

"Thank you," Mimi said as Rubina handed her the water. "Can you get the pills out of my bag?"

Rubina did as she asked. "How many do you want?"

"All of them." There was a large handful of pills left.

"Really Mimi? What type of pills are these?" she read the label. "Oxycontin? Where'd you get these?"

"When I had my hip surgery last year."

"If you take them all…" Rubina paused, "you'll die."

"I know. I'm going to take these pills, fall asleep, and never wake up."

"No! You can't Mimi," Rubina said and started to cry again.

"It's alright Ruby. I can feel my body failing; I know I'll be dead from this flu soon. I don't want to be in pain and I want you to be the last person I see."

Rubina continued crying. "Don't cry baby, its ok," Mimi said, then "give me the pills sweetie."

Rubina wasn't sure what to do so she hesitated. Her grandmother's eyes gave her a look like 'I know what I'm doing,' and Rubina reluctantly shook the pills out of the bottle and handed them to Mimi. "Before I take these," Mimi said, "I want you to know something."

"Yes Mimi?"

"I always loved you, you and your mom. I'm sorry things didn't work out better for you," Mimi said, and looked Rubina directly in the eyes. "But now you have a chance to remake your life how you want to. You need to be strong, no more tears, to get through what's to come. I have faith in you, have faith in yourself. I love you."

With that Mimi downed the pills in three large gulps. "Let me hold you, like I did when you were little, until I fall asleep."

"Ok Mimi," Rubina said and lay down on the bed with her grandmother.

| **19** |

Chapter Nineteen

Tyreke sat in his room watching his best friend Cedric sleep. Cedric was still alive, he was still breathing, but he was sick. Tyreke panned across his bedroom, saw the bookshelf with schoolbooks, posters of basketball and football players, pictures of cute girls cut from magazines. It was his first bedroom he had all to himself. Now that he had shared it with Cedric he didn't want it to become his room alone again.

He saw his old basketball in the corner of his room. It needed air, was dirty, and had lost its grip. His mother had bought it for him when they moved to the neighborhood and he had taken it to the park. That's when Tyreke met Cedric, playground basketball at the park.

"Shit man, you foul me like that again and I'm going Brother Theo style on your ass!" Cedric said and threw the ball at Tyreke. Pick-up basketball in the park sometimes got heated, but it was in good fun, and when they were done hours later both were sweaty and tired. Cedric approached Tyreke and said, "This is a nice ball. It yours?"

"Yeah."

"Here," Cedric said and spun a pass to Tyreke, which he couldn't handle. The ball stopped at the chain-link fence, and Tyreke went to pick it up. Cedric followed.

"You new here?" Cedric asked.

"Me and my mom just moved in with my aunt. She lives over there," Tyreke pointed to a tenement building across the street.

"Cool, I'm Ced. Short for Cedric."

"Tyreke."

"Let's go over to the water fountain; someone fixed it last week."

"Ok."

Tyreke, already six feet tall at twelve towered over his shorter and pudgier new friend, but still he walked behind Cedric. As they walked home Tyreke asked, "Who's Brother Theo?"

"You don't know? My brother told me about him. He runs this neighborhood and the Admiral Ray projects over there. He's a bad ass, rolls with two gold pistols, wears a long black duster and a bulletproof vest. He leads the Disciples."

"Hmm."

"He's a crazy killer. Kill you if you look at him wrong. Kills women, kids like us. A real bad dude. Always wears a crisp white baseball hat. You mean you ain't seen his guys around the neighborhood?"

"Don't know."

"He's got some on the corner up there. See their white hats, white armbands? That's them."

"Ok."

"You don't want to fuck with them. I heard they took one guy who was stealing from them and cut his balls off, then fed them to him. Nasty shit. Heard Brother Theo killed some lady who bit him while they were screwing. Cross the street if you see them just in case."

"Ok, I will."

"Hey can your aunt cook?"

"I think so, why?"

"Can I come over for dinner?"

"That should be cool."

Tyreke smiled at the memory and spun the basketball in his sizeable hands. Only sixteen years old, due to his size and stubble of facial hair, he could pass for nineteen or twenty easily. As he rubbed his chin hair he saw Cedric stirring under the covers. "Ced, you up?"

"Yeah," Cedric said and rubbed his tired eyes.

"How you feeling?"

"I'm doing. What you doing with that ball? You want to play?"

"Shut up man. I was just thinking about that first time on the court."

"When that ball was new."

"A lot of things used to be new Ced."

"Yeah."

| 20 |

Two Days (before the End of the World)

This is Jonas Johnston with a breaking news report. It appears that protests in front of the South General Hospital have now turned violent. For the last few days, the number of protestors demanding a vaccine and care for their sick loved ones has been growing in front of South General Hospital. Up until moments ago these protests had been relatively peaceful, however gunfire has erupted and fighting has ensued between the National Guard and the armed militia.

I apologize to our viewing public as we have no video but we do have audio contact with our reporter at the scene, Ginger Fontaine. "Ginger, can you hear me?"

"Yes, I can. Can you hear me?"

"Yes, just barely. Ginger, is that gunfire in the background, and more importantly are you alright?"

"Yes, it is and I am fine for now Jonas. My producer Glen and I are hiding on the second floor of a nearby office building. We lost our cameraman in the commotion, and he is nowhere to be seen.

We do have an excellent view of the chaos going on in front of South General Hospital."

"Can you tell us how this all started?"

"We were taping an on-air segment for the five o'clock news when a shot fired from the crowd hit a National Guardsman in the chest. In retaliation or possibly confusion the National Guard opened fire on the crowd. We were told they were using rubber bullets, but by the blood on the ground I don't know if that's true. All I know is that there are unmoving bodies, people screaming and crying, and shooting continuing between the troops and the militia, all in front of South General."

"Wow. I'm speechless Ginger..."

"It's a surreal scene here Jonas--"

"Ginger, what was that?"

"Someone's shooting at us...get down Glen!"

A window shattered. The microphone hit the ground with a loud thud. "Ginger, Ginger are you there? Are you ok?" Jonas said.

From farther away a man's voice said "Get back, get to the back of the building away from that window!"

"Ginger?" Jonas asked. There was no response. Only the crying, shooting, crumbling could be heard from Ginger's microphone. The station cut to a commercial about dish soap.

They returned three minutes later.

This is Jonas Johnston, back with you here on KRTV Morning News. We apologize for having to go to commercial abruptly moments ago. We have lost contact with reporter Ginger Fontaine, her producer Glen Richards and cameraman Barry Howell. We hope and pray they are alive and that they will be back here with us as soon as possible. I've just been told police have been called to the scene and should be there shortly.

For our listening public: It is advised to stay indoors if at all possible. Please do not go to South General Hospital for any reason.

We are still monitoring the microphone of our report team and will bring you any further information as we receive it. Take care of yourself out there.

| 21 |

Chapter Twenty-One

"Move, Move!" Major Jackson yelled at his squad. Their numbers were dwindling; he could see that clearly. They needed to get off the street. "Head for that garage door," he ordered. They crouched and moved behind bombed-out cars, past the dead and the dying. "Go, go, don't stop 'til we get inside!"

Jackson brought up the rear, firing at the last militiamen as he made his way into the empty garage. He dove inside and went skidding across the slick floor of the automotive station. Jackson got quickly to his feet. His men stood around him, waiting. "Secure this area. Everyone move away from any windows. Radio, what do we got?"

"I saw at least three pockets of gunfire out there. That's at least three healthy shooters."

"How 'bout us?"

"We got four healthy including you, three are sick, the rest of the squad are missing...or dead."

"Ok Radio, take the sick out of sight. Keep them away from windows. Find an office or something."

"Yes sir."

"Crudo you're our best remaining shot. Take the sniper rifle and head to the roof. They won't see you coming."

"Yes sir!"

"Hermes, go back outside, find a good spot. In two minutes, start firing. Doesn't matter at what, just keep yourself safe. We want to distract them so Crudo can hit 'em. You got it?"

"Yes sir."

Hermes made it back outside and crouched behind a cherry red pick-up truck. He scanned the scene through the scope on his rifle. He didn't see anything moving. Maybe they had got them all. Didn't matter though, he had his instructions. Hermes leaned against one of the pick-up's large tires and shot five rounds into the sky. Almost immediately he heard the return fire hitting the pick-up, the windows shattering. Hermes covered his head to block the falling glass.

He couldn't see Crudo, but he knew in about thirty seconds Crudo would see whoever was shooting at them. It didn't even take that long. "Hey Hermes, up here," Crudo was standing on top of the building, looking down at Hermes.

"I got those fuckers! Woo-hoo!" Crudo said, then to Hermes "You know from up here I could piss right on you?"

"Go fuck yourself," Hermes said and gave Crudo the middle finger.

"Yeah, you know where you can stick that," Crudo said laughing. "Get back inside and I'll tell you all about my sharpshooting."

| 22 |

Chapter Twenty-Two

James watched the anarchy from his window. It was surreal, but he couldn't look away. Not that he had anything else to do anyway. He watched the looters first, throwing bricks, trash cans, whatever could be used to break glass through shop windows. He watched the looters carry away televisions and microwaves, computers and vacuums, why didn't these people understand, these items, these things wouldn't help them, not even in the short term. But it didn't stop them. The police didn't stop them either as James did not see one cop in his time watching. They had bigger fish to fry he assumed.

Next it was the fires. Overturned cars for no apparent reason set on fire, like their sports team had just won the championship. But there were no riot police. He heard on the news the worst fighting was happening at the hospitals. Even though the news had said there was no vaccine, no cure for the Rabbit Flu people still went to the hospitals. Maybe they went for painkillers, anything to ease the pain of dying of Rabbit Flu.

James continued watching the streets but as of now they were empty. The life was sucked right out of the neighborhood. It was like the aftermath of a tornado, broken glass, overturned cars, somebody had even taken to cutting down the trees. James had watched the man with a chainsaw cut down a large birch; even the other looters and rioters gave the man with the chainsaw a wide berth. But he wasn't long for the world; he was shot and his chainsaw stolen.

Now he looked at the birch tree that was one quarter cut, and wondered if that was enough to take it down. James didn't think so, as it was still standing with the body of the chainsaw man lying face down underneath it, dried blood covering his head and the ground around it.

But at least in his apartment, behind the thin window pane, he was safe. At least he felt safe. The moans, coughing and dying that was going on within his building was another story. He had barricaded the door with his sofa but the sounds still crept in.

James knew those people were in pain but couldn't bring himself to help. What could he do really? He didn't have a cure. James didn't know his neighbors, one of the perks of living in the city he always had thought. He had manners, would say hello if he saw a neighbor in the hallway, would hold the entryway door open for the old ladies with their groceries and the young mothers with their multiple kids. Friendly but not friends he would say. But still he didn't know them and felt no empathy toward them. They were just a few of the billions dying; he couldn't help them, he couldn't save them all, so why bother trying to help a few?

His parents only lived a couple of hours away by car, but when he called them, they told him not to come. It was the last time he spoke with them or any other person for that matter.

"It's alright James, it'll probably pass," his mother said.

"Mom, seriously no it won't. I want to be there with you."

"The roads are backed up with traffic for miles they say and there are riots everywhere. You'll never get here."

"So what? I'm coming over."

"James, no," his father said, also on the line, "You're not sick. We are. We have the symptoms. There's nothing that can be done. We won't have you die for nothing."

James was crying. "I love you guys so much," he said.

"We know son," his mother said, "We love you too much to let you risk your life. Your father and I agree on this. And who knows? Maybe we'll get better. You never know with these things."

"Mom, you're always being positive. I love you."

"I love you too. I'm going to go lay down, your father wants to speak with you alone."

"I love you mom," James said through sobs.

"James?"

"Yeah Dad?"

"James, you're my only son..." his father said, "...and now is going to be the most important time of your life. Your whole life you're been preparing for this time, even though you didn't know it. I have faith you're going to make it through; you're a survivor, don't forget that."

"Thanks Dad," James said.

"We don't have much time. I want you know I love you, and I'm sorry if I didn't say---"

The call dropped, and the line went dead. "Fuck!" he said. He tried to call them back but got the horrible "all circuits are busy now. Please try your call again later." He hated that voice. James threw the phone across the room. It crashed with little fanfare. "Fuck! Why the fuck is this happening to me?"

| 23 |

Chapter Twenty-Three

"What the hell happened out their Major? You were there to keep the peace, not kill Americans on television!" the Lieutenant Colonel yelled from Central Command, hundreds of miles from the remaining troops in the city.

"I know sir. Things got out of hand. They fired at us first."

"I don't care! It turned into a bloodbath, and now it's all over the national news."

"I am sorry sir. It couldn't be helped."

The Lieutenant Colonel coughed loudly and then cleared his throat. "I take it you are in a secure location Major?"

"Yes sir. We have sustained injuries and casualties however sir."

"How many men do you left?"

"Four healthy sir, including myself. Three sick sir." Major Jackson said.

"How long do you think the sick ones have?"

"I don't know. Not long sir."

"You're going to move on without them. Your orders are to secure a location in one of the tallest buildings in the area with visibility of the South Highway. Do not allow any people to leave the city. Anyone seen trying to leave you need to shoot to kill on sight."

"Sir? If they are able to move at this point, they're probably not infected."

"Major we are taking no chances, understood? Let me reiterate: Shoot to kill on sight. After seven days we will send in choppers and pick up the remaining survivors in your squad. Once you arrive transmit that location to us."

"Why seven days sir?"

"Not that I have to tell you, but in these circumstances I will. Our scientists have determined that that seven days from now the disease should burn itself out, and we may be able to save some of the rural citizens. We're trying to prevent the spread of the Rabbit Flu to the countryside."

Jackson was silent. 'So, killing people who were shooting at them at the hospital was a bad thing, but shooting people trying to simply leave the city is a good thing? What a world…' he thought.

"So now you know. Do what you've been ordered to do and wait for further instructions. Good luck Major."

Jackson's father, grandfather, two uncles, one great uncle, and two cousins were all in the National Guard. He was a soldier and he followed orders. He protected his state, his country, and his fellow citizens so he understood and would do what the Lieutenant Colonel ordered. Jackson took the Lieutenant Colonel's message to his men. "We're to monitor South City, prevent anyone from leaving down the southern highway. Those are our orders men. Now, Radio, tell us what you know about South City."

"South City has a thirty-block radius, to the north is the Downtown, north of that is North City, to the northwest is the West City, and we got water to the east. Populated mostly by blacks and Hispanics, some left over Irish and Italians that didn't leave during the white flight, and the Admiral Ray projects. Mostly tenement buildings built right on top of each other. Three gun shops, four pawn shops with weapons, twenty liquor stores, one hospital, two large grocery stores, a lot more smaller convenience stores."

Radio took a deep breath. Jackson said, "Good, continue."

"As of the last census there are around two million people living in south city. If the Rabbit Flu is as effective as we've heard, that it would take out 99% of humanity that would leave about 20,000 people in the area. If 99.9% than only 2000 people. If 99.99% only 200. If 99.999%..."

"Ok Radio, I think we get it."

"That doesn't include those that died in fighting with us, or by other means."

"Understood. Now our orders are to find an appropriate spot to watch the South Highway," Jackson said.

"There's a building on the corner of Grand and East Avenue; should get us the best view."

"Alright men, let's move out."

"Wait, Major, what about them?" a Private named Hermes motioned to the room where coughing and low moaning and dying was coming from.

"They're sick. You know that."

"What about the shot?"

"The shot?"

"You know, the vaccine they gave us before we left."

Every solider upon departing the base was given a shot, told it was a Rabbit Flu vaccine, told they would not get sick. Jackson started with thirty soldiers guarding the hospital. Half were sick within hours of their arrival, dead days after that. A few of his men fought it longer but now they were going to die in the backroom of car repair shop. Now he had four healthy soldiers including himself, and if what Radio said was right about the numbers then maybe the vaccine did work, at least partially. But Jackson didn't have time to worry about that.

"It doesn't work, far as I can tell."

"Then why'd they give it to us?"

"Don't know, maybe to keep us sane."

"But it had to have worked. I mean, we're still alive. Four healthy soldiers, what are the chances? I mean, if the Rabbit Flu kills 99% of everyone living, there's no way the four of us are still well. The chances are astronomical."

"I'm not a math major Hermes, but I know that we're alive and not sick," Jackson said as he lit a cigarette, "Our brothers over there are not going to make it. If the odds fall in our favor this time, I'll take it. I don't know what else to tell you."

"But…"

"What do you want to do? We can't carry them; we can't wait with them. You want to shoot them, put them out of their misery?"

"Well…no."

"They're comfortable in these beds; they're not going to live much longer, at least if what we know is true. I'll go with you. We'll offer to shoot them if they want us to. We owe them that."

"Yes sir."

Hermes and Jackson asked each dying soldier what he wanted. The dying soldiers asked them if they were going to be left there, in the auto body shop, to die. Jackson didn't lie. He told them "Yes." He asked if they wanted him to shoot them, and each soldier nodded. He shot each one in the temple, and the three shots reverberated in the large shop.

Hermes stood, frozen in place as he looked at his dead fellow soldiers. "C'mon Hermes, those shots are going to draw attention," Jackson said, "We have to move out."

"Yeah, alright," Hermes said as he fingered the gold cross around his neck and prayed silently to himself.

The day (before the End of the World)

Good morning, this is Jonas Johnston. As far as I can tell we are the last remaining network on air, in which case, I welcome all of our viewers.

We still have not heard word from our missing reporting team. In fact, our entire crew and staff are all not here today, and as such I am running this show on my own today. It's been a while since I've done this, so no make-up and only one camera unfortunately. I apologize in advance for my candor, I know the Rabbit Flu has infected and killed your loved ones, and mine as well. But I feel it is my duty as reporter of the news to provide you as much information as I can.

Let's start with what we know, which isn't as much as I would like, but it is what it is. Worldwide death and dying tolls from the Rabbit Flu are believed to be in the billions however it has been extremely difficult to confirm these numbers. We have not had any international correspondence for days including electronic mail. Internet websites from Europe, Asia, and Oceania have not been updated in the past 24 hours, and servers have gone down as well in the Eastern Hemisphere.

We have had no word from the CDC for last two days, and rumors abound as to if and when a vaccine will be released, and also what is happening inside the CDC facility in Atlanta. Early this morning I received a message from our Atlanta correspondent saying:

"Two days ago, at around 9:30am, a caravan of four vehicles, two official town cars with tinted windows and two portable lab stations, came through the entrance gates for the Center of Disease Control. We were unable to ascertain what they were doing or who or what they were transporting. Since then, there has not been any person or vehicle going into or coming out of the facility. Gates are locked; there are no visible guards. Calls and emails have not been returned from CDC officials."

That message was left overnight. I have been unable to get in contact with the reporter who left the message.

Rioting across our nation centered on hospitals and pharmacies searching for an unconfirmed vaccine caused many unnecessary deaths. However now it appears the Rabbit Flu has taken hold of the population and quiet has ensued across our city and our country.

Moments before I came on the air a fax from the President of the United States addressed to all news outlets came through. The President in Hawaii, in conjuncture with the Vice President in Washington, have now declared martial law for the entire contiguous United States. A little late in my opinion as I don't know who will enforce the law but that our President and Vice-President are still alive and well, we should all take as a good sign.

Specific instructions include: the cessation of television, radio and internet communication except for official government use, restricted use of interstate highways except for military personnel, a dusk curfew, and a warning that visibly armed civilians will be shot on sight. Martial law goes into effect immediately for those watching. As such this will be the last KRTV Channel Six broadcast for the foreseeable future.

For those of you out there listening, those of you not sick, keep your head up. The world is not over for you. Actually, it will just be beginning. It will be your job to re-build our great nation. You are not alone. Work together, take care of each other, see the massive amount of death and do not add to it. God bless you, God bless those infected, God bless America, and God help us all.

| **25** |

Chapter Twenty-Five

Jonas left the news studio knowing it would be his final time seeing it. His technical director had left two days earlier to be with his family, and Jonas had seen no one since. He put on the final newscast alone and hoped it provided some kind of comfort to his viewers if any of them were still out there watching.

He took the stairs down the twenty-three floors to the mezzanine; no one was around. He saw the metal detectors, a necessity following September 11th, unused. Jonas remembered all the people that would line up every morning to pass through the metal detectors on their way to work. It was like going to the airport every day. He remembered Shauna the homely security guard who he would say hello to every morning. He hadn't seen her in a week.

He stopped by the café which still had rolls and muffins in a plastic display case and took out a banana nut muffin. It felt weird to him not paying for it, but this was the new world he told himself and things you want you can take. 'Money becomes worthless, only living has any value anymore.' It was a weird realization.

He nibbled on his muffin as he left the lobby. It was a short, five-block walk to his condo, but all the while his ears were assaulted by ambulance sirens and car and store alarms. It felt like a war zone like when he was a much younger reporter in Split during the Yugoslav wars in '93. Broken glass was all over the sidewalk, but it was like that on the way in. The smell of burnt toast permeated the air. He saw many crashed cars but no people. They were around, he just knew it. They had to be. Somebody else had to be alive.

His wife was dead in their bed; she died earlier that morning before he came in to do the last newscast. He didn't want to leave her there but he felt he had an obligation to the living. Jonas knew that when he returned to their condo she would still be there, under the sheets, dead. He couldn't bury her. He didn't see a point in it and would rather leave her in their bed, peaceful and pure.

He had left his bedroom door closed when he had left earlier and it was still closed when he returned. His thoughts turned to Ginger, Glen and the cameraman. He was a new cameraman and Jonas couldn't remember his name. It aggravated him. 'What happened to them? Hopefully they're alive,' Jonas thought but deep down he knew their chances of survival were the same as his wife's.

He thought about Ginger. They had slept together but only a couple of times, before she called it off. Now he felt bad for his wife. His dead wife.

He went to his liquor cabinet and took out a bottle of expensive whiskey. Normally he never drank more than two glasses. This evening, he planned on having more than two. He poured himself a large glass, added a couple ice cubes, and sat on his way too expensive couch. Then he poured himself another and said "I'm getting drunk tonight," before downing it.

| **26** |

Chapter Twenty-Six

Tyreke was standing on top of his one-hundred-year-old brownstone apartment building looking at the streets below. The flat black asphalt roof with ancient chimney stacks, abandoned chicken coops and the remnants of a homemade garden remained. Large puddles dotted the roof due to rain from the night before.

Tyreke put his hand on the rusted guard rail and peered over the side. Usually, the hot dog vendor or the ice cream man would be on the sidewalk, kids would be playing basketball on the asphalt court, women and men and kids would be moving, going to work, school, to hang out, get lunch. But today nothing was moving, only a gentle breeze swaying the trees below.

After surveying the city from two sides of the roof Tyreke sat on an ancient wooden chair that had always been there, looking at nothing. He remembered watching his mother sitting up here before, legs crossed, thinking and smoking long, thin cigarettes. As a child he would sneak out after her, making sure she didn't hear the door open and then close again behind him. She didn't know he was watching her and it gave him a glimpse of his mother he usually never saw. There was something regal about watching her think and relax, so peaceful and pure to young Tyreke.

Tyreke still had on his school uniform, navy blue polo and khaki shorts, white socks and even whiter sneakers. School had been closed for two days but Tyreke hadn't thought about changing his clothes.

His mother had taken his younger sister to the hospital two days ago, and hadn't returned. Tyreke knew something was wrong. It was sitting in his stomach churning as he played video games, read books, checked on Ced. His mother told him not to leave the apartment; that she would be back for him. She hugged him so hard he felt he might pop. Then she took his younger sister and they left.

She said they'd be back but that wasn't true. She had lied, not on purpose, so Tyreke didn't hold it against her. He knew they were both dead. That feeling was ever present, and he didn't want it to be true, but it was. At least he still had Cedric but who knew for how much longer.

Cedric and Tyreke were best friends since they met, brothers from another mother, they would say about each other. Once people started dying Tyreke prayed that Cedric would be ok. More than his mom, more than his half-sister, more than himself even, Tyreke wanted his best friend to live.

Cedric got sick later than most but was still sick. He had spent the last couple days in Tyreke's bed, in pain, slowly dying. Cedric never knew his dad, and his mom had her own problems, so for the last year Cedric slept on Tyreke's floor. When Cedric got sick Tyreke gave him his bed.

Tyreke was a head taller than most kids his age, and everyone wanted him to play basketball. He enjoyed playing; the problem was he wasn't very good. But that didn't stop everyone he knew from talking to him about it. It was expected that he would be a great basketball player.

Everyone expected it, from his aunties and uncles to the kids at school, the corner store shopkeeper, even his mother, everyone except his best friend Cedric. They would go to the park to shoot around, just be kids, and there would always be someone to challenge Tyreke to a game. "What's up big man?" They would say, "I bet you got game, what's say we play?"

"Nah, man, I'm just fooling around," Tyreke would respond.

"Seriously man, you a giant, I bet you can ball, let's play," they would continue to try and convince him.

Cedric, a foot shorter than Tyreke, would step in. "My man says he doesn't want to play, so he's not going to play. Leave him be." Cedric moved in front of Tyreke.

"Who the fuck are you little man?" The man saying it was over six feet tall, standing with another guy about that same height.

"Cedric, that's who," and he lifted up his shirt to reveal a shiny silver gun.

"Alright, bro, we just wanted to play, no need for all that." Cedric intensely stared at them with a slight grin as they slowly backed away.

"You don't have to do that," Tyreke told him after the other guys were gone.

"It ain't no thing," Cedric said, "we were just goofing around anyways."

"Yeah, yeah, I know," Tyreke said as he took the last shot of the afternoon, the ball hitting the rim with a thud.

Tyreke loved to remember that story. He didn't want to have to grow up so fast. But now it wasn't up to him and he knew it. Sitting on the roof, like he always did, almost stopped time. There wasn't a building full of dead of dying people below. His best friend wasn't one of them, wasn't sick. 'Why couldn't this be?' he thought. 'What am I going to do? Why am I not sick and Cedric is? He's tough enough to handle this, I'm not. This isn't fair.'

Once these questions and thoughts came to Tyreke he knew he had to go back inside to face his current reality. He looked at the poorly painted wooden door that led back into the apartment building, sighed, and turned the rusted handle.

| 27 |

Chapter Twenty-Seven

Rubina woke up before the sun came up with her dead grandmother's arm still over her. Her arm had become cold and clammy but it didn't bother Rubina. She slipped out from under her grandmother's arm and stood over her. She looked like she was sleeping and Rubina gave her a kiss on the cheek and said, "Goodbye Mimi, I love you," with tears on her cheeks.

Rubina wiped her tears away with her hands and pulled the blanket over her grandmother. She turned out the light and closed the door. She used the wall to support herself on the way to her bedroom. Adorned with high school pictures, the cross-country team, her friends, parties, her dressed as Strawberry Shortcake for Halloween when she was seventeen, and there was her best friend Mae as Supergirl.

'Mae, shit I forgot about Mae!' Rubina thought and was awakened from her stupor. Mimi had occupied her thoughts and actions completely. Mimi was her mother, father, everything. But now Mimi was gone, and she had forgotten about her best friend. 'What kind of a friend, what kind of a person am I?' she thought as she ran through the house looking for her phone.

"Please, please pick up," Rubina said as she listened to the phone ring. 'C'mon, it had to work,' she told herself, 'It just had to.'

The phone finally did pick up, on the fifth ring. Rubina heard it pick up, but no one said anything. "Mae, Mae you there?" Rubina said.

Almost an inaudible "yes" came through the phone.

"Mae is that you? It's Ruby."

"I'm here," Mae said weakly.

"You don't sound good. I'm coming over."

Rubina stepped outside her grandmother's house. The air was dry and there was a slight breeze. Summertime was almost here but it didn't feel right. It was quiet but not silent. Far off car alarms and business alarms were singing. Rubina saw no people, no apparent life. The streets were empty, all the cars parked neatly on the street or in their driveways. Rubina went to her car and started the short drive to Mae's.

She stopped at a red light, and looked around. There were no other cars, but she heard an engine far off. Straight ahead a small speck became larger, and she could tell it was a jeep, going fast. Really fast. Heading right toward her. 'What the fuck?' she thought and almost dropped her cigarette. Instinctively she put took her foot off the brake, still looking up at the red light.

Rubina sped up moving to the farthest right lane, and the on-coming car followed her.

It was getting closer, faster. She put her hand on the horn, trying to get them to stop, to not hit her. The other was car was heading right for her. Rubina said, "fuck it then," and as the jeep approached, she cut the wheel, and was on the sidewalk, knocking over a restaurant's outdoor plastic tables.

The jeep missed her, hit the curb, and landed upside down in a sandwich shop. She drove the car off the sidewalk back onto the street and stopped. She adjusted the rearview mirror and looked at the jeep. Smoke was coming from the engine and a man fell out the driver's side door. He was bleeding and the smoke was getting worse. He was crawling away from the wreckage and Rubina saw his face. Blood was running from a gash on his forehead. What haunted her for days was the fact that he was laughing a maniacal laugh, like a cartoon villain. Rubina hit the gas and left the man to his fate.

"Mae, where are you?" Rubina didn't knock, just entered her friend's small apartment.

She got no response and found Mae in her bedroom. Mae was lying on her side in bed, her back to Rubina. Rubina touched her on the shoulder and said "Mae, hey Mae wake up."

Mae made a small sound and Rubina sighed. "Thank god."

"What time is it?" Mae asked as she rubbed her eyes.

"Seven-thirty. You are not going to believe what just happened to me."

"You're not sick?" Mae asked.

"Don't think so. I feel fine."

"That's some bullshit, ain't it?" Mae said, tried to laugh but coughed instead. "Hand me that glass of water would you?"

Rubina did and Mae took three large gulps. "I've never been so thirsty."

"It's ok, I'm here," Rubina said. "What can I do?"

Mae shrugged and said "The news didn't say anything about what to do if you get the Rabbit Flu..."

"What about the hospital? I know they said there's no vaccine but maybe they have something and they didn't want to tell everybody."

"I don't know. Maybe. The news said there was rioting and shooting there."

"You think you can even make it to the hospital?"

"I can try."

"But there's probably no one there, definitely no doctors," Rubina said.

"Probably not, but you don't know for sure. If there's a chance…"

"I know what the news said."

"But you're not sick! Fuck you! I'm fucking dying, I know it, and you can't do this for me? What kind of best friend are you?"

"Fuck me! Fuck you! I almost got killed by some psycho coming over here, for you! My grandma's dead, lying in her bed! Shit!" she said and pounded her fist on the bed.

"I'm sorry Ruby, I didn't know…"

"It's alright Mae, I'm sorry too," Rubina said.

Rubina fidgeted with her keys, Mae twirled her hair around her finger like a little girl. 'It's not my fault, it's not my fault,' Rubina thought. Then she said "Fine. I'll take you. The hospital is what, like three miles away? We'll have to drive."

"Ok," Mae said, "Hey Ruby?"

"Yeah what?"

"Thanks."

"You'd do the same for me, I hope. You want me to put together a bag for you?" Rubina asked.

"Yeah sure," Mae said and slowly got out of bed.

"Where's your suitcase? In the closet?" Rubina started looking through the closet.

"It's in the back," Mae said as she took clothes out of her dresser and laid them on the bed. Rubina stopped her and said, "I got it, why don't you go to the bathroom, get anything you'll need."

Rubina helped Mae into her car and they drove to the hospital. The streets were still empty as Rubina drove. She told Mae what happened to her earlier. "And he was smiling? That's fucked up Ruby."

"I know, right? It was fucked. Glad we don't have to drive by there."

As she drove still obeyed the traffic lights even after her experience earlier. The rules were in place for a reason and it was just instinct that she didn't want to break them. They got within a mile of the hospital when they ran into the traffic jam. All the lanes, even the ones supposed to be going the other way were packed with abandoned cars. It didn't matter the make or model, Lexus', BMWs, Hondas, old Buicks and Cadillacs, all empty, some with their doors wide open.

"Looks like we weren't the only ones with this idea," Rubina said, "Can you walk a bit Mae?"

"I think so."

Rubina saw the first dead body, face down, blood soaking the blue flannel shirt of the dead man. "Mae, look!" Rubina said.

Mae saw the body and said, "I heard about this on the news. My Lord…"

"Holy shit! There's more up there." Rubina didn't want to sound excited, she wasn't, but this whole experience was new and her voice couldn't hide it.

"Oh, that smell, it's awful," Mae said and covered her nose with the sleeve on her shirt.

"Be careful where you step," Rubina said.

"Ew, gross, I don't even want to look down."

More dead bodies greeted them as they neared the bright red Emergency Room sign. There had been no clean up attempt, no attempt to do anything.

A little girl no more than five was dead right outside the Emergency Room entrance, still holding a blonde doll, one eye open, still faced the sky above. A large professional looking video camera was missing its lens and looked somehow lost. A soldier was crumpled on the steps; his right leg below the knee was missing. No National Guard troops or militiamen or even police remained. No one was alive outside the hospital.

They reached the automatic doors into the emergency room and went inside. The low moaning began as soon as they walked inside. People were lying on the floor, slumping in chairs, some not moving at all. It was like they were zombies or heroin junkies maybe. Rubina ushered Mae to the front desk, but no one was there. "Hello? Hello?" she called and looked around.

"No nurses. No doctors either," a young girl in a pink hooded sweatshirt said. She looked about fifteen years old and a blond swatch of hair hung coolly on her face. She was using a washcloth on the forehead of man who looked old enough to be her dad.

"Oh," Rubina said.

"Stay out of room 103, we cleared it out. That's *our* room. All the others, there's still people in them, but…"

"I get it. Thanks," Rubina said, "You want to lay down Mae?"

Mae nodded. Rubina walked arm-in-arm with her friend, glancing in the open doors as they walked down the hallway. She saw bodies lying in the beds, under clean white sheets, not moving. Rubina hoped they weren't dead, but she knew better.

They went to the first room they saw, room 101. There were two beds, both with bodies in them. "They're dead, aren't they Ruby?"

"Why don't you sit in the hallway while I clean out the room, get the bed ready, ok?" Rubina said and helped Mae into a plastic chair in the hallway.

Rubina closed the door to the room, and checked under the sheets. She wished she hadn't. They weren't disgusting or bloody, but they were dead. One was a teenage boy, couldn't have been older than thirteen. In the other bed was a petite middle-aged woman, and by their faces Rubina thought there was a good chance they were related.

Rubina wasn't strong enough to lift either, so she pushed the woman's body onto the floor as gently as she could. Then she dragged it under the bed of the teenager, and she pulled the curtain closed around them. 'Out if sight, out of mind' she told herself.

Then she looked through drawers and found clean sheets. She stripped the bed the woman was in and threw the sheets under the curtain. Rubina made the bed and then went to get Mae. She helped Mae into bed and pulled the covers up over her. In moments Mae was sleeping and Rubina was left with her thoughts.

| 28 |

Chapter Twenty-Eight

Nadia cried as she pounded on the steering wheel. She was in her yellow Nissan on the parking level of her boyfriend's condominium building. She'd been taking care of her boyfriend but this morning he died. Rabbit Flu had gotten him like so many others. She didn't know what to do with his body; it was too heavy for her to lift, and in the city, where was she going to bury him?

She had been watching the news reports and she knew what was going on just outside. It wasn't safe outside, at least it didn't seem to be. She watched from the windows as the streets got quieter and quieter, fewer cars every hour, even less people. The news told her not to take him to the hospital; it was too dangerous. Nadia had wanted to ignore the news reports and take him to the hospital but he had said no, that if he was going to die, he wanted to do it in his own bed. She held him last night and when she went to sleep, he was alive. In the morning, this morning, he wasn't. He was gone.

The depression set in almost immediately. Nadia blamed her piece of crap father that had left her with her mentally unstable mother. She hadn't seen her mother since she turned eighteen two years ago. 'They're both probably dead from the Rabbit Flu, and it served them right,' she thought, 'but I'm still pissed. And scared. I don't want to be left alone. Anything but alone.'

Pete had been there for her. Even if it wasn't the best relationship, he still would hold her, tell her everything was alright. He was there for her. But now he was dead, everyone she probably knew was dead or dying, at least if the news was telling the truth. Nadia couldn't and didn't want to deal with the loneliness, not anymore, not after Pete died.

The keys were in the ignition; she could go anywhere she wanted. But Nadia knew that wasn't true. She was stuck; this was the end of the line for her. The fear wouldn't let her go. Maybe she wouldn't get sick, but maybe she would? The news didn't say. She didn't want to die like Pete and all those other people did. At least Pete went in his sleep. Better that than to die by a bullet or worse.

She was there for Pete, her smiling face comforting him, her warm body next to his, keeping him warm. But who was here to comfort her, to tell her everything was going to be alright? 'No one,' Nadia thought, 'Better to just do it myself.'

She had the pill bottle; prescription sleeping pills Pete had been using for insomnia. She knew they were strong; he told her he took half a pill whenever he couldn't sleep. Nadia knew if she took them all she wouldn't wake up.

'Dying was easier than living,' Nadia had read that somewhere, and absolutely agreed. The time was rapidly approaching. There was no reason for a note, no loved ones to say goodbye to or give a reason to. Whoever found her would understand, how could they not? She felt an easing calm come over her and she smoked a cigarette with the window down. 'My last smoke,' she thought. She took the contents of the pill bottle with a flat, twenty-ounce soda that she had bought days earlier.

She tapped on the steering wheel waiting for the pills to kick in while her tears dried on her cheeks. Nadia wanted to extend her legs fully but they were too long for her tiny car. That always annoyed her about the car but it didn't matter anymore.

Nadia finished her cigarette and flicked it out the car window. She was getting tired. "Goodbye cruel, cruel world," she said, then "God how stupidly cliché I sound…" Her eyes slowly flickered before closing completely.

THE DAY AFTER THE END OF THE WORLD

Part II: Fallout

| 29 |

Chapter Twenty-Nine

Franklin would wake every morning to the 6:30am local news coming through static from the AM dial on his clock radio. He'd hit the snooze button initially, but the second time he would lie with his eyes closed and just listen, well at least he did, before the Rabbit Flu. But the Rabbit Flu was nothing new as the news always was about death. "One man died in a train accident early this morning. Two people overnight were shot and killed in a convenience store robbery. An elderly couple died in a house fire on the 7300 block of Wellington..."

Death to Franklin was a constant, even if most things in life weren't. Death and taxes, wasn't that the old saying? Franklin paid his taxes on time, but sometimes he felt he was simply waiting to die.

Franklin would check his computer every morning while he ate breakfast wanting, rather needing, to know the overnight death toll. He didn't need names, hell the news reporters rarely provided names anyway, and it wasn't like someone Franklin knew was going to die since he knew too few people. But the deaths, the myriads of ways people can, do and will die was fascinating to him. He didn't think he was all that out of the ordinary. If people as a whole weren't interested, he would say obsessed, with death, there wouldn't be so much information pertaining to it. It wouldn't take up so much of the news anyway.

Fighting off death with anti-aging techniques, ancient Chinese secrets to extend lifespan, Viagra to extend a man's penis, so we can go on fucking and making more babies and extend the whole human race. 'Didn't matter everyone was going to die sometime, and the more spectacular, the more unique and special the death, all the better,' he had often thought.

Franklin knew it was all right there, out in the open. Death led the news, didn't matter if it was the morning, afternoon or evening editions, in every media market in the US. Franklin would watch the news and think to himself, 'that's not the way I want to go. No sir, I want to go in my sleep. Once I'm old and ready. Comforting to think that instead of 'I want to get in a car wreck going eighty miles an hour and be decapitated by the passenger door of the car I hit.'

Franklin was a customer service rep for a large health insurance company. He worked from home, and only went to the office for training on new policies and plans every ten weeks. He ordered clothes, food, movies, books, paid his bills, did his banking, escorts, everything online because he couldn't deal with mass groups of people. It took a lot for him to attend the training meetings but he made good money and lived frugally.

Once he heard about the first death from Rabbit Flu he placed a food order for one months' food, instead of his usual one week. After their first encounter the food delivery guy knew to leave the delivery at the door and knock three times. Then he left and Franklin always watched him through the peephole. Once Franklin heard the elevator doors close, he opened his condo door.

The last order took him three trips to bring all the food inside. 'Just in case. Always better to be prepared,' he thought, 'And now if

I don't have to leave the condo nothing is forcing me. At least for a month, maybe two. But then what?' Franklin put the last thought out of his head as quickly as he could. 'One day at a time,' he had to remind himself. But that thought didn't give him solace, and he kept thinking about it. 'What if I do need to leave?' If so, he had to check his car.

He walked toward the elevator as he normally did. All the doors were closed as usual but he heard the soft meows and whines of pets. 'How long until they eat their dead owners?' Franklin thought. He couldn't feed them all even if he wanted to, and on top of that he was allergic, so he wasn't even contemplating the idea and put the pet sounds out of his head.

The wide hallway with its fifteen-foot-high ceilings and burgundy carpeting felt unusually stuffy and there was an odor like something he hadn't smelled before. It wasn't a good smell. Franklin covered his mouth and nose with his hand and headed for the stairs.

When he arrived at the garage level Franklin was winded. He couldn't remember the last time he had used the stairs. He had purchased an all-in-one piece of exercise equipment, used it for a month, and now it became a place to hang up clothes. 'What was the point of working out?' he reasoned to himself, 'I'm not trying to attract a mate.' Franklin was happy with his daily masturbation, once in the morning, then again before bed, with the occasional escort girl on special occasions, like his birthday. Anything else took more effort than he was willing to exert.

Franklin was surprised to see only his forest green Cadillac and a yellow Nissan on the whole level. He almost hoped for a huge SUV, or a pick-up, even better a monster truck, something to get him away if need be.

But by not trying his neighbors' doors Franklin had not dealt with the possible dead body problem. He hoped that everyone had just disappeared, vanished without a trace. He never wanted to come across a human carcass, and when he looked over into the Nissan, he never wanted his mother more.

| 30 |

Chapter Thirty

Cedric had been moaning in pain all morning and Tyreke couldn't take it anymore. He heard faint moaning and cries for help from all over the building the last couple of days. 'Like a bunch of dying cats,' Tyreke thought. Even in the summer heat he had to close the windows to keep the noise out. Today though the sounds coming from the other apartments ceased, and the Cedric's troubled breathing was the only sound he heard.

Tyreke figured he would have to leave the apartment soon. He assumed that eventually the electricity would go out, and he wouldn't be stuck here in the dark, on the fifth floor, not with all the dead bodies and the smell and the fear. He wanted Cedric to come with him but knew that wasn't going to happen.

Cedric was lying in a ball, with his knees in his chest, shivering. Tyreke put a black and red checkered blanket on him and made sure it would stay, tucking it under Cedric's shrinking body. Cedric hadn't said much in the last twenty-four hours, but he had to have the talk with him. Tyreke couldn't sleep listening to the wails of Cedric that went on intermittently all night.

"Ced, hey Ced," Tyreke said softly while nudging Cedric on the shoulder to try and wake him up.

"Wah, what?" Cedric said.

"Man, you alright?"

"Man, I was dreaming," he mumbled as he went to sit up.

"What about?"

"What about what?" Cedric said, rubbing his eyes.

"What was your dream about?"

"Oh yeah, right. We were in school in Mrs. Shawberger's class, and I'm in the back of the class, you know? And Janice, you know that cutie Janice? She keeps turning around, first she's smiling, giving me the eye, and then she starts talking, but like no words came out. Then she was screaming, but I still couldn't hear her. I tried reading her lips, but right when I figured out what she said I woke up."

"What'd she say?"

"Don't remember."

Tyreke sat in an old rocking chair that he and Cedric had found in a dumpster, rubbing the short stubble of hair on his head, rocking slowly.

"Why did this happen?" Tyreke asked out loud. "Why?"

"Man, there ain't no answer for that," Cedric cleared his throat and sat up in bed. His cornrows had begun to unravel, and his hair began to look like spider webs. "'What will be will be,' I heard that somewhere." He paused for a moment. "I can't take this pain anymore. It hurts everywhere. My head, my chest, my muscles, everywhere. I'm dying Ty, I can feel it."

"Don't say that."

"But you know it's true. I know it's true. I thought maybe both of us would make it. Then we could do whatever we wanted, no parents, no rules, no school."

"That would be sweet..." Tyreke's voice trailed off.

"But that's not how it is Ty. I wish it was. Goddamn I wish it was," Cedric said, "But I need you to do something for me. I know you don't want to, but right now what you want doesn't matter."

Tyreke stared at his friend and noticed how hazy Cedric's eyes had become, how he could barely keep them open. Cedric's voice lowered, "I need you to kill me."

"No!"

"What did I tell you? What you want doesn't matter. I need you to do this for me."

"Why? You'll get better, I know it."

"You don't know shit man," Cedric said, "Here, use this."

Cedric took his gun from underneath the pillow and handed it to Tyreke. Tyreke had handled the gun before but this time it felt different, maybe because this time he was actually going to use it.

"I don't want to be in pain anymore," Cedric said, "Do it when I'm sleeping. Then you need to get out of here and don't come back."

Tyreke was crying, large tears falling down his smooth cheeks. "But I never shot anybody before. And now you want me to kill you, to kill my best friend? I can't do it."

Cedric sat up straight and raised his voice, "You *can* do it. And you *will* do it. I need you to. Your mom is dead, my mom is dead, your sister is dead. Same with everyone in this building. They're all dead Ty."

"I know, I know."

"And I'm going to die too. It's the truth, man. And it's not fair, but it is what it is. I'm tired and hurting bad. I'm going to take a nap here and I don't plan on waking up. You're my brother and I love you." Cedric had never said that before, but Tyreke knew he meant it. Cedric extended his hand, and Tyreke took it.

Tyreke wiped his tears on his shirt and said, "I love you too brother. Don't worry about me. I'll do what I have to do."

They held hands for a moment then Cedric's hand went limp. "See, I got no strength left," Cedric said.

It made Tyreke smile, and the expression it left on his face was something he hadn't felt since all this began.

| **31** |

Chapter Thirty-One

Jonas woke up the next morning with a serious hangover. The bottle of whiskey was empty and there was a broken vase on the floor and a brick through his TV. 'I did that? Where did I get a brick?' Jonas thought as he rubbed his head.

He went to the bathroom and found some aspirin which he took. Jonas saw the door to his apartment open, thought he remembered closing it, and went to close it again. He was about to close the door then noticed the door across the hall was open. As far as he could remember it wasn't before so Jonas went exploring.

The people that lived across the hall Jonas knew as Bob and Peggy but no more. In a condominium building with more than one hundred units Jonas barely knew any of his neighbors. He and his wife were always friendly with a nice smile and a hello but they never went farther than that.

He walked into their condo with a knock and a "Hello"; it looked like his own condo only backwards. The walls were painted a dull yellow and their décor was antique. He liked their wood slab butcher block with real chop marks from use in their kitchen; in his own they had a modern one with much less character. There was also a substance that looked like vomit on the butcher block and the floor. Jonas gingerly touched the substance, felt its freshness, and realized he had been here the night before.

A glass table was in pieces in the dining room along with a broken vase with dying carnations and Jonas stepped carefully over the glass and went down the hallway. All the doors were closed except the last one and he had no desire to open closed doors if he could avoid it. Jonas went into the open room, a study; the walls were decorated with sports memorabilia. He saw a picture of Bob and Peggy with the governor along with a pennant from the last World Series.

Jonas remembered that game, that night. He was not a sports reporter and was off that night, but he went downtown to the victory celebration with his wife. They watched the ninth inning with friends at a bar and got a little tipsy. Once the game was over people poured into the streets. There were no fights, no looting, no fires, no overturned cars, just happy celebrating their teams' win. It was surreal the energy he felt pulsating through the mass of people was unlike anything he ever felt before. Everyone pulling in the same direction, everyone happy. He was sure it was very different from the energy outside South General Hospital just days earlier.

The study was dimly lit and Jonas didn't immediately see the body lying face down on the floor. Once he did he saw the brains and blood caked to the black and silver hair of his neighbor, Bob. The carpet was a deep blue and hid the rest of the blood fairly well but Jonas still vomited the remaining contents of his stomach onto the carpet.

Jonas wiped his mouth and saw the gun on the floor, the gun Bob had used. He picked it up and upon examining it noted four bullets left in six bullet chamber. Immediately Jonas figured that behind one of the other closed doors in the hallway he would find Peggy with a bullet in her brain too. First he thought, 'Did Bob kill her, then himself?' then 'How long had they been dead? I never heard the shots. I must've been working. God, I hope she didn't hear...'

The gun he put in his pocket and closed the study door behind him. He left their condo quickly and went back into his own. "Shit," Jonas said and rubbed his jaw and throat, his hangover still not yielding.

| 32 |

Chapter Thirty-Two

Theo watched his monitor and saw Clint standing on the stoop outside Theo's office staring up at the small camera that was watching him. Theo watched Clint hit the buzzer, and Theo buzzed him in. Clint was alive and Theo was genuinely surprised. 'Did it work, the hand biting? The news had said it wouldn't, but Theo was alive, and Clint was alive, and that couldn't be a coincidence,' Theo thought.

Clint came in Theo's office looking ragged and tired. "How are you doing Clint?"

"I'm good."

"Not sick I hope."

"Nope, just tired."

"You sure you're not sick?"

"Yeah, I've seen the sick people. I'm not coughing, don't have a fever, no lesions. I'm alright."

"Good, good," Theo said, "Did you do what I asked?"

"Yeah, but the results..."

"What about them?"

"That rabbit bite everybody, but not everybody's alive. That shit is weird."

"Where is Sally Jesse?"

"She's with the guys. They like her."

"She's not hurt, is she?"

"Hell no, I said she was your rabbit, you know the guys won't fuck with your shit."

"Who's left?"

"There's Tay and Serge, your cousin Shaun, and those young pups from over there on Third Street. Seven including me."

The young pups from Third Street. Theo knew about them, heard that they were regular gangsters, even though they were barely old enough to be in high school. He had never met them, but he had known their mother. Too well.

Theo responded, "That's better than expected. The rabbit biting worked." He didn't expect it to work, but he was willing to try anything. He needed the manpower to accomplish what he wanted.

"Hurt like hell though. But if it kept us alive and shit, man a little bite never hurt nobody too bad. We lost most of them to the Flu anyway."

"Better than nothing. Where are they now?"

"I left them at the Spot, you know. They're drinking, smoking, carrying on. They beat on that homeless bum Test; beat his ass to death. He was sick anyway…"

"He wasn't going to be of any use to us. But no more killings, not unless I give the order. We need all the people we can get," Theo said and reclined in his chair before continuing "Any word on D'Mo?"

"Nothing, he's still in jail far as I know. We busting him out?"

"Leave that to me," Theo said and put his cigarette out in the gold ashtray on his desk, and then continued, "Clint, I have a plan.

And I'm going to need your help. With D'Mo in jail, and what we have left, you're getting a promotion."

"Cool."

"You've done well so far, but now I'm really going to need you to step up. Do you think you can do it?"

"Fuck yeah. I mean, yes sir," Clint said and sat straight up in his chair.

"You're going to be my number two," Theo said, "So my first question is can you handle the guys down at the Spot, get them in line?"

"Yeah boss, no problem. This will help." Clint pulled out a large gun from his pants and fidgeted with it.

"Sober them up, make some coffee, wait them out, whatever you got to do to get them ready to work. Can you do that?"

"Yeah."

"You sure? Because if you can't, I *will* replace you."

"I got it boss, don't worry."

"Being boss means I have to worry. Once they're ready to go, I want to go to the nearest hospitals, Downtown and South General. I want this done as soon as possible."

"What about those army guys, aren't they at the hospitals?"

"Last I saw on the TV it looked like everyone down there was gone. But be careful, you never know."

"Gotcha. What do I got to do?"

"People searching. Men, women, kids. Don't kill anyone unless you absolutely have to. Anyone not sick we're going to assume isn't going to get sick, so we can use them. We need supplies, like medication, bandages, that kind of stuff. Clean out the pharmacy, take it all, even if you don't know what it is. Bring back an ambulance too. You follow me?"

"Yeah, yeah boss. No problem."

"Here, take this, you're going to need it," Theo said and handed Clint a high-tech walkie-talkie.

"Walkie-talkies? This is nice boss," Clint said as he fidgeted with the buttons on the walkie-talkie.

"This is going to be our means of communication. I have one for each remaining man we have. I'll be on channel four. Remember that, because I'm only going to communicate with you. Have the men use channel two."

"Got it."

"Once you've secured the hospital, hit me up. Channel four. One last thing, I want you to send my cousin to meet me at the police station where they got D'Mo locked up. Got it?"

"Yeah," Clint said, still focused on the walkie-talkie knobs and buttons.

"Clint?"

"Yeah boss?"

"What are you waiting for? Get the fuck on."

Theo wasn't sure if Clint would work out, but if he didn't, Theo had no problem replacing him, and if he had to do it, it wouldn't be the first time.

| 33 |

Chapter Thirty-Three

"All these pills, so little time, eh?" Rubina said, returning to the hospital room with her arms full of pill bottles.

"So funny," her friend Mae said.

"I know, I know. You want some of these? They should help ease the pain."

"You have any Vicodin? I've taken that before."

"Yep I do. How many you want?"

"Four."

"You sure?"

"I'm sure. Can you get me some water?"

Rubina did so and Mae took the pills with a gulp of water that made her cough. "How are you feeling Mae?"

"Not great," she managed between coughs.

"There's a lot of dead people, most of the other rooms have dead people in them," Rubina said, "its freaking weird."

"Who else is here?"

"In the hospital?"

Mae nodded.

"There's that girl we saw coming in. She's taking care of some guy, I didn't get their names. I didn't see anybody else, but I thought I heard other people behind the closed doors but I'm not checking them."

"Ruby, can you get me some more water?"

Rubina refilled the plastic water cup and handed it to Mae. She took two big gulps and then looked Rubina in the eye and said, "Ruby, I don't want to die."

"I don't want you too either."

"Will you hold me? I'm so cold."

"Of course, move over."

They fell asleep like that, Rubina holding her friend.

***

A couple hours later Rubina awoke to loud yelling coming from the entrance foyer. "Check the bodies." "Who's alive?" "Where do you think you're going?" Deep voices, men's voices, yelling. "No! Leave me alone! Don't hurt him!" she heard a girl scream.

Rubina, startled, fell out of bed and onto the floor with a thud. She was far enough away from the entrance that no one heard her, at least she hoped so. She made for the bathroom, hid in the tiny shower and pulled the cream-colored curtain closed. But the yelling was getting closer. "Shit," Rubina said quietly to herself, "what about Mae? I hope she's already gone," Rubina prayed.

They were getting closer; there were less screams and more, deep yelling. Rubina was not leaving that bathroom. "Go through every room, we need as many survivors as we can find." She heard one say, and he was definitely close.

The bathroom door was closed, and Rubina was losing it not knowing, just hearing, what was going on outside the room. She made herself as small as possible behind the shower curtain. "Fuck, fuck, fuck!" she whispered. She didn't want to be caught more than anything she had ever wanted.

"No one in this room!" she heard one yell; he had to be in the next room. She knew they were coming; knew they would find her. She had no idea who she was hiding from, and that made her more freaked out. Rubina started crying. "No!" she said in a tiny voice to herself, "stop crying. You're tougher than this." But the tears kept coming.

She could hear someone on the other side of the door, checking the room. "This one's dead," he said, referring to Mae, her best friend alive no longer.

The bathroom door flew opened with a kick. He opened the curtain and she saw a large man with an automatic rifle. Rubina screamed and made for the door, but the man grabbed her. "Where you going sweetie?" he said. "Got one!" he yelled to the others.

"Aargh!" Rubina bit his arm, and he dropped her. "Ow, bitch, that fucking hurt," he said as Rubina scampered out of the bathroom and made her way into the hallway. "Hey, we got a live one, get her!"

Rubina looked left, toward the foyer, saw two guys with guns standing around a few other people, including the teenage girl in the pink hooded sweatshirt from earlier. No one was to her right so she took off running that way. "Don't shoot her! Brother Theo wants them alive," she heard one yell to the others.

As she ran, she could hear his loud footfalls on the sterile tile floor running after her. Rubina ran cross-country back in junior high, and was running like she hadn't in years. "She heading outside, what are you guys waiting for, go get her!" Rubina heard the large man yell, still chasing her, then "I got dibs, I saw her first."

Rubina wasn't thinking anymore, her flight response had taken over, and all she could process was what path to take to get away. She came to a fork in the hallway, and instinctively went left. She made it to the end of the hall, into a stairwell. There was a door that said EXIT or stairs to go up. In an instant she chose the exit to the outside.

Rubina didn't see anybody once she was outside the building and she stopped for a moment to catch her breath. The hospital was designed in a cross, and now she was at the left end. She figured the men had come in through the front, so she ran along the building toward the backend. There was a forest just beyond the back of the hospital and she figured if she could get there, she would be safe.

As she ran through the long grass Rubina didn't turn around but she could hear a car's engine and it was getting closer. For a moment she thought back to Sunday School and the story of Lot's wife turning around to view Sodom and Gomorrah burn.

As the car's engine got louder, closer, she finally turned around and saw a dirty yellow jeep driving on the grass toward her. She could hear them yelling at her but she couldn't make out the words they were saying. Rubina ran faster, her breathing getting heavy. She hadn't run like this in forever and now was just hoping to reach the forest before the jeep reached her.

Rubina looked again to see the jeep almost next to her. "Stop!" the man in the passenger seat yelled. Their eyes met for a moment, and Rubina knew by looking at him if she was caught, it wasn't going to be good. "Get closer!" she heard the passenger yell to the driver.

The woods were rapidly approaching and the car would crash into the sizable forest trees if it kept going at the same speed. She could feel the car's heat, it was so close. Rubina could feel the grass getting longer around her legs; the woods were less than one hundred feet away.

Rubina looked to the left, and the jeep was near enough they could knock her over with it. She looked over; the passenger was standing on his seat and he jumped at her. Rubina avoided taking the brunt of the two-hundred-pound man but he caught her left foot and she went tumbling to the ground. She was only twenty feet away from the dense forest, and got up fast but then collapsed. She was done, and the driver, who had stopped the car, was now standing over her.

He was breathing heavy and said "You're fast," just as he hit her in the head with the butt of his gun and Rubina was out cold.

| 34 |

Chapter Thirty-Four

Jonas went into the bathroom and looked at his face. The stubble of a five o'clock shadow was already starting. He decided it would be a while until he would shave again so he shaved. The shaving cream felt cool on his skin; he used a new razor and only cut himself once. "Not bad," Jonas said as typically when he shaved with a new razor he would have multiple cuts. The cuts would be covered up before he went on air by the makeup girl, Marlene.

Marlene the curvy redhead with the nice tits and large nipples, Jonas remembered, when they hooked up one lonely night at a fancy downtown hotel. Jonas told her later that it was a one-time thing and she had accepted that but was still cold to him, even when she applied his makeup. Poor Marlene, dead Marlene, he assumed.

Once Jonas finished shaving, he took a shower and put on clean clothes. 'What do I do now?' was the constant question on his mind. 'Do I even care? Does it even matter?' typically followed it.

Jonas knew that even with endless food and supplies that were on almost corner of every block in America people were still curious creatures, and a society that was always go-go-go doesn't just stop. Even a deadly Rabbit Flu wouldn't stop it. If he was alive then there had to be others. Did he want to find them? Jonas wasn't sure. But he thought it would do him some good to get outside and take a walk. It was a nice day and maybe it would help him figure out what to do.

Jonas went into his bedroom; his wife's body was still lying peacefully under the covers. The gentle breeze coming in through the open window rustled the sheets ever so slightly. He went to the bed and pulled the sheet down over his dead wife's face. She looked like she was sleeping but her skin was starting to change colors, becoming bluer. He gave her a kiss on the forehead, whispered "I love you", and covered her back up.

He already missed her touch, her soft hands, soft skin. He already missed kissing the nape of her neck as she slept, missed telling her 'I love you' while she slept, and even in her sleep she would say it back. He wasn't a good man, not a faithful husband, didn't deserve her love and affection; she knew all this and loved him anyway. Jonas left the room quickly and closed the door.

Jonas decided to take the neighbor's gun just in case; he put on a beige windbreaker and set out. He left his apartment building and started walking. He had no place in mind, didn't know who or what he might find, but began to feel more confident in not knowing what was to come. Jonas had walked three blocks when he saw them. Other people. Two men and a woman it looked like. They saw him and immediately froze. Jonas kept walking toward them; he saw one of the men had an assault rifle, and pointed it right at Jonas. "Freeze!"

Jonas did as he was told and they approached him cautiously. "Who are you?" The man with the rifle asked.

"Name's Jonas," he said and was surprised they didn't recognize him, 'maybe they watched channel 2,' he thought.

"What are you doing out here?"

"Taking a walk."

"That's…weird," the woman said.

"Maybe so," Jonas said, then "Uh, You mind not pointing that gun at me? I'm not armed."

The man with the assault rifle lowered it to his side. "What are you guys doing out here?" Jonas asked.

The woman spoke up, "We're leaving the city. Nothing left here. Going to Florida."

"Shut up Maureen. We don't know this guy."

"No problem," Jonas said, "You don't know me, that's true. But I can tell you I'm harmless. My wife died two days ago. The Rabbit Flu killed her. I'm out here just trying to think things out."

"Well we won't keep you."

"Ok then. I'm just going to keep going the way I was going."

The man with the rifle watched Jonas walk away with an intense stare. "Hey wait," Maureen said, "If you're hungry or need shelter or other people, there's a church on Third Avenue. They have food-"

"Maureen what did I tell you? Shut the fuck up."

"You shut the fuck up," Maureen said, "Where's your common decency? We're not coming back here, so why shouldn't I tell him?"

"Fine. Whatever."

"So like I said, it's over on Third Avenue and Grand, I think. Run by some tranny they called Sister."

"Thanks," Jonas said, "Hey, can I ask you a question? Why did you leave there?"

"They're going to stay in the city, try and rebuild or something. We don't want to stay through the winter; it'll be too cold then. But they fed us and gave us a place to sleep for the night. Seemed like alright people but something felt odd. You might want to check it out."

"Thanks again. Good luck," Jonas said and turned his back to them and proceeded on his path. 'Sister?' Jonas thought. He remembered a transvestite nicknamed Sister from back when he used to hang out at lesbian bars with his lesbian sister, before he got his anchor gig, before he got married.

The Sister he remembered used to wear a long gold chain and slightly too big gold-plated cross but he had no idea she was religious; he thought it was part of her ensemble, part of her 'look.' But she wasn't stupid, that much Jonas remembered. He remembered talking about politics and religion and literature with Sister. It started to make sense to Jonas that if she survived the Rabbit Flu she would probably have followers. 'Well at least now I have something to do,' he thought and began to whistle again, this time a happier tune.

Chapter Thirty-Five

The four remaining soldiers settled in the corner apartment on the fifteenth floor of a gothic high-rise; one corner faced the South Highway, the other faced the city. They set up the sniper rifle to watch the South Highway, and waited.

"This…is…fucking…boring. I hate waiting, reminds me of being over *there*. Remember Radio? All we did was wait. Wait, wait, wait," Crudo said.

"Is it better shooting those people at the hospital then?" Radio said.

"At least there was some action."

"That shit sucked man."

"What do you mean?"

"You know, shooting innocent people, our fellow Americans?"

"Those people weren't innocent. Not once they decided to join a militia, and they shot at us first, remember?"

"Yeah, I was there, I remember. But they weren't all redneck, hard ass looking dudes. There were women there, old people, kids…"

"Some of them had guns, same as the rest."

"How do you know that? You see them all?"

"Didn't have to."

"Shut up. Both of you," Jackson said.

"What's up your ass Major?" Crudo asked.

"Nothing soldier. Watch your tone."

"Hmmph," Crudo said, "I'm going to go take a shit. Hermes, it's your turn to watch."

While Crudo was in the bathroom their monotony was finally interrupted. "Major, we have three civilians walking southeast on Monroe toward the on-ramp for the South Highway," Hermes said.

Jackson looking through binoculars saw them, two men and a woman and said, "People are approaching the highway."

On a normal day they could have been tourists, or day hikers, but this wasn't a normal day. "Confirmed three civilians Major. Two men, one visibly armed. One woman, apparently unarmed. How do you want to proceed Major?" Hermes asked.

"Keep watching. Our orders are to shoot anyone trying to leave. They aren't there yet."

"But you know where they're going," Radio said.

"Keep watching. Don't do anything until I order it."

"Yes sir."

"Sir they are approaching the highway," Hermes said as he lined up his shot.

"Hold steady."

"Sir they are now walking on the South Highway."

"Hold Hermes."

"Sir they are proceeding down the highway, approaching the gridlock. Once they reach the cars it will be too hard to shoot all of them."

"Do it Hermes. Do it now!" Jackson ordered.

Blam. blam. blam. Three efficient head shots. Jackson watched through the binoculars as each body hit the ground. He felt the thump of their bodies hit the pavement. He saw the blood running from their heads. "Good shooting soldier," was all he said.

"Thank you, sir." Hermes set the sniper rifle down and went to the bathroom to vomit. He almost knocked Crudo down on the way.

"Watch out Hermes. Hey, what the fuck just happened?" Crudo said as he emerged from the bathroom.

"Some people trying to leave. See for yourself," Radio said and handed him the binoculars.

Hermes came out of the bathroom and wiped his mouth on his sleeve. Crudo said, "I can't believe I missed that. Damn you're a good shot Hermes, you're like Lee Harvey or some shit. I underestimated you bro."

Jackson sat on the couch and put his head in his hands. "You alright sir?" Radio asked.

"I'm fine."

"No seriously Major, you look like you got something on your mind," Radio said.

Jackson thought for a bit on what he wanted to say to his men. They were still his men, and he was still responsible for them, and they deserved his honesty, even if it was harsh. He cleared his throat and said, "Here's the deal. It doesn't matter what happened before. Not anymore. You get that Crudo? Life isn't going to be normal anymore. Why don't you think on that? Start thinking about our fucked-up future instead of our fucked-up past."

| 36 |

Chapter Thirty-Six

"Where are you? Why won't you answer? Don't be dead, seriously don't be dead!" James was yelling into his phone, leaving a message on his psychiatrist's voice mail.

"What am I supposed to do? I need you, need someone to talk to. You're probably dead. You know I was joking about the end of the world and all that, you know that, right?" James was pacing around his apartment.

"I'm talking to my dead psychiatrist's voicemail. What am I doing talking to your voicemail, you're never going to hear it. But if I talk to your voicemail and not myself then I'm definitely not crazy, right?"

James imagined how she died. His therapist. 'Was it painful? She wasn't married, at least if she was, she didn't wear a ring. Maybe she had a boyfriend, girlfriend, mother or father, someone to take care of her as she died. Probably not though. He hoped she wasn't stupid enough to try the hospitals. James imagined her having a condo. One with floor to ceiling windows and maybe a bidet in the bathroom. He imagined her fat ass trying to maneuver a bidet, and it made him laugh. But it couldn't save her. Nothing could.'

"I thought I would catch up on all the books I've been meaning to read, watch some movies I haven't seen, start working out, eat my canned food, live in peace," James said into the phone. "But I don't want it. I don't, I don't want to die like those people. They never had a chance. No one had a chance with this stupid Rabbit Flu."

'Rabbit Flu, really?' he thought, 'What a joke. Wasn't the human race tougher than that? Well humanity would carry on; he was alive for one and there had to be others. Maybe Rabbit Flu just thinned the herd. Dead bodies everywhere, even if I can't see all of them. But I know they're there, behind closed doors. I can see those three by the highway. Dead, bullet in the brain, but where did the shots come from?' James couldn't tell. It happened so fast. He heard the shots then looked through his telescope. He saw the dead bodies, blood flowing from their heads onto the black asphalt.

"What kind of life is this? I'm fucking scared. I don't want to leave this apartment ever. And I don't have to, do I? I've been preparing for this for a while. I have food to last me for a long while. The power still works. If I leave, if I go outside, I'll get shot...or worse. That's not going to happen. I'm not leaving."

"I'm not going to kill myself; I knew you might think that. No way. I survived so there must be a reason. It sure would help if I had a reason to keep living. I need one bad. Why don't I have girlfriend, or kid, or even a dog or a cat or even a fucking rabbit? Then I'd have a reason. But I have nothing. No family alive. No friends alive. They've all left me. I'm on my own. But I'm not going to do it. Fuck it, I'd rather have someone else shoot me in the head than do it myself. Does that make me a coward? I don't want to die. I just need...some kind of direction."

The phone cut in: 'Thank you for your message. Good-bye.' Then the line went dead.

"Fucking voicemail, now I have to call back, listen to your stupid message, start all over. I'm not doing it though. Fuck it, fuck you for not being there, a lot of help you are," and threw the phone at the wall and watched as it broke into pieces. "What am I going to do?" James sobbed into his hands.

| 37 |

Chapter Thirty-Seven

Theo waited behind some large bushes and watched Shaun pull up in front of the police station in a forest green SUV. Shaun was only seventeen and he was family. Theo wanted him close if at all possible. Clint was older, more established, but Theo knew if Clint couldn't hack it as his number two Shaun would be next in line.

Shaun sat in his SUV and Theo snuck up on him. "Get the fuck out bitch!" Theo said and bashed through the driver's side window with the butt of his automatic shotgun.

"Holy shit!" Shaun said and then saw it was Theo. "What the fuck man?"

"What bitch? You need to be on your guard always. Especially now. I hurt you?"

"Nah, man, I'm ok," Shaun said and got out of the car and cleaned the glass off himself.

"Come here," Theo said and he hugged his cousin, "Good to see you alive cuz."

"Yeah, you too," Shaun said and Theo released him, "We busting D'Mo out?"

"That's the plan. You packing?"

"You know it."

"Damn," Theo said.

"What is it?"

"I was hoping if anyone was in there they'd come out when I busted your window, but they didn't. Not sure what cops would still be holed up in there, but there might be some. Watch yourself."

Theo approached the front door with Shaun close behind. He stopped at the door and motioned for Shaun to go in first. Shaun opened the door quickly and slipped in. He aimed his gun as he surveyed the room. Nothing moved. "Doesn't look like anyone's here," he said as Theo walked in the station behind him. "Stay low, and go left," Theo said.

They walked down the left corridor, under a sigh marked OFFICES. They examined the first room, nothing special but a desk covered in papers, a computer, and a small fish tank. "Look at this stupid shit," Shaun said as he looked around the office. "Fucking pigs."

"Keep quiet, I thought I heard something," Theo said. They both stopped and listened, but heard nothing. "Let's go to the next room."

Shaun went first out of the office, and as he did blam! a loud gun went off and a bullet whizzed by his head. The next one hit him in the arm. "Down!" Theo yelled and pulled Shaun to the floor. Shaun howled from the wound in his arm. "You alright?"

"Yeah, I'm ok, that fucker got me in the arm."

"You see where it came from?"

"Yeah, that way," Shaun motioned to the right.

"Ok, I'm going to go back through the office, try to get behind him. If he comes near the doorway, blast his ass."

"Got it."

Theo went around the desks, through a door that led him to a row of interrogation rooms. The first door was open, and a person was tied to a chair, its back to Theo. The person wasn't moving, but from the back of the head he knew it was his brother, D'Maurice. Theo felt his neck for a pulse but he was dead, and his face and arms had deep gashes now a dark crimson color. 'Torturing my brother? Oh shit am I going to fuck that dude up,' Theo thought, and was interrupted by more gunfire. "Shaun!" Theo yelled and ran back into the offices. "I got him cuz," Shaun said.

Theo helped Shaun up by his good arm. He looked in the hallway and saw the cop's body lying face down. He was still alive, wheezing and breathing heavy. Theo took his shotgun and from point blank range shot off the cop's left leg. His scream was a sound Theo had heard before. "Shut the fuck up you stupid motherfucker," Theo said, and shot him again.

"Damn Theo," Shaun said, nursing his arm.

"Fuck, man. This piece of shit killed D'Mo."

"D'Mo's dead?"

"Yeah, man, and someone cut him up."

"Fuck, man, let me shoot this piece of shit," Shaun said and unloaded the rest of his clip in the cop's back. "He still breathing?"

Theo nodded. "He won't be for long," Theo said and put the shotgun up to the back of the cop's head. He pulled the trigger and the cop stopped breathing.

In his deepest voice Theo bellowed, "Anyone still in here I'm going to kill. You pissed off Brother Theo you stupid fucking pigs. If you're still alive, you better come out now and maybe I'll let you live."

Theo wasn't expecting a response but got one from a woman's voice, "Please, please don't kill us," but it was muffled, like she was in a room with the door closed. "Where are you?" Theo asked.

"In one of the cells. That psycho locked us in. Please let us out of here."

"Stay here," Theo told Shaun.

"Where are you going?"

"Quiet," Theo said and put his finger to his lips implying silence.

Theo walked back toward the main entrance, and saw the CELLS sign down the opposite hallway. He carried his shotgun ready to shoot anything that moved, and slowly walked toward the cells. The cell doors had a small window to look out at eye level, and Theo saw a face in the second cell trying to see him. "Hey, hey you still out there? Don't leave us in here! Please!"

Theo ignored the voice and returned to Shaun. "What about this bullet in my arm? It fucking kills."

"Better to leave it in."

"What?"

"Yeah, bullets are so hot when they're fired, they're sterile, and I don't know any doctors still alive. It'll hurt like a bitch for a while though."

"Shit man, you serious?"

"I ever lie to you?" Theo said, then "I'll drop you back off at the Spot once we're done here. Clint should've gotten some hospital supplies, hopefully some painkillers too. But don't let anyone try to take out that bullet. You'd probably die."

"But it hurts man."

"Don't be a pussy. Wait here, I'm going to go find a first aid kit or something."

Shaun nodded. Theo made his way to the back of the police station, where they kept the cars, guns and ammo. He had expected a garage full of police cruisers and enough guns and ammo to start a small war, but he found nothing. It was a big empty lot, no cars, no guns; there was however a lot of ammo left. Theo found shotgun shells and filled his pockets. He then went looking for and found a first aid kit. Theo took the walkie-talkie out of his back pocket and radioed Clint. "Clint, you there?"

"Yeah boss, I'm here."

"Where you at?"

"Just finishing up here at the hospital. Found some people, had to chase this one bitch down, but we got her. Got an ambulance too, like you wanted."

"Good, good."

"What should we do with them? And the ambulance?"

"Meet me at the Spot. Shaun got shot."

"Damn, he alright?"

"He'll live. You get some painkillers?"

"I got all kinds of pills. Cleaned out the pharmacy."

"Good. Leave the people you got tied up in the car; I got just the place for them."

"Ok boss."

Theo then went back to Shaun. "I found the first aid kit. There ain't much, but at least we can wrap it and sterilize it. But it's going to hurt cuz."

"Any painkillers in there?"

"Yeah, but not strong ones. Here, take these," Theo said and handed Shaun four pills. Theo patched up Shaun the best he could, with Shaun groaning and gritting his teeth the whole time.

"See, good as new."

In the background they heard the locked-up people continue to call for help. "What do you want to do about them?" Shaun asked.

"They're not going anywhere. Right now I'm going to have a smoke. You want one?" Theo sat down and took an antique silver cigarette case from his inner coat pocket, lit one for Shaun, handed it to him, and then lit one himself.

When Theo was done he put the cigarette out on the floor, crushing it under his boot. "You alright? Don't pass out on me."

"Yeah, yeah, I'm cool."

"Let's get out of here," Theo said, "Here let me help you."

Theo helped Shaun out to the car, and put him in the backseat. They drove to the Spot with Shaun wincing at every bump in the road.

| 38 |

Chapter Thirty-Eight

Tyreke walked by Cedric's room, heard him alive, sleeping but still breathing, and proceeded to the bathroom. He washed and dried his face, then stared into his own eyes in the mirror. 'Can I do it? Can I do what needs to be done?' Tyreke thought. He brushed his teeth out of instinct, and his mouth felt cool while beads of sweat started to form on his forehead.

Then he paced in the kitchen, back and forth, fighting the internal voice that told him not to kill, not to murder his best friend. 'Cedric is going to die anyway, everyone's dead, he'll be one of them soon, why isn't he dead yet? I don't want to do what must be done. I don't want to kill him…This isn't fair. None of this is fucking fair. Why won't he just die so I don't have to do what I don't want to do?' That last thought was keeping him back, keeping him from doing what Cedric wanted.

Tyreke opened the refrigerator and went for a can of soda, but not before he saw a can of light beer, and took that out instead. He opened it and took the first sip; it tasted bad but made even worse by the fact that he had just brushed his teeth. That didn't stop him from drinking it as quickly as he could, and he finished it with a bellowing burp and satisfying "ahh."

He set the beer on the counter and took Cedric's shiny silver gun out. Tyreke didn't even know what type of gun it was, but that didn't stop him from examining it, feeling its weight, its power, in his oversized hands. He knew what he had to do, knew it needed to be done. "Fuck it," he said to no one.

Tyreke walked into the bedroom; he saw Cedric sleeping quietly. Tyreke felt his heart rate speed up and felt his neck for his pulse. His heart was beating so fast it frightened him a little. To calm down he took a deep breath and sighed.

'Here we go son, you can do it,' he heard his mother say in his mind. He put a pillow over his best friend's face, and raised the gun. His heart was beating so fast and loud he thought it might explode. His mind was telling him 'just do it, get it over with. It'll all be easier after.'

"Ced, I'm so sorry," he said through tears. Only the pillow separated the gun from his best friend's head. His hand was shaking, time was dragging, almost stopped. "I love you brother," he said and pulled the trigger twice. The kickback startled him and knocked Tyreke back, and he tripped over some books stacked on the floor.

Blood started slowly running from under the pillow onto the sweat soaked sheets, then onto the dirty yellow ochre carpet; Tyreke knew he was never going to lift up that pillow. He left the room and closed the door quietly as if Cedric was still alive, and just sleeping. But Tyreke knew he wasn't and went to lie on his mother's bed and sobbed until he fell asleep.

| 39 |

Chapter Thirty-Nine

A young woman no older than nineteen with bright pink and purple hair was covered in blood and bile vomit from chin to crotch as she sat in the driver's seat of the yellow Nissan, her head titled slightly to the left on the headrest. "Dead girl, is that what the Rabbit Flu does to a person?' Franklin thought. He stumbled to the nearest support post and dry heaved.

Franklin began taking deliberate deep breaths, in and out, and once his breathing slowed down, he felt embarrassed. A fifty-four-year-old man scared of a young girl.

Without millions of people, it was amazing the clarity of Franklin's hearing. He strained his ears to listen into the car, and thought he heard breathing, but couldn't be sure. He cautiously re-approached the Nissan.

Franklin tapped on the glass softly, got no response, and then rapped on it with his knuckles. Her skin was a cool tan; she looked Mediterranean, with purple eye shadow and faded red lips. But she wasn't dead, 'she was breathing, she was alive, thank god,' Franklin told himself. He tried the door but it was locked.

That woke up the woman, and she opened her eyes slowly, disoriented. She looked down at the watery puke and yellow bile and tiny blue pills on her chest, then looked at Franklin, and then screamed.

"Take it easy," Franklin said and tried the car door handle. It was locked. She screamed for about ten more seconds, then burst out of the car, ran to nearest support pole, and dry heaved, just as Franklin had done moments earlier.

Not wanting to startle her further Franklin followed her slowly. "Are you ok?" he asked.

The girl stood up and dusted herself off. "Um...no... I don't...so... no. I'm covered in my own puke, have a killer headache, and really need a shower. Can you help with any of that?"

"I can. First, what's your name?"

"Nadia. My boyfriend lives in this building. Or he did."

"Franklin," he said, and extended his hand, which Nadia tentatively and limply shook. Franklin continued, "My condo is on the twenty second floor. Elevators are out, so if you're boyfriend lives on a lower floor, you could shower there."

"There's a slight problem," she said as she pulled her yellow puke covered raincoat over her head, and threw it under her car. Nadia reached in the center console and took out her menthol cigarettes, and proceeded to try and light up, but she couldn't get the lighter to light. It just flicked and flicked, her hands shaking. Franklin took the lighter from her. He touched her hand for only a brief moment, and he felt her warmth. She was alive, and he wasn't alone anymore. He lit her cigarette, cupping his other hand around it, and handed it to her.

"Is your boyfriend...?"

"He, he died," she said and started to cry.

"I'm so sorry."

"Thanks," Nadia, said whipping the tears out of her eyes with her coat sleeve.

"Can I ask, what were you doing in the car?"

"None of your business mister."

"You're right, it isn't my business. But you do know what's happened, right? The Rabbit Flu?"

"Yeah, I know, that's what killed my boyfriend," Nadia said and flicked her finished cigarette, "you said you could help with a shower?"

"Sure, let's go up to my condo."

"I'm going to need some clean clothes, but he's still there."

"What do you mean?"

"I mean my boyfriend, he's still in the apartment, and I need some clothes."

"Ok, so do you want me to go in there and get them?"

"You read my mind."

They walked up the stairs to the apartment, Nadia leading the way. Once at the door Nadia bent over to retrieve the key from under the mat and gave a Franklin his first feeling other than fear since he had gotten up that day. She was a cute, albeit young, woman save the vomit, and he could tell she was wearing a bright yellow thong. 'She accessorizes her panties and coats,' Franklin thought, 'What a weird world, after a deadly flu kills most of humanity I come across the prettiest girl I've seen in ages...' Franklin shook his head.

"Key under the mat? Isn't that too easy?"

"Not anymore, and you'll see, Pete didn't have that much stuff, you know, worth stealing," Nadia said, "There's a purple bag in the bedroom, should have all I need."

She opened the door and let Franklin inside. He found her bag in the bedroom, saw her boyfriend under the covers, grabbed the bag quickly and met Nadia back in the hall. He closed the door behind her and they walked up the rest of the steps to his twenty-second story place.

"This is a nice place Franklin, or do you like Frank?"

"Franklin."

"Ok. Franklin, you have a nice place."

"Well thank you Nadia."

"Your bathroom?"

"That way, second door on the left. There should be a towel under the sink."

"Thanks, I'll be done in a bit."

Franklin sat on his couch knowing that his situation was different now. He was responsible for Nadia now, when before he just had to worry about himself. Franklin was an only child, never had a girlfriend he loved (or at least felt that love returned), but now he had a new feeling, one of protector. What Nadia was thinking who knew? He figured from the puke, the pills, that she had tried to commit suicide. But she seemed alright now. Maybe he could be her reason for keeping on too, at least he hoped so.

His thoughts were interrupted by gunfire somewhere in the city below. Franklin went to the window to look, but didn't get too close. He heard the water go off, and Nadia came out of the bathroom a viridian-colored towel wrapped around her petite body.

"Franklin? What was that?"

"Shhh. Gunshots, I think. But sound echoes off these big buildings, so who knows where it came from."

"That's messed up," Nadia said while combing her hair.

"It is. Hey haven't you heard all the gunshots the last few days?"

"Yeah, I guess, but after a while with the sirens and all I tried to block it out."

"That I understand. But yesterday it seemed to all stop. Up until now that is."

"Franklin, do you have a gun?"

"No, do you?"

"Sure don't."

"Did your boyfriend?"

"I don't think so, and I'm not looking."

"Ok, ok, but maybe we should think of getting one."

"Not a bad idea. I have to finish getting ready, make-up, you know?"

"Sure."

Franklin wanted to tell her that makeup wasn't necessary, but thought the better of it.

Nadia came out with her hair up, wearing a powder blue tank top and jeans, with powder blue eye shadow to match. Franklin wondered if she was wearing a powder blue thong too. Nadia lay down on the couch, looking up at the ceiling, "So now what?"

"That's a good question. I don't know. Internet, TV, radio, nothing is on. Power still works, but who knows for how long? I have enough food for at least two months, after that..." Franklin said.

"And then what?"

"Don't know," Franklin said, "I wasn't planning for the end of the world."

| 40 |

Chapter Forty

Jonas found Sister's church amid a row of random shops and saw a man out front with a large assault rifle. It didn't look like a church as it sat in a row of other stores and bars. The only thing that gave it away was a hanging sign with a large black cross on it and a Biblical quote underneath it. That and a guard with a large rifle pacing under the sign.

He waited in an alley, taking care that the guard wouldn't see him until he wanted him to. He pondered if it was a good idea to take the gun with him. He finally decided it wasn't so Jonas took gun out of his pocket and placed it quietly in a large green dumpster in the alley. Then he approached the church. Jonas got within thirty feet when the guard said, "Hey you, yeah you, get down on the ground."

"What? I'm just walking here."

"Don't give a shit. Get down or I'll blast you."

"Alright, alright no problem," Jonas said while motioning with his arms for the guard to be calm.

Jonas got down on his knees and put his arms at his side. The man approached cautiously and said, "Put your hands behind your head."

Jonas did so and the guard asked, "You have any weapons on you?"

"Nope."

"I got to check you anyway," and the guard patted down Jonas from neck to feet. "Alright, you can get up."

Jonas walked in front of the guard to the church. He went to open the door, but the guard stopped him. "What now?"

"Last thing, got to make sure you ain't sick. Strip."

"Here?"

"Yeah, there's no one around. What, you modest?"

"No, but if you're worried about the Rabbit Flu, um, everyone who got it is dead already."

"Doesn't matter, Sister's orders."

"Fine," he said, and took off his clothes, down to his underwear, noting that the guard referred to Sister.

"You know those lesions are down there too," the guard said.

"Seriously? Do I look sick? Do I have any lesions on my pits?"

"Sister's orders," the guard said again, "You want in, right?"

Jonas took off his underwear, standing naked in the street was not something he ever expected to do. "Lift up your ball sack," the guard said.

"This is degrading, you know that? You satisfied? Get a long look."

After the guard finished checking he said, "Can't be too careful, you know? Get dressed. You can go in; head downstairs."

He entered the front door and it opened into a cafeteria where two men sat at a table, shoveling food into their mouths. Both men looked at Jonas quickly, not making eye contact, then went back to eating. From behind a kitchen door a man in faded army fatigues approached Jonas. Jonas could see the gun on his hip. "What's your name?" he asked.

"Jonas."

"Have a seat. My name's Danny, I'm the meet and greet committee," Danny said and motioned to a chair for Jonas to sit.

Danny took the seat directly opposite and pulled out a pad of paper and a blue pen. "You got ID?"

"Why would I need that?"

"Not what I asked, I asked-"

"I heard you. No, I don't have ID. What would I need it for?"

"Funny guy. Ok. How old are you?"

"Forty-three."

"What you been doing since the Flu started?"

"Trying to stay alive. What have you been doing since the Flu started?"

"You are a smartass, aren't you," he said, and didn't wait for a response, "Hey, you look familiar, where do I know you from?"

"Channel Six news probably."

"Yeah, that's right, you're that news guy. You know that blonde lady, with the huge cans?"

"Ginger Fontaine?"

"That's right, Ginger, she's a good-looking lady. What happened to her?"

"Don't know."

Jonas didn't know what happened to Ginger; that was true. He wasn't exactly sure what had happened at the hospital, and if there was one place in the city to avoid, it was the hospital. His thoughts drifted back to Ginger, Ginger with whom he had worked with for nine years. Ginger whom one Christmas party had blown him in the bathroom. Ginger who was probably lying dead on the street outside the hospital. Ginger…

"You hungry?" Danny asked.

"I'm good. Had a big breakfast."

"Mr. Jonas, where have you been staying?" Danny asked.

"My condo, until today. Ran into some other people, they said I should check this place out. And here I am."

"How many people did you run into? Where'd you see them?"

"Three. Two men and a woman. They said they were heading south. They told me about this place."

Danny took out a notepad and started writing. "Were they armed?"

"One guy had a rifle; that was the only gun I saw."

"Go on," Danny said.

The other men finished eating, and Jonas watched them file up the stairs, into the chapel. "What's going on with them?" Jonas asked.

Danny looked up from his notepad and said, "You're lucky, you know that? It's time for our evening service."

| **41** |

Chapter Forty-One

Rubina rubbed her eyes but still couldn't focus. She saw shapes and colors all fuzzy. She was lying down, but it wasn't her own bed; that much she could recognize by the thin, lumpy mattress. She sat up, rubbed her eyes once more, and began to regain her focus.

The girl in the pink hooded sweatshirt from the hospital was balled up on another bed trying to keep warm by pulling her jean skirt down over her blue, fishnet covered, legs. She wasn't facing Rubina. The room was oversized with two sets of bunk beds on either side of the room. 'Am I in jail?' Rubina thought, "But that doesn't make sense. I remember the hospital and Mae, poor Mae, and running and a yellow jeep…"

A man, or a man's body, was on the floor face up. She couldn't tell if he was breathing. A woman with dirty blond hair in a purple coat was leaning over the body, sobbing. She looked to the other bun bed and saw the girl with the pink hooded sweatshirt had turned over and was now staring at her. "Hey," the girl said, "you're awake."

"Yeah," was all Rubina could say.

"You alright?"

"I'll live," she said and rubbed her head. Rubina's hair was sticky, and looked at her fingers and saw the flaked blood on them.

"They must've hit you hard. I thought you were dead," the girl said and went to sit next to Rubina.

She whispered into Rubina's ear "they took her, once we got back here. When they threw her in here she ran to that guy and has been like that since. She won't talk or nothing. I think that guy might be dead."

Rubina shook her head. "What the hell happened?"

"You don't remember? I was at the hospital-"

"I remember you there."

"I was taking care of my boyfriend; he was sick. Then these guys with guns came in and grabbed me. Then I saw them chasing you through the hospital. They found the lady and that guy in another room. Then they brought us here."

"Was your boyfriend...?"

"Dead? Yeah..." the girl said and started crying.

"I'm sorry. I lost my best friend..."

Rubina and girl held each other, sharing each other's sadness for a moment. When they separated Rubina noticed the girl's oversized hoop earrings covered in shiny stars and the silver unicorn that hung around her neck. Once no more tears would come the girl asked, "I'm Emmalee. What's your name?"

"Rubina," she said, making her first eye contact with Rubina but only for a moment. Rubina still noticed her pale green eyes; they made Emmalee look more beautiful than she actually was.

"You know you almost got away. You ran pretty fast," Emmalee said.

"I used to run cross-country back in high school. I thought I was tough. I needed to be, to get away. Now I'm stuck in here. I'm sorry Mimi, I know you said I had to be tough, but I wasn't."

"Who's Mimi?"

"My grandma."

"Oh."

The woman in the purple coat mumbled something that Rubina couldn't hear. "What was that?" she asked.

The woman turned around and looked at them. Her bottom lip was cut, her face had purple bruises and cuts on it, her dirty blond hair disheveled, but underneath Rubina could still tell she was an attractive older woman, like an actress. "It's bad, real bad…," the woman said.

"What is?"

"This place, these people."

"What people?"

"Those men that took us, that beat up Glen…"

"He's alive?"

"He's breathing, I can hear it if I listen real close…"

"Who are you?" Emmalee asked.

"My name? It's Ginger."

"Are you ok Ginger?"

"Not really, no, no, I'm pretty sure I'm not ok."

"Do you want to tell us why?" Rubina said, but in the back of her mind she had an inkling of what had happened to Ginger.

"I…They…they're bad people. We're in trouble. You two are in trouble. Big trouble."

"What do you mean?"

Ginger stood up. She looked taller than Rubina had originally thought, and was wearing a professional skirt and knee-high black leather boots. The skirt had jagged edges on the hem, like a child had used it as construction paper for a collage. Ginger kept trying to pull it down, "I know what you're thinking. They cut it. My skirt. They said I was a 'bad girl.' I'm forty-two years old for christsakes." Ginger shook her head.

Rubina now was almost certain what had happened. She hoped, wished, prayed that Emmalee didn't. "Did they rape you?" Emmalee asked.

"Emmalee!" Rubina said with a surprisingly motherly tone.

Ginger nodded her head. "I'm Ginger Fontaine, I'm an award-winning Channel Six new reporter. I am somebody. Those men, those pieces of shit…treated me like, like I was nothing."

"I knew I knew you from somewhere," Rubina said quickly wanting to change the subject, for Emmalee's sake as well as her own, "My grandma Mimi had a thing for that news anchor, Jonas something."

"Jonas…" Ginger said.

"How'd they catch you, Ginger?" Rubina asked.

Ginger dabbed her eyes with a cloth from her pocket and said, "We were doing a report on the protestors at the hospital, when someone started shooting and all hell broke loose. We lost our cameraman. Oh Barry, Barry I hope you're all right…".

"Then what happened?" Emmalee asked.

"Yeah, right, sorry. Glen was shot in the leg, but we waited until it had been quiet for a while and then went into the hospital. I tried to take care of him, but there were no doctors, no nurses-"

"We know, we were there too," Emmalee said.

"Shitshitshit," Rubina said. "We got to get out of here. Like asap."

"Where would we go?" Ginger said, "Everything has gone to hell. There's no society, no laws, these guys are going to use us. I heard them talking about you two…"

"What did they say?" Rubina asked.

"I don't think you want to know."

"Yeah, I do. Tell me lady," Rubina said.

"They said they're going to use you two, and any other women they find, to restart the human race. They want to start making babies as fast as they can they were saying. They said they only wanted *to fuck* me though," Ginger said through tears, which made Emmalee start crying.

"C'mon ladies," Rubina said, "we need to figure a way out of here. Anywhere is better than here. Ginger, did you find out anything else about them?"

"They have a leader named Brother Theo. He's their boss, and if he's really alive, we're all in trouble."

"How many?"

"Of them? Only three I saw."

"Only three at the hospital too," Emmalee said.

"Ok, good. Three's what we're dealing with. And they have guns. But I almost got away from them at the hospital, so I don't think they're too smart. This Brother Theo might be though, so we need to get away from here quick."

"I'm with you Rubina," Emmalee said.

"Ok," Ginger said.

Rubina could feel her heart beating faster. She was getting excited. Her chance at redemption might be coming. "We're going to have to attack them when they come in. Bite them, scratch them, kick them in the balls, whatever we have to do. I don't think they'll shoot us, at least if those plans they have for us are true."

"Hey, I have this," Emmalee pulled out a six-inch hunting knife, "It was my boyfriends'. He gave it to me. You want it?" Emmalee handed it to Rubina.

"They didn't search you?"

"Not well. I had this on my arm," Emmalee showed Rubina the arm holster, "They just wanted to grab at my boobs. Fuckers."

"Damn right," Ginger said.

Rubina had never stabbed anyone. In her life there had been people she had wanted to stab, like that pretty bitch from high school that always picked on her, or the one manager who would sometimes pat her butt, but the physical act of stabbing someone was foreign to her. She was talking tough and with the hunting knife she would need to act tough too. She took it from Emmalee. "This will come in handy," Rubina said and inspected the knife, then practiced stabbing the air.

"When were they last here?" Rubina asked.

"Not sure exactly, an hour ago maybe?" Ginger looked to Emmalee for confirmation.

"Seems about right. They said they'd be back with food and water," Emmalee said.

"Ok then. We have to be ready. One of you needs to cause a scene, to distract them. Then I'll come up from behind and stab one of them in the neck."

"You think that will work?" Ginger asked.

"Don't know. Hope so. If there's two of them both of you need to distract them," Rubina said.

Ginger nodded. Rubina said, "Can you do that Emmalee?"

"Yeah."

"You sure?"

"I'm sure," Emmalee said.

"Good. Now we wait."

Chapter Forty-Two

"Clint, Clint you there?" Theo spoke into the walkie-talkie.

"Yeah boss, I'm here. We're at the police station. Shit man, what happened?"

"There was a cop. You find his body?"

"Yeah, but he wasn't a cop. At least that's not what the people in the cell said."

"You didn't let them out, did you?"

"Hell nah."

"Good, leave them there. Meet me at the Spot. Bring D'Mo's body with you. We're going to bury him."

"Right boss, we'll be there soon."

Theo poured himself a shot of whiskey and downed it quickly. Then he poured another. Shaun was sleeping on a gaudy purple couch, snoring. 'At least he's alive,' Theo thought. Things were going better than expected, but not perfect. Nothing was going to be perfect, but Theo was adept at adapting. Any good leader of men had to be, and Theo knew he was a good leader. No, a great leader. A great leader who was ready to take his men and humanity to where it needed to go. He was in charge of the city now and he no doubt of that fact.

After a while Theo heard his men pull up. He would use them to further his goals of power and he knew they were ready to be used, like a bricklayer used his bricks. He was hoping Clint would be the mortar that held them together. He hoped. Clint came in first and saw Theo behind the bar. "Boss, how are you doing?"

"Fine, Clint," Theo said.

Serge, Tay and the young pups from Third Street followed behind Clint. Tay said, "Shit man, I thought Clint was bullshitting us. Good to see you alive."

"Alive and kicking Tay."

"Is Shaun…dead?" Clint motioned over to Shaun.

"He's sleeping; he took one in the arm. He should be fine. Now sit down, all of you," he ordered and they followed.

"You all are lucky. Each one of you," Theo began, and they all intently stared at him, "You've been chosen for a specific purpose. You know what that is?"

The men were silent.

"I'll answer the question. You're alive to help me save our city. This is our city, and we're not leaving. You're all going to have important parts in rebuilding. That's why the rabbit bite chose you, and not our dead friends."

Theo walked around the bar as he spoke placing an empty shot glass in front of them. "If you don't want to be part of this, there's the door." No one moved.

"Good to see you men and willing and able. Clint here is in charge when I'm not. His orders are *my* orders. If you disobey him, you're disobeying me. Those of you that know me know I don't play like that and you *will* get dealt with. By me personally. Understood?"

The men nodded and Theo continued, "Alright then, Clint, pour us some whiskey, we're going to toast."

Clint did so and handed each of them a shot. "Raise your shot glass in the air. To a new world, *our* new world."

Each downed their shot; Theo slammed his on the table, and the young pups did likewise, shaking their heads from the potency of the whiskey. "Relax now men, you did well today, but tomorrow's another day. No day is going to be easy, but you stick with me and you'll do fine for yourself."

Theo set the whiskey bottle on the table where Serge, Clint and Tay sat, then he glanced at the young pups as they stared at him. He could tell they were in awe of him, and it made him smile. They sat in a booth, their arms resting on the table. Theo grabbed a chair and pulled it up to the booth. Then he sat down. "You boys like whiskey?"

"I've had it before," one said and the other two nodded their heads.

"What are your names?" Theo asked, but he already knew, but at this point he didn't want them to know. It hurt his heart to see them, they looked so much like their mother.

"I'm Markus, this is John-two, and he's Ptolemy."

"You know I knew your mother..."

Theo remembered her soft features, her braided hair, her full lips. He was too young to deal with her being pregnant. He didn't know if they were his or not, back then he wasn't the only guy sleeping with their mother. But as he examined the pups' faces, he thought he could see a resemblance.

When he went away to prison their mother would visit him, tell him the boys were his. He told her to screw off, he couldn't do anything from a jail cell for them. Two years into his sentence he heard she had overdosed on smack. Her mother, the boy's grandmother, had to raise them. Once he was out of prison every month he'd deliver an envelope to their grandmother's mailbox with a note attached: use this to take care of the boys. He still wasn't sure if they were his, but he felt obligated to help out.

Now he was not surprised the boys survived the Rabbit Flu as he was even surer that they had half his blood running through their veins. It made more sense that members of his own family would have lived, like Shaun and Tay, his half cousin.

"She was a good woman, just fell in with a bad crowd," Theo said.

"Hey man, don't talk about our mom like that," Markus said.

"Yeah," the brothers echoed.

"What'd you say?" Theo rose from his chair, snapped out of his memories.

"Nothing," Markus said.

"Thought so. Listen to Clint, like I said earlier what he says is what I say, got it?"

They nodded. "If he tells me you're doing a good job I can use you on other things, more important things. You feel me."

"Yeah."

"Ok then," Theo said and rose from his seat, "Clint, come with me back to the office."

Clint followed Theo to his office at the Spot while Tay and Serge did another shot and the young pups gathered around Shaun, now awake, inspecting the bullet hole in his arm as Shaun told them what happened at the police station.

Theo owned the Spot, but hadn't used the office in months; the cops had gotten word he was owner and were trying to or already had bugged the place, but that didn't matter anymore. Only Clint and his other top lieutenants knew where he lived, and he was going to keep it that way for the time being. Theo sat down behind the desk with Clint sitting across from him.

"How did things go at the hospital?"

"It went good. The ambulance is out front. Found six survivors between the two hospitals. We put them in other cells. This one white bitch tried to run, but we caught her. We got a bunch of medications and supplies in the back of the ambulance. You want me to take it anywhere specific?"

"Park it out back, keep it off the street."

"Will do. What's next boss?"

"You know El Supermercado? The one on fifth?" Clint nodded.

"I want you to take it. We can use it for food supplies. If there's anybody there take them to the police cells. Then get some paint and black out the windows. Have the kids do that. I want you to close all the entrances except one, so there's only one way in and the same way out. I want this done immediately. After that's done send Tay and Serge with food and water for the prisoners. Have them stay there and guard it overnight."

"Can do boss."

"Leave the young pups at El Supermercado for the night. They should be able to handle guarding that. You stay here with Shaun tonight, make sure whatever he wants, he gets. Now I'm going to go back to my place and I'll be back in the morning. You're the only one that knows where that is, and I want you to keep it that way, got it?"

"No problem. I won't tell none of them."

"Where's D'Mo's body?"

"In the ambulance."

"Ok, check the basement; I think there's some shovels down there. Grab a couple and we'll bury him. I'll meet you out back."

"Sure thing boss."

Theo nodded slightly to Tay and Serge on his way out; both nodded back. He didn't acknowledge the young pups, but as he walked past they got quiet. Once outside Theo opened the back doors to the ambulance and looked at his brother's bloody, dead, body. "Man D'Mo, I bet you wouldn't have gotten the Flu either. Why'd this have to happen?" Theo said aloud to himself.

He lit a cigarette and sat on the chrome bumper of the ambulance, waiting for Clint. Shortly thereafter Clint emerged with the shovels, old and rusted, and carefully placed them next to D'Mo's body. Theo finished his cigarette and flicked it into the street, then said, "Let's go."

| 43 |

Chapter Forty-Three

Jonas followed Danny up the stairs, into the chapel. The same men who were in the basement earlier were there, along with a couple of women and the guard from outside. No one spoke and Danny led Jonas to the third pew from the front. He saw, at the altar, a person standing with their back to them. The figure had long braided hair, a black vest with white shirt sleeves sticking out from it, tight blue jeans and black boots. The figure turned around to face the congregation; Jonas saw the same lightly freckled face, hoop nose ring, bulging Adam's apple that he had known years before. The same Sister. Sister began speaking, "Praise God that you can all be here today."

"Praise God," the congregation responded in unison.

"Rejoice in the fact that God has chosen you to begin his new human race. We are the new Israelites, God's chosen people, and he has led us here. We're the living children of God. Billions of others were not worthy, but we were. Praise be to God."

"Praise God."

"We were chosen to survive God's wrath. And we have seen his wrath. I've seen many die firsthand, and I know all of you have too. Our God is a vengeful God, and humanity had gotten lazy in its reverence. But he is also a loving God, and that is why you are here. God loves each and every one of you. He brought you to this place, so we can survive, and rebuild, humanity in His image. Praise be to God."

"Praise God."

"But it will not be easy. No sir, it won't be. But we are ready to work, yes we are. We can do it. We will rebuild the human race, in God's image. It will be beautiful and it will be because of God. Praise be to God."

"Praise God."

"I know I don't look like a normal servant of God. And before the Flu I was not an overly religious person; that is true. I took drugs, drank, had sex with whomever whenever I wanted. But that was wrong. I know that now. God proved this to me by allowing me to live, to survive this Rabbit Flu, and he came to me and told me I was to lead his people through these troubling times. And I promise all of you here today I will.

I was misunderstood most of my life. Back in school I was the quarterback, senior class president, then manager at my job, made good money, had a nice place. But I was never happy. I was only happy when I looked as I do now. God understood this; I had many conversations with him during those times, he understood me like no one else did. For helping me get through that extremely tough time of living I made a promise that when God needed me, I would be there. God needs me now, and I am here to do his work.

You are not here by accident. God has a plan for all of us, and if we work together, we can achieve his goals. Together we are stronger than we are apart. That is why God brought us together. All of you are loved by God, and loved by me."

"Today will be a good day. We will prosper and grow. Go about your daily jobs knowing that God loves you, he chose you to do his work. Let us pray," Sister said and led the congregation in the Lord's prayer, ending with "Amen."

Sister finished and left through a door off to the right of the altar. Danny said to Jonas, "C'mon, Sister always wants to meet the new people."

Danny knocked on the door Sister just went through and said, "Sister, we had a new guy come in today. You want to meet him now?"

"Yes, that's fine. Come in, the doors not locked."

They entered the small office; its walls were adorned with pictures, some of real people, others of Jesus, his mother Mary, and crosses of all shapes and sizes. The walls were thin particle board; everything was hung up on push pins. There was a wooden desk in the middle of the office and a set of ancient wooden chairs that faced Sister. She motioned for the men to sit down. "Sister, this guy showed up today. He's on the TV news."

"Jonas…Jonas Johnston? I remember you…do you remember me?"

"Of course, you're why I came here."

"I knew God would bring someone like you to me, someone from my past. It is good to see you," Sister stood up and embraced Jonas.

Sister noticed Danny staring, his mouth slightly agape as he hadn't seen Sister embrace anybody, not in his time as part of her congregation. Sister said, "Danny, you can leave us."

"Are you sure?"

"Jonas is an old friend. I'll be fine."

"Alright, I'll be outside," Danny said and closed the door behind him.

"He's protective of you," Jonas said.

"They all are. I'm the reason they're here, the reason they're still alive."

"Oh really?"

"Yes really. I can't believe I'm speaking to you."

"Me neither, to be honest."

"How's your sister?"

"Don't know. She moved to Phoenix last year with her girl-friend. I haven't heard from her, not since the Rabbit Flu started. So, I don't know."

"I'm sorry Jonas. Me and Shel fell out of touch a couple years back. I had some rough years for a while there. We were such good friends back then, me and her."

"I remember."

"Well, anyway, do you want a drink?"

"Sure, what do you have?"

"Up here I have brandy. You want?"

"Sounds good."

Sister poured them two glasses about half full. She took an ice try from the mini-fridge next her desk and dropped two cubes in each glass and handed one to Jonas. She raised her glass to cheers, and Jonas did likewise. "To old friends," she said, "and new beginnings."

Jonas nodded his head and sipped his brandy. He said, "This is some kind of set-up you have here. I always thought the crosses and religious stuff was a shtick."

"Back when I knew you before it was. But not anymore, not since I started this church about a year ago."

"A year? Wow..."

"We started just meeting at the Y. But the church grew, and I rented this space."

"Doesn't seem like a church space, what with all the bars and stores and such around."

"It doesn't matter what is going on outside, what matters is what happens inside."

Jonas swirled the brandy around in its glass, looking around the room. Jonas thought the weak would always find comfort and safety in religion, and Sister would probably use this to her advantage.

Sister didn't take her eyes off of him. She said, "Sorry to cut our reunion short, but I have some things that need doing. It is so good to see you Jonas, it really is. I'm sure this is a lot to take in. Rest assured I'm glad you're here. We'll talk more later, that's a promise. Let Danny get you set up with a bed, some fresh clothes if you want. Danny?"

Danny opened the door immediately. "Yes Sister?"

"Find Jonas a bed, introduce him around. I have some things I need to take care of."

"You got it. C'mon newsman."

| 44 |

Chapter Forty-Four

"Is there anyone else in other cells?" Rubina asked.

"Don't know. Haven't heard anything," Ginger said.

"Maybe we're the first prisoners," Emmalee said.

Rubina went to the door and said, "Hello? Hello, anybody out there?"

Rubina stood hoping, then a muffled woman's voice, "Who's there?"

"We're in another cell," Rubina said, "Are you alright?"

"We are for now."

"What's your name?"

"Betsy. What's yours?"

"Ruby."

"Betsy, we're getting out of here," Rubina said, "We're going to jump those guys."

"Let us out if you do. Please don't leave us here."

"We'll try. But now you need to keep quiet."

"Ok."

***

They had been waiting for hours. Rubina was thinking clearly as the pain from the knock on her head was finally subsiding. "Where are they? They said they were coming back, right?" Rubina asked aloud.

"That's what they said," Emmalee said.

It was so amazingly quiet once all the people were gone. As such every sound was amplified, so when the women heard a car pull up, Rubina knew it had to be them. "You hear that? Sounds like voices."

As the men approached, the women could hear their conversation. "You want to help me bring this food inside?" "Quit bitching Tay, it weighs like nothing. I'll wait out here. Hurry the fuck up."

"Two of them it sounds like," Rubina told the other two women, "only one's coming in though. Get ready." They both nodded in response.

"Bitches your man is here," the man said as he opened the cell door. He had the assault rifle slung over his back, and he was carrying a box of food in both hands. "Hey you," he motioned to Emmalee "here, come take this."

Emmalee got up from sitting next to Rubina and went toward him. He wasn't the one Rubina bit which she took as a blessing. Emmalee tripped on her way to get the box of food falling in front of the door. "Stupid bitch, what's wrong with you?" he said as he turned his back on Rubina and grabbed Emmalee's arm to help her up.

Once his back was turned Rubina lifted the hunting knife over her head and stabbed him straight down the back of the neck with a force she never used before. The knife stuck in his neck.

"Fuck!" he yelled as he turned around to face Rubina. "You fucking bitch!" He said as he swung his arms behind him, trying to grab the knife out of his back. Blood squirted from his neck across the jail cell, hitting the women. Emmalee shrieked.

The man turned to face Rubina and the rage mixed with pain on his face was something she had never seen before. It momentarily distracted her but she regained her bearings when he lunged at her. Rubina sidestepped him and he ran into the wall, face first. He continued to reach for the knife and turned to face Rubina again. This time she took two steps towards him and kicked him right in the crotch. He tried to scream, but it came out a whimper and he dropped to the floor.

Rubina heard the car horn. "Let's go!" she said and ran toward the partially open door. They made it out and slammed the cell door, locking the man inside. "What about Glenn?" Ginger asked and grabbed Rubina by the arm.

"What? Let go of me! There's no time. We have to get out of here," Rubina said.

The car horn blared again, this time longer. Then they heard the car door slam. "Fuck fuck fuck," Rubina said, "where's the fucking exit?"

"This way," Emmalee said and led them through the office.

They ran in front of the glass entrance door and saw the other man coming toward the entrance. The women quickly went past the entrance door so they wouldn't be seen. "Alright," Rubina whispered, "once he's past us run like hell out of here."

Ginger and Emmalee nodded. "Hey, what's going on out there?" Rubina heard from the other cell. Betsy. "Let us out!"

Rubina ignored her. There was nothing she could do at the moment about the people in the other cell.

"Dude, what is taking you so long?" Serge said as he entered, walking right past the hiding women taking no notice of them. Once they saw him turn the corner and head for the cells they ran for the exit.

Serge looked in the tiny cell window and saw Tay lying on the floor in a pool of blood, a knife sticking out of his neck. "What the fuck?" he said and looked around but the women were already out the door.

"Look! The jeep is still running, go, go!" Rubina said.

Rubina and Emmalee were faster than Ginger, who was lagging behind. "C'mon Ginger, hurry up!" Emmalee said as she neared the jeep. Rubina looked back and saw Serge was coming for them, gun drawn.

"You stupid bitches, I'll kill you for what you did to Tay!" Serge yelled and began firing at them. Rubina made it to the driver's seat when she heard Emmalee scream. Rubina didn't see Ginger fall, didn't see the blood running out of her side and head as she hit the pavement, she just saw the door to the jeep that she opened and got inside. She heard the bullets hit the car and saw Emmalee in the passenger seat, her head between her legs. Rubina hit the gas and drove with her head down as Serge became smaller in the rearview mirror.

| 45 |

Chapter Forty-Five

James didn't *have* to leave his apartment. He was prepared, almost neurotically so with enough food to last him for a year, if he rationed. The emergency food collection began one day while shopping at the store, buying just a couple extra cans at first, and his collection grew.

Bags of salt and rice, vitamins, canned green beans and spinach, corn and peaches, black beans and pinto beans, corned beef hash and condensed milk, Twinkies and ho-hos for a treat, cases of bottled water and Spam among other things, James kept in his apartment pantry to last him at least six months he figured, just in case. In case of what he didn't know for sure, but better to be safe than sorry he always told himself.

A fallout shelter would have been best, because if anything, nuclear war would have probably gotten him first. Living on the third floor of his apartment building however didn't allow for a fallout shelter and he figured he'd be dead anyway in a nuclear war. But just in case of disease, war, famine, aliens or something else like that happened, he'd be ready, he'd be prepared. Now that couldn't be farther from the truth. 'Prepared? No one could prepare for this.

Even the government wasn't prepared. Hell, they were less prepared than I am,' James thought.

It wasn't just food he kept in his abnormally large pantry for a two-bedroom apartment. James had a four-person tent, top-of-the-line sleeping bag, grill with gas attachment, a dozen extra gas tanks for the grill, a hand powered radio one of his exes had bought for him as a present (which was a great present, too bad she was a lousy girlfriend), a case of matches, a case of lighters, and one 9mm handgun.

James knew that if the apocalypse ever came to America having guns would be necessary tools of survival. He had that idea in common with the second amendment gun nuts. He would go to the shooting range about once a month, to practice and let off frustration. It was exhilarating and calming at the same time. His psychiatrist told him people who suffer from depression shouldn't own guns, but he knew himself; he wasn't the suicidal type.

His parents had been hippies, free love and peace and against the war, and as such were anti-gun. They were not happy to hear he had a gun license and had purchased the gun. "Why do you need a gun?" his mother had asked when he told her he bought it.

"For protection, obviously," he told her over the phone.

"But James, we're peaceful people and we raised you to be a peaceful person, too. Guns only bring bad news."

"I know mom but I didn't buy it to hurt anyone. I keep it locked up in my pantry."

"But still, I'd rather, me and your father would rather you didn't own one. I read somewhere that something like eighty percent of all home invasion deaths by gun are by the homeowner's gun, not the robbers."

"What have I been telling you mom? Don't believe everything you read. And I didn't buy the guns for protection against a robber. What stuff do I have to steal?"

James did a quick inventory of all the things he had of "value" in his apartment, could they want his nineteen-inch TV? Or maybe his five-year-old laptop? Or his used furniture he bought at the Goodwill? The only thing he had of any value was an antique telescope which he figured most robbers wouldn't know what to do with.

Funny thing was there was a robber in his apartment a few months before. He was sick, had a fever, and had stayed home from work. Well, the crackhead who broke into his house, one with only his two front teeth, hadn't expected him to be home. He was groggily going to the bathroom when he saw the robber, and the robber froze. "Who the fuck are you? Get the fuck out of my apartment asshole," James had said.

"Back off man, I have a knife," the robber said and grabbed a bunch of quarters off the coffee table. James' laundry money.

"Just get out man," James said and puffed out his chest.

The robber said nothing more and was gone, along with quarters. James laughed to himself as he recalled the story then became sad again when he thought back to his parents. They were right, he didn't even time to get the gun, much less use it to kill some crackhead who stole his laundry money.

His parents were gone now; he knew it, and more so he felt it. In his bones, in his being, he knew his parents were dead. 'I need to forget them. It's better to forget them. Better for me. I need to prepare. To go on. It's what they wanted,' he thought.

'First things first,' he told himself, 'I have to figure where those shots came from.' There had been more gunshots days ago, but that had subsided. Those last shots, the ones that killed those poor people on the highway, those were unique, and they didn't sound like the normal handgun shots. Something more powerful about them.

Now that it was dark he could see what apartment lights were left on. They had to be in one of the near buildings, but what if they weren't facing him? How could he tell? James looked out cautiously from his window with the lights out in his apartment. He didn't want anyone knowing he was here.

He saw many apartments with the lights still on but no one moving; he imagined people didn't care about turning the lights off as they were dying of Rabbit Flu. He looked for movement, first just using his eyes and when he saw nothing, he used the telescope. It didn't take long until he saw them. Men in green military fatigues standing in a corner apartment, ten stories above him. James quickly hid under the window. He then slowly peaked out again at them. 'It had to be them, had to be, they killed those people.' James shuddered and realized, 'I have to close all the blinds, I can't let them see I'm here or they'll kill me too.'

As quietly and calmly as he could James closed all the blinds, never standing, crawling on the ground from window to window in his apartment finally crawling into his bedroom, into his bed. He fell asleep with the 9mm handgun under his pillow.

Chapter Forty-Six

"Won't the government save us?" Nadia asked Franklin as she lay on his comfy tan couch with her feet up.

"I don't think so, not this time," Franklin said from his navy-blue recliner.

"Why not?"

"Why do you think they will?"

"Umm isn't that their job? Isn't that what we pay taxes for and stuff?"

"I don't mean to burst your bubble but I don't think the government is out there. And I don't think they'll save us."

"Why not?"

"After what happened at hospital, soldiers shooting civilians and then they declared martial law..."

"What's martial law?"

"It's basically when the army takes over. That's what they did at the hospital I guess, and the last thing on the TV was the newsman saying that's what the Vice President in Washington said."

"I don't really follow politics. But if the Vice President is still in Washington, maybe we should go there."

"I hadn't planned on going anywhere, at least not for a while," Franklin said.

"Why not?"

"I ordered a bunch of food a week ago, just in case. Enough for two months maybe longer."

"You knew this was going to happen?"

"No, but it felt better to be prepared."

"I don't know Franklin. I think we should leave. If not Washington maybe somewhere else."

"Nadia I'm going to be honest with you. I didn't leave this apartment more than once or twice a month and then only for work meetings before the Rabbit Flu."

"Oh. What did you do?"

"I was a customer service rep. I could do it from home," he said and motioned to the headset with a microphone attached that sat next to his computer. "Speaking of that, I've been wanting to do this for a while."

Franklin rose from his recliner and went to pick up the headset. He dropped it on the floor and crushed it beneath his foot, enjoying the crackling sound of it breaking. "Feel better?" Nadia asked.

"Actually, I do."

"Franklin, don't you understand, we're free now. Free to do whatever we want. Don't you get it?"

I do, but I wasn't the one who tried to kill myself..."

"Hey! Shut up, I don't want to talk about that."

"Ok fine."

"And I didn't, did I?" Nadia said, "But now I feel alive, really alive. It's weird but I've never felt this, this life force that's running through me. Don't you feel it too?"

"I don't feel any different, not really, than last week before this all started."

"I'm not going to stay here, that's for sure. I want to live! I know that now. We can go anywhere, we don't have to go to Washington."

"But you don't know what's out there, what else survived. What if it's bad, what if bad people survived. I'm not...prepared for that."

"C'mon Franklin, really? What have you got to be scared of?"

"I don't have to justify myself to you, kid."

"I'm not some kid, I'm twenty years old, and not scared of life like you!" Nadia got up from the couch and made her way quickly out of his apartment, slamming the door behind her.

"Nadia, where are you going?" Franklin asked, but she was already gone.

Franklin didn't chase after her but he did wonder if Nadia was coming back. She was in such a bad way earlier it would surprise him if she didn't. But she was young and pissed, so he let her be. He heard her knock loudly on another condo door down the hall, but he didn't follow. He just sat on his couch, opened a magazine about computers, and waited.

'What the fuck is his problem?' Nadia thought as she walked down the hall with purpose. 'This is what I'm left with,' Nadia thought as 'this old man, well not that old but well, in his forties, who now that the world is open to us, doesn't want to leave his apartment. Great.'

She tried the door handles to the other condos but they were locked, until she arrived at apartment 2202. She knocked loudly then turned the handle and opened the door and went inside.

The smell hit her as she entered, from what she didn't know, and didn't want to. All the windows were closed and the stuffiness of the condo exacerbated the horrible smell and she crossed the orange carpeting to a window and opened it. She breathed in fresh air and sighed. Nadia thought, 'I mean, I'm scared too, but at least we're two people instead of alone. I can't be alone, not again. I'll have to apologize, I know that. I don't want to not like Franklin, he seems like an alright guy, better than some asshole.'

There was no one in the main living room, which was connected to the kitchen and dining room, just like Franklin's place. The walls were painted an awful purple, and there were old movie posters in frames adorning the walls. There was also an antique grandfather clock that hadn't been wound. The time on it read 4:40. Nadia went to the kitchen and began opening cabinets, looking for something to drink. Finding nothing she went back into the living room and sat on the couch. 'I bet he's worried about me, worry if I'll come back. I will, but not without any booze.'

Nadia surveyed the living room again, and this time noticed an old record player sitting on top of a burgundy cabinet. She opened the cabinet, finding only records. 'Who listens to records anymore?' she thought, but then realized she didn't want to know the answer. Eventually Franklin came into apartment 2202 quietly while Nadia was looking in the record cabinet.

"Nadia?" he said softly.

"Fuck!" she said and fell on her behind. "What the fuck Franklin, you scared the shit out of me."

"I'm sorry for before," he said as he helped her up.

"Me too," she said and sat on the couch. She motioned for Franklin to sit as well, which he did in an old rocking chair. He rocked slowly back and forth, looking at Nadia, then said, "I want you to know I'm not scared, I just, I don't know, I'm set in my ways. Like I told you I ordered a bunch of food just in case. But that's stupid. What am I going to do after the food runs out? Or when the power goes out? I don't know."

"It's ok."

"Thanks," he said and for a few moments both were silent while they looked around the apartment.

Then Franklin said, "So what were you looking for?"

"Booze."

"You should've asked. I have a case of Cabernet Sauvignon in my apartment."

"Wine, right? Is it white or red?"

"Red."

"Cool. Let's get out of here. I didn't find anything to drink here, and this smelly, old timey condo is giving me the creeps," Nadia said as they left condominium 2202.

| **47** |

Chapter Forty-Seven

"We got to go back, we can't leave those other people, and what about Ginger?" Emmalee said after they had driven a while.

"I know, I know, but do you want to go back there?"

"No. But we left them…"

"Hey, I stabbed somebody! I fucking stabbed and probably killed that guy back there. Shit…"

"It's ok. I'm sorry. You're tough," Emmalee said and rubbed Rubina's shoulder. "Do you know where we are Rubina?" Emmalee asked.

"Yeah, this is my grandma's neighborhood. She's lived here for years. What were you doing down here?"

"My boyfriend lived downtown. We went to the South General when they said the Downtown hospital was closed."

"What about your parents?"

"I don't know…I ran away a couple of weeks ago."

"Seriously? Why aren't they looking for you? A girl that looks like you going missing, I'm surprised it wasn't all over the news."

"What do you mean 'a girl like me?'"

"You know, white, cute…"

"You're not a dyke are you?"

"No, I'm not. But you know the media always makes a big deal out of cute white girls that go missing."

"Oh, well not me, I guess. I actually told them I was leaving. They're getting a divorce, or they were...they didn't have time for me."

"That can't be true."

"You'd be surprised. They knew I could take care of myself."

"Did they know about your boyfriend?"

"I told them I was going to stay with him, but they didn't know him, like, personally."

"Crazy," Rubina said shaking her head, then to change the subject, "Hey, check if they left anything in the back seat, would you?" Rubina said.

"Check out these guns," Emmalee said and held up a large assault rifle. "Is this an AK?" she asked.

"Don't know, but it should come in handy," Rubina said, then "You hungry?"

"Yeah, starving."

"We should get off the street. Who knows if the other guy or that Brother Theo is looking for us, and the sun's going down. There's a convenience store just around the corner; we can get some food there."

The windows were all busted out of the convenience store. The place was trashed. They heard mice or rats or squirrels making little squeaking noises. "Keep to the higher shelves, less critters," Rubina said.

Emmalee went to the cooler and opened the door. A cool breeze hit her. "Stuff is still cold," she said.

"You need a bag?" Rubina asked, and they proceeded to load up on supplies.

They each carried two plastic bags of canned weenies, beef jerky, candy, potato chips, ice cream, energy drinks and soda, all the essentials. "Where to?" Emmalee asked once they were back in the jeep.

"Only place I know is my Mimi's house. We can stay there tonight and figure things out in the morning."

Rubina parked three houses down from her Mimi's, so in case the gang was looking for them they would assume the wrong house and that would give the women enough time to react and get out of there. Hopefully.

Mimi's house was among many single-family brick homes with plastic awnings, mostly widowers and Eastern European families. It didn't matter now that everyone was gone, but Rubina always missed the old days when she was a kid and her grandfather was alive and every Sunday the family got together for dinner, and she saw her aunts, uncles, and cousins and ate until they were uncomfortable, then watched football with her grandfather. But when he died, the family drifted apart, and she saw her aunts, uncles, and cousins only on rare occasions of weddings or funerals, Christmas and Thanksgiving. That was all over now.

Once they entered the house Emmalee said "It smells like old people."

"So?" Rubina said.

"Just saying."

"Well keep it to yourself. I need a shower, what about you?"

"Yeah, this blood is so gross."

The women showered, Rubina first, then Emmalee. Once they were both finished Rubina said, "Let's eat and then I'm going to bed."

They ate their convenience store dinner and afterward Rubina showed Emmalee the house. "You can sleep in this room," Rubina pointed to the spare bedroom that Rubina's aunt had lived in until she was thirty-six.

"It's not your grandmother's room, is it?" Emmalee asked.

"No, it's that room," she said, motioning with her hand to a closed door on the other side of the hall.

Rubina had left Mimi's door closed with her still inside. Now that Emmalee was with her she could think about burying Mimi, probably in the backyard. 'We could do it,' she thought, 'But do I want to? Is that what she would want? She seems perfectly fine in her own bed, in her own house.'

Mimi had bought a plot in the neighborhood cemetery next to her husband, Rubina's grandfather Walter. There just was no feasible way for her and Emmalee to take Mimi's body there, not with those gangsters still out there. But Mimi's body would start to smell; that was a fact.

Rubina had come to the realization that she couldn't stay in this house forever. There was a whole world out there. Hell, she'd never even seen most of America or even the Pacific or Atlantic oceans. She'd been to the Gulf of Mexico once, got really sunburned, but it was still the best vacation of her life. The water so warm it was like a bath, the sand so white and soft under her feet, the relaxation she had felt knowing that she didn't have to do anything.

She really didn't want to stay in the city much longer. 'I'm sure they'll be other problems, other bad people out there, but I know that they're out there. I'm going to find someplace else to live. I'm going to leave Mimi right where she is, at peace.'

"I think I'm going to crash, I am so freaking tired," Emmalee said, "Is it cool if I leave the door open?"

"Yeah. I'll leave mine open too. If you hear anything, anything strange, scream to high heaven, ok?"

"Ok," Emmalee said, "Hey Rubina?"

"What?"

"Thanks."

| 48 |

Chapter Forty-Eight

By nightfall eleven bodies littered the Southern highway, dried blood in pools sticking to the hot asphalt. Hermes and Crudo had done the shooting, all sniper bullets through the head. "There should be less activity at night," Jackson said.

"The bodies lying there should be a pretty good warning," Radio said.

"Me and Hermes are fucking deadly with that sniper," Crudo said and went to high five Hermes, who didn't high five back, "Don't hate the player, hate the game."

Jackson returned to his game of Solitaire while Hermes flipped through a car magazine. "Sir, there's something that is worrying me though," Radio said.

"What is it?"

"We've had no communication from Central Command since we got here."

"Maybe it's our location?"

"I thought of that, but I went to roof earlier, got nothing. Went to the building across the street, nothing. Sir, the last communication we had was yesterday inside that body shop near the hospital."

"What are you getting at Radio?"

"Something's happened. Maybe they got the Rabbit Flu too."

"I think they've abandoned us," Hermes said.

"Wouldn't be the first time…" Crudo said.

"Shut up Crudo, you're not helping. Let me think…" Jackson paced the room, thinking, 'should I tell them what the Lieutenant Colonel told me? Will it do any good?'

"Now what are you thinking Major?" Radio asked.

"Sir, if I could speak honestly…" Hermes said.

"Fine."

"Sir I don't feel right anymore about killing people just trying to leave. I was in New Orleans when we had to prevent people from leaving the city. This is America sir, and it's not right. I mean, if you give the order, I'll do it, no question. But if we're all that's left…"

"We're not, that's for sure. Your opinion is taken into account Hermes. Central command isn't all dead either, and we have orders. Radio, keep trying Central Command."

"But what if we can't get a hold of them? What if they're dead from the Rabbit Flu too?"

"I doubt they are. They're smarter than us, remember that. And we're all alive, that vaccine or whatever shot they gave us has kept us alive-"

"But not all of us," Crudo said.

"Radio, anything from Central Command yet?"

"Still nothing sir."

"Major, I think it's time you come clean with us," Crudo said.

"About what?"

"About what the Lieutenant Colonel told you in the body shop. I know he told you something, you're as easy to read as a kid's book."

"I told you already, he told us to find a spot to watch the Southern Highway and prevent anyone leaving."

"But why?"

"You think I asked why? That's not what a soldier does. We follow orders. You all know that."

"But I think you asked why, or he told you why. Just tell us man, we deserve to know."

Jackson knew telling them wouldn't change anything. He already had a lot of innocent blood, innocent American blood, on his hands. It was easier when they were in some god forsaken country on the other side of the world, but this was his home, these were his fellow soldiers, his fellow Americans, and he finally relented.

"The Lieutenant Colonel told me what I told you, don't let anyone leave. The why? It's because they figured if we don't let anyone leave, we might save the rural citizens. Rabbit Flu, he said, is supposed to die out in seven days, then they'll come get us. That's what he said."

"So why didn't you tell us?" Crudo asked.

"You know why. And besides, what does it matter?" Jackson said.

"Because we're killing innocent survivors," Hermes said.

"I have to agree with Hermes sir," Radio said.

"Yeah, I'm all for shooting at people shooting at us, but this has gotten way too easy," Crudo said.

"So what? We haven't heard from Central Command for a day and half and you guys are ready to abandon our orders? Not going to happen. But as leader of this unit I do have a plan."

"Alright, now we're talking," Crudo said.

"Tomorrow morning, if we still haven't heard from Central Command, Radio you and Hermes are heading to Central Command. It's about 250 miles southeast of here, right?"

"Yes sir."

"Once there you'll report back to us. Hopefully you can get some more answers. I'm going to stay and do the job we were assigned. Since there's four of us, we'll split into teams of two. I can't trust you to not go off the reservation Crudo, so you're sticking with me. Hermes, you're going with Radio."

"Yes sir."

"Now you two get some sleep. Crudo, you got the first shift watching the highway tonight. Wake me up at two hundred hours. I'll take over then. Everyone understood?"

"Yes sir."

| 49 |

Chapter Forty-Nine

Jonas was shown the common room; there were green cots lining the walls, each with a folded blanket and fluffed pillow on them. It reminded Jonas of a youth hostel he had stayed in while studying in Paris as a much younger man. There was an ancient drinking fountain in the corner that he was surprised still worked when he tried it. The water was cool but with a slight metal taste to it. The tile on the floor was cream and looked clean but worn. Jonas was sure that if he was standing on it barefoot it would be cold.

Danny showed him where to find extra clothes; they were in large red plastic bins, every bin had a sex and a size, like WXL for women extra-large, and ML for men large, and so on. Like he told Sister earlier he was happy in his clothes so he ignored the bins.

Right after dark Danny came back into the common room, along with the rest of the congregation. They all took a cot, but Danny came over to Jonas. "How are you doing?"

"I'm fine. Thanks."

"Sister wants to see you."

"Now?"

"Yes now. Come on."

Danny led Jonas back through the chapel, into Sister's office. "Thank you, Danny. Sleep well."

"Good night, Sister," Danny said as he left.

"He's loyal," Jonas said.

"Yes, he is. Danny's been with me since I started the church," Sister said then changing her smile to a more humorless look "I have a serious question for you and I want you to take your time thinking before you answer. Ok?"

Jonas nodded. Sister continued, "I want to know if you think that the Rabbit Flu was an act of God, and if so, the act of a malicious God punishing the sinners of humanity?"

"Like Old Testament God you mean?" Jonas asked.

"Yes, you could say that."

"I don't know really. I think maybe we had it coming."

"What do you mean?"

"Like humanity had it coming. It was bound to happen at some time in human history. I'm more surprised it wasn't a nuclear war or something like that. But do I think it was an act of God? I don't know, it could be, I mean I won't discount the possibility-"

"Are you a religious person Jonas?"

"I'm not."

"Not even after the Rabbit Flu has just wiped out most of humanity?"

"That's not going to make me turn to religion Sister. Religion didn't save the billions of Muslims or Christians or Taoists or Jews or any other religious people that died from the Rabbit Flu."

"Then why are you here, talking to me?"

"I told you earlier, we were friends once upon a time. I figured my wife is dead, just about everyone I know or knew is dead, so I went looking for a friendly face."

"You're a pragmatist Jonas Johnston. I like that about you."

"Thanks, I guess."

"No, I really mean it. I want your help. You're smart, resourceful, a true man of the world. But there are other people working to bring about your demise. Yours and mine, these people they seek to control what's left of humanity. I think, no, I know I can provide a better, more positive way."

"Who exactly are you talking about?"

"Who indeed? That's what I want you to find out."

"Alright, I'm game. But I'm not buying into all the God and religious stuff to be honest with you."

"I wouldn't want you to be any other way. Right now, I have a job for you to do. Electricity and lights are still on, right?"

"As far as I can tell."

"I want you to take these night vision binoculars, and this map, and go around this area, South City," Sister pointed with a manicured nail, "I want you to mark where you see lights, or more specifically movement, people. Don't get too close, I don't want you to get hurt."

"Why do you think I'd get hurt?"

"Like I said, there are bad people out there."

| 50 |

Chapter Fifty

Theo and Clint buried D'Mo in a cemetery about a mile away from Theo's home; then he sent Clint to El Supermercado and planned his next moves while eating a small dinner and then went to bed.

The one rule he never broke was getting nine hours sleep. It seemed like a lot, maybe more than most need, but he knew himself, knew what he needed, and sleep was important to him. Theo was awoken by the crackle of the walkie-talkie. "Boss? Theo? You there?"

Theo rubbed his eyes and grasped for the walkie-talkie which was on his nightstand. "Clint what the hell do you want?"

"Boss we have a problem."

"What is it?"

"Boss, Tay is dead. Those bitches we picked up at the hospital stabbed him."

"What? It sounded like you said Tay is dead."

"He is. Tay's dead."

"Fuck. Didn't you search them?"

"Tay and Serge did. Or at least I thought they did."

"How many got out? All of them?"

"Only three, and Serge killed one of them. The others were in another cell."

"Feeding the prisoners shouldn't have been difficult. God-dammit," Theo said, "Any other problems?"

"No boss. Everyone else is here, at the Spot, all accounted for."

"What about Shaun?"

"He's sleeping."

"You sure? Is he breathing?"

"Let me check," Clint said then returned to the walkie-talkie, "Yeah boss, he's breathing. He wanted some Oxycontin so I gave him a couple pills. You said to give him anything he wanted."

"Fine. Are the pups alright?"

"They're fine. They painted the windows at El Supermercado real good."

"Are you done there?"

"We were working on shutting down the entrances like you said, but that was when Serge showed up and told us about Tay. After that we went back to the jail and gave the food to the people in the other cell. We made sure they weren't going to try to escape, and they didn't. Then we all went back to the Spot to check on Shaun, and now I'm telling you."

"So…you didn't finish it up?"

"We're almost done. I figured we'd finish it tomorrow. Serge needed a drink and the pups were worn out. But we'll be back there tomorrow, no problem."

"It is a problem Clint. You fucked up. I told you to leave the pups at El Supermercado. Why didn't you do that?"

"I figured we needed them at the police station. You want me to take them there now?"

"No, nobody should fuck with that place. But get there early tomorrow, like dawn. No drinking tonight, you got it?

"Yeah boss."

"Drop off the pups and Serge, then I want you to come see me. Alone. Understand?"

"I understand boss. But it wasn't my fault. Stupid fucking Tay."

"Be here tomorrow. Early. I'll be waiting."

| 51 |

Chapter Fifty-One

Franklin poured two large wine glasses halfway full and brought them into the living room. Nadia was sitting on the couch, and Franklin made like he was going to hand her the glass, but then held it back and said, "Hey, didn't you say you were twenty? I don't think you're old enough."

"I'm old enough now, don't you think?"

"I was just kidding," he said and handed her the glass.

"Can I smoke in here?" she asked.

"Before all this I would've said no, but now, who cares? Light up."

Nadia did so and Franklin took a seat in his recliner, and began speaking, "Nadia, I'm fifty-four years old-"

"You don't look it," she said with a smile.

"Thanks. Anyway, I've seen a lot in my life, but nothing prepares you for this. For every person you know or ever did know being dead."

"I know; it's fucked up."

"That's what I'm saying. My life before, I was self-sufficient, like I said earlier, I barely left this condo. And I was happy, at least I thought I was..."

"Well I wasn't. I didn't like my job, but it paid the bills. Now there's no more bills to pay, nothing tying us down here. I think we should leave."

"I guess…" Franklin said as he drank more wine.

"Franklin, look at me," Nadia said and stared at Franklin who looked back into her stunning blue-green eyes, "We're going. We don't have to go today, but tomorrow we're leaving. If you want to help decide where we go, that's fine. But I'm not going alone, and I'm not leaving you here. It wouldn't be right."

He looked at Nadia's painted fingernails, then down her toes, noticing the matching polish. Nadia was too cute, too young, too much, for Franklin to turn down. 'She needs a protector, I mean look at her. She's fragile, she'll never make it out there on her own,' he thought.

"Fine," Franklin said, "but first, where do you want to go?"

"I want to see the ocean. You know I've never seen the ocean? I've seen rivers, and the big lake, but never an endless ocean. I want to do that."

"I think we can make that work."

"Why, is there somewhere you want to go?"

"Nope. I've been most everywhere, and I'm not just saying that to sound like a jerk."

"You're not a jerk. Where all have you been?"

"When I was ten me and my mom went to Mexico City and Cancun. I just remember swimming in the ocean and the hotel pool. I remember my mother wearing a red and white polka dot swimsuit," Franklin closed his eyes and pictured her.

He continued, "Her family was well-to-do. She didn't work, just raised me and took me around the world. We went to Europe, Russia, China, Japan, Australia, New Zealand, too many places to remember. But Mexico, that was my favorite trip. It was so differ-ent from the other places. I remember seeing a boy with a llama. I could tell he loved it. Like a boy and his dog but more so. I wanted something to love that much."

"You want to go to Mexico? I could do that, just as long as we see the ocean."

"Mexico's on the ocean. At least parts of it."

"Oh."

"It's ok. But first we need to make a list and then go to a store and get supplies for the trip."

"What kind of list?" she said.

We need to be like Thoreau, you know?"

"Huh?" Nadia looked at him.

"You know, Walden, Henry David Thoreau?" Still nothing on Nadia's face. "Seriously? What do they teach in school nowadays?"

"Nothing important. If you say we need a list like Thoreau then I guess we do," Nadia said, a little hurt by Franklin's implication.

"You want more wine?" Franklin asked.

"Yes, please."

Franklin went to the kitchen and brought back two more glasses, this time three-quarters the way full, and a pen and paper. "Well in *Walden*, before he 'ventured into the wilderness,' you should know he made a list. So that's what we should do. Of what we'll need, and what we can carry."

Franklin continued, "I figure we'll need mostly camping supplies. Propane tanks, portable stove, matches, lighters, a compass, sleeping bags, a tent-"

"Why are we sleeping outside? There should be plenty of empty houses for us to sleep in."

"Just in case, you know," Franklin said, but he was thinking more about the dead bodies inside those 'empty' houses. "What, you never been camping?"

"No, what's that make me some kind of freak?"

"It doesn't. Just means you're not the outdoorsy type, that's all," Franklin said and finished his second large glass of wine. Then he continued and decided to tell her what he was thinking, "Maybe you're right. But I don't want to go into houses where there are dead people."

"Me neither, that's true. And what if they come back to life, like zombies or something?"

"Be serious. I don't want to disturb the dead. There will probably be hotels along the way, and there shouldn't be too many dead people in them hopefully. But I don't know how far we'll get every day, and I still think we should be prepared."

"Alright Franklin, let's go camping."

Franklin continued to add items to the list, including vitamins, first aid kit, short wave radio, flashlights, batteries, socks, twine, binoculars, fresh water tablets, hunting knife. As he wrote Nadia rose from the couch and took the two glasses into the kitchen. "We've finished one bottle," she said, a little tipsy, "You want more?"

"Sure," Franklin said, chewing on the pen.

She came back with two more glasses, and set Franklin's down in front of him. "I think it's done," he said and handed the list to Nadia.

She read the list over and said, "All important stuff. But you're missing something."

"What?"

"Protection. You know like a gun or something."

"I've never used one."

"Neither have I. But you said there might be bad people out there. We heard those gunshots earlier, so other people are out there."

"You're right," he said and wrote down 'gun' on the list.

They drank more wine and Nadia smoked more cigarettes. Franklin looked more and more appealing to her. 'He was an attractive older man, well, at least not ugly,' Nadia thought, 'I want this. I want to make him happy. If he's willing to leave his house for me at the very least I can try to show him I appreciate it.'

After the second bottle she rose from the couch and sauntered her way to Franklin, just as she would've if she was still working in that rat hole strip club. But this time it was different. They wouldn't let her drink at the club, being under twenty-one and all. When she did drink she usually didn't drink much, but now the wine was getting to her. "Do you have any music Franklin?"

"Nothing you'd probably enjoy," he said, "and we don't want to draw attention, even way up here."

She turned her back to him and began to sway her hips, slowly and sensually. Franklin didn't say anything, he just watched, his eyes transfixed on her. Nadia inched closer to him until she lost her balance and fell in his lap, laughing at herself. "That was sexy, up until your wipe out," he said, laughing along with her.

Their faces came together and they kissed. "I don't want to be alone Franklin," she said in between their passionate kissing. "Don't worry, you won't be," he said and carried her to his bedroom.

TWO DAYS AFTER THE END OF THE WORLD

Part III: Destruction and Preparation

Chapter Fifty-Two

The sun was rising and its rays of warmth and light began to cover the city. Tyreke was surprised he had slept at all, but he had, and had woken up in his mother's bed, clutching her favorite red housecoat. Once fully awake he made his way to the refrigerator where he drank some milk directly from the carton and finished it. He didn't look toward his bedroom, where his best friend lay dead. Dead by his own hand. Once he started thinking about that he quickly left the apartment and headed for the roof.

He looked out across horizon down at the city below and sighed. 'What do I do now?' he thought. He heard Cedric's voice in his head, 'You have to move on, get out of this city, find other people.' "But where Ced? Where do I find them? How do I know if I can trust them? Dang…" he said aloud.

As if answering his question he saw them. Three teenage boys, younger than himself, walking toward the gas station. He ducked, instinctively not wanting to be seen, and just peered over the ledge. The neon OPEN sign was on in the gas station window and it struck Tyreke as odd. He couldn't place the boys, rather how he knew them, but their white armbands and crisp white baseball hats that shone in the sun, those he recognized. The sign of Brother Theo's Disciples.

Tyreke continued to watch as the boys entered the store. Once they were inside, he stood up and continued watching. He wasn't scared of them because they looked younger and if there's anything kids typically don't fear its kids younger than themselves.

They were being loud inside, breaking things and yelling. Normally he wouldn't have been able to hear what was going on inside the store, what with the traffic and people. But now he could hear everything. Then he heard a scream, tinged with fear. It only took minutes until he saw the boys push through the glass doors back out into the street carrying something. They were carrying a body.

He couldn't make out the face of the body, but by the way the head hung he was sure it was dead. 'Probably one of the clerks,' he thought. The boys dropped the body on the ground and proceeded to kick it like they would a soccer ball, but with such force that Tyreke again became apprehensive and wanted to hide. But this time he didn't, he just continued to watch them desecrate the clerk's body. Finally tired from kicking, they spit on the body, one last gesture to show their disgust for the clerk.

One of the boys lit what looked like a cigarillo, but Tyreke realized it was a blunt once he saw them pass it around. His fear was subsiding and his intrigue grew. A part of him wanted to go to them, to see what they were doing, to share in the smoking of the blunt. He didn't have a choice once they saw him. "Hey, hey you," one called and pointed, drawing the other's attention.

"Yeah?" he responded in his deepest voice.

"Come down, man, you want to hit this?" they motioned with the arms for Tyreke to come and join them.

"Alright," he said loudly and made his way down the stairs, out the door to where they were.

'They won't hurt me,' Tyreke thought and he had no reason to believe this thought, but his instincts told him they were ok, even with the dead clerk's body still on the ground. The boys watched him approach, still passing the blunt between themselves.

As Tyreke approached, he recognized the boys. The pups from Third Street they were known as around the neighborhood. They had a bad reputation even though they were only thirteen years old. He also knew them because they sold Cedric the gun. The gun Tyreke used to kill his best friend. 'Fuck! I forgot the gun upstairs,' he thought but knew he couldn't go get it, at least not at that moment.

The leader of the triplets stepped forward and said, "What's up man?" and extended his hand. Tyreke shook it, then did the same with the other two. "Who are you man?"

"Tyreke."

"Cool, cool. I'm Markus, this is John-Two, and this is our little brother Ptolemy."

"Fuck you! I came out like three minutes after you Markus," Ptolemy said.

"Still, you're the youngest," Markus said and laughed, then "Here Tyreke, hit this."

Tyreke took the blunt to his lips. He'd only smoked weed a few times with Cedric, and had liked it, and also, he wasn't turning it down now. "Thanks," he said.

Tyreke passed it to Ptolemy, and Tyreke fixated on the body of the clerk. Markus noticed and said, "You want to kick that fucker? You must know that asshole, always watching us in his stupid store, thinking we were going to steal something-"

John-Two said, "But we were trying to steal stuff," and laughed.

"Yeah, I know, but fuck him and his fucking store," Markus said and spit on the dead clerk, then "Kick him Tyreke, right in his fucking face, man it feels good."

Tyreke didn't want to, didn't see the need to, but same as with the blunt he did it. Twice, and then noticed the blood on his all-white shoes and winced. The other boys didn't notice. Markus passed him the blunt again and Tyreke took it, inhaling slowly. Then Markus asked him, "So what's up with you Tyreke? You look familiar…you go to TJeff?"

TJeff stood for Thomas Jefferson high school, the school Tyreke and Cedric attended. But he hadn't seen the triplets there. "Yeah. Did you guys?"

"Only for a bit, but there ain't no school can hold us," John-Two said, then continued, "You still got the uniform on, that's weird."

"I didn't feel like changing, that's all."

"I feel you," Markus said but still stared at Tyreke with a quizzical look. "Now I remember, you're friends with Ced, right?"

"Right. He was my best friend."

"He dead?"

"Yeah."

"Fucking sucks man. Our grand-mom is dead, our aunties and uncles too. Now we just have Brother Theo. You like these hats? They're tight, right?"

"Yeah, they're cool. Brother Theo's alive?"

"Sure is, we saw him yesterday," Markus said as he finished the blunt, and flicked the rest into the street. "Hey Tyreke, man, you want to come with us?"

He was wondering if they would ask him that. He didn't want to go; he never wanted to meet Brother Theo, not after what he had heard. He heard Theo had a face full of silver stud piercings, lining both his lips, his eyebrows, his chin, two in his nose. He had heard one time some cop pulled one out of his lip, and then later they found that cop with his tongue cut out and eyes full of acid so he couldn't identify Theo. Tyreke didn't know if it was true, but he was in no hurry to meet him. Still, what other choice did he have?

Go back upstairs, with Ced's dead body? No thanks. "Yeah. If that's cool, that is."

"Yeah man, we got a sweet set-up. With Brother Theo, we're going to own this city. Own this motherfucker!"

All the boys laughed, including Tyreke, who, while uneasy, felt safer than he had since the Rabbit Flu began.

Chapter Fifty-Three

Franklin woke up, alone, to static coming from his alarm clock. He thought the static was odd, but not too much so as he hit the snooze button and went back to his dream. Ten minutes later the same static, no news, no music, just static again came from his alarm clock. He hit the off button, threw the sheets off himself and stumbled to the bathroom. His head hurt and his eyes ached. He managed to lift the toilet seat before pissing for what felt like forever. Once done he washed his hands and face, slapping his cheeks lightly for effect.

He walked to the kitchen, wearing only blue plaid boxers and a white t-shirt, went to the refrigerator, took out the orange juice and drank from carton. He walked with the carton into the living room and dropped the orange juice with a thud. "Shit!" he said.

"Good morning, Franklin," Nadia said, stretching her arms and yawning from the couch.

"I…I forgot you were here."

"Yeah, it's weird, isn't it?" Nadia said and sat up. She had a blanket on top of her, and Franklin tried to remember if last night really happened. 'If it did, why's she on the couch?' he wondered to himself.

"Do you need some help cleaning up that OJ?"

"Um…no, I got it," he said and went back to the kitchen to get a towel. Nadia followed.

"What's for breakfast?" she said as she started going through his cabinets.

"I have some cereal in the cabinet above the stove, there's also maybe some oatmeal…" he said as he cleaned up the spilled orange juice.

Once finished he went back into the kitchen and saw Nadia still going through his cabinets. She was wearing a too big for her, sky-blue t-shirt with unintelligible markings. It wasn't Franklin's. And she wasn't wearing any pants. When she reached for the top shelves, Franklin noticed himself staring at her legs as her oversized t-shirt just came past her butt.

She turned and faced him, box of bran flakes in hand. "Bran flakes? Franklin, you are so boring."

He quickly looked away, toward the fridge. "Like I said there's oatmeal too."

"No, that's even more boring. This is fine. You have some sugar and a bowl?"

"Yeah, in that cabinet there," he pointed.

"You want some too?"

"Sure."

They ate at his kitchen table, flakes crunching in both their mouths. "Nadia," Franklin said, "we were together last night, weren't we?"

"You don't remember?"

"It's just, you were on the couch when I woke up."

"Yeah, so? I don't want this to get weird between us. I mean, we just met, and my boyfriend, he's dead like fifteen floors below us or something. It's just a lot, you know?"

"I understand."

"Don't be hurt Franklin. Please?"

"I'm fine. Just hung over and my head hurts."

"You want me to get you some aspirin?"

"That'd be great, it's in the-"

"Bathroom. I know because I took some this morning. I'll be right back."

Nadia returned with the aspirin and a glass of water. "Thanks," Franklin said.

"When do you want to leave?" she asked.

"You still want to go?"

"Um…yeah. You don't want to?"

"I just didn't know if you still want to go, you know, with me."

"Franklin, stop it. Nothing is changed or different between us. I wanted last night to happen. To feel normal, like nothing was wrong…"

"So where do we stand?"

"We're both adults, right? I don't regret last night, do you?"

"Of course not, at least not what I remember."

"The simple answer is I don't know. We're the only two people we know are alive. Let's just see where life takes us, ok?"

"Ok," Franklin said. He would half to live with her answer for now. He didn't know exactly what he wanted but for now he knew he wanted to be with her and to protect her.

Nadia could tell he was thinking and asked, "You good?"

"Yeah. I'm fine with what you said."

"Good deal. Let's get dressed and blow this popsicle stand."

Chapter Fifty-Four

James awoke that morning feeling better than he had over the past few days, past few weeks even. Something about that morning, he couldn't tell why, gave him a calm that he hadn't experienced except when he was really stoned. Like stoned on pot from Amsterdam stoned. Euphoric and not caring about the present situation, James ate a bowl of corn flakes sitting on his couch watching the events, or non-events as it were, from his living room window.

He wanted to eat some pure sugar cereal, something like Cocoa Puffs like he used to eat as a kid when he would stay with his grandparents, but all he had was corn flakes. He was trying to be healthy, eat better, exercise and such, but what did it matter now? He wanted to eat deep dish pizza, cookies and cream ice cream, lasagna, sweet and sour chicken, burritos the size of a person's head, but he didn't have any of that. Trying to be healthy before the Rabbit Flu killed most of humanity was not serving him well this morning. In any case he did what he could and covered his corn flakes in sugar and ate two bowls.

Nothing was happening on the streets. In his early morning euphoria even the soldiers in the other building didn't faze him.

The soldiers were quiet, unmoving, when he checked his telescope. They didn't take notice of him, or if they did, they didn't bother with him. They only killed the people on the highway. 'People trying to leave, that much was obvious,' he thought, 'but why?'

He contemplated this as his finished his second bowl of cereal. 'Why don't they want people to leave? Is it some kind of government conspiracy? It wouldn't surprise me. The government was always doing shady stuff, shit it wouldn't surprise me if they were behind the Rabbit Flu. For what reason, that I don't know,' he thought.

James brought his bowl into the kitchen and put it in the sink. Then he took a shower, put on fresh clothes, and resumed sitting, watching. 'There can't only be me and some army guys left, there just can't be. And they can't kill everybody, can they? I mean the government has fucked with the average person's life enough. Why can't they just leave us regular people alone?' he thought.

Being in a corner apartment, James had views on two sides of his building. One side faced the soldiers' building. The other faced a more commercial district consisting of a video store, commercial coffee shop, two-story book store, sporting goods store, movie theater, and an electronics store. During the days leading up to the end of the world he watched as looters ransacked each place, first the electronics store, then the sporting goods store, then the video store, however never the bookstore. It didn't surprise him, 'I mean, who reads anymore?' he had thought at the time. It made him laugh as he recalled his cleverness.

Then he heard it. A car. Then he saw it. A forest green Cadillac was driving down the road. He felt the sudden urge to want to yell, to scream, for them to stop, to turn around, to go back from where they came. He wished he had a sign, more specifically a big white poster board with large block letters, to warn them about the soldiers, the murdering soldiers. But he had nothing. There was nothing that he could do. So, he watched.

James saw the car stop in front of the sporting goods store, Randy's Sports Emporium, and sighed. 'At least they're not headed for the highway, or else those soldiers would kill them for sure,' he thought. He quickly moved his telescope to the window facing the car and could make out an older, bald man along with an attractive twenty-something girl. "Damn, she's fine," James said aloud.

'How'd he manage that?' he thought, then 'Maybe it's his daughter. Has to be, or else why would she be with him? It wouldn't be crazy to think two people in the same family survived, right? Genetics and what-not.' He watched as the man knocked away the remaining glass in one of the large front windows of the store and then he helped the girl climb in.

Then it hit him, 'I know what I have to do. I have to go to them. To warn them and to see if maybe they'll take me with them. That's why I was so happy this morning, because something new, something exciting is going to happen. Fuck my old life, and my bullshit hang-ups, and that stupid bitch of a psychiatrist with her prodding and coddling and stupid suggestions. I need to act now. Who knows if I'll get this chance again?' he thought, 'and that girl is hot.'

Chapter Fifty-Five

Crudo watched through the sniper scope as Radio and Hermes approached the South Highway. The sun had been up for about an hour and its rays were blinding, so Crudo squinted and watched as best he could.

The dead bodies were still there. The two soldiers gave them a wide berth as they passed them. Then he saw Radio and Hermes look up toward the sky, looking for something. Crudo waved, but it wasn't him they were looking at. Then he heard it. At first a tiny whistling sound but it grew louder.

"Jackson, you hear that?"

"Hear what?" Jackson said and approached the window. Jackson picked up a pair of binoculars and looked down at Radio and Hermes.

"What are they looking at?"

"Shhhh. Don't you hear that? It sounds like a jet or something," Crudo said.

Jackson took his binoculars and panned over the sky. "I see it. Look," he said to Crudo.

"Shit that is a jet! And it looks like one of ours," Crudo said, "What's it doing? Is it here for us?"

"Don't know. Nobody told me if it is."

They watched the jet get nearer, watched it fly closer, lower, until, "What the fuck? Did it just drop something?" Jackson said, and a moment later the South Highway exploded, knocking them to the floor. "Holy shit!"

Jackson got to his feet first and dusted himself off. There was no dust on him; it was just his natural reaction. He returned to the window and looked down at the highway. He could only see dust, large clouds of dust drifting upward. He couldn't see Radio or Hermes. Crudo stood and said, "They dropped a fucking bomb on the highway. What the fuck?"

Jackson didn't respond. He moved quickly to his radio and tried to contact Hermes and Radio but all he got was static. He kept trying until Crudo came behind him and grabbed him by the shoulder. Crudo said, "Major, they're dead! Quit messing with that radio! They're fucking dead!"

Jackson pushed him and Crudo stumbled to the floor. Crudo stayed there, put his head in his hands and mumbled to himself. Jackson began closing the windows to prevent the smoke from getting in. "Crudo help me close these windows. Crudo! C'mon man, help me with this."

"Yeah, yeah, ok," Crudo said as he got off the floor and began closing the other windows.

Once the windows were closed the smoke became so thick they couldn't see out them. They sat on the couch, stupefied. A few moments later they heard another explosion, this time a bit farther away. "Another bomb? What are they doing? Do you know Major? If you do you better tell me."

"I don't, honestly. I already told you they were trying to save as many people as possible, and that we weren't supposed to let anyone leave. I didn't think that meant us too…"

"Fuck…I want a beer. You want one?"

Jackson nodded. Crudo opened the fridge and felt no cool air. He also noticed the kitchen clock was off. "Jackson, we have no power. They knocked out the power too. What the hell is going on?"

"How about those beers Crudo?"

"What…oh yeah." Crudo grabbed two beers from the fridge and brought them back to the couch. "At least the beers are still cold."

They drank their beers in silence, and Crudo smoked a cigarette. Once finished he got back up and went to get two more beers, which they drank quickly. "So, now what Major?"

"I don't know."

"We ain't much of a unit anymore, are we?"

"What does that mean?"

"Just what I said. Now we're just two guys in a fucked-up situation. Our guys are dead, and the highway is gone. No more unit, no more command. It's just us."

"Thanks for pointing that out, asshole," Jackson said and smiled.

"Well brother, glad to know we're in this shit together. I wouldn't want to be stuck with anyone else. Well maybe a runway model with big tits, but you're a close second."

"Thanks man," Jackson said as he rose to look out the window.

Smoke was still everywhere but was beginning to clear, enough so that they could make out the large crater filled with concrete, blood and steel was where the South highway used to be. Their fellow soldiers disappeared, as did the bodies of the dead civilians, as did the South Highway from the city.

| **56** |

Chapter Fifty-Six

Even though Jonas had little sleep he still awoke with the rest of Sister's people and went to breakfast. They ate eggs flavored with salt and pepper and grape jelly toast. Jonas ate alone while the others sat at a table talking quietly, indiscriminately about their daily tasks. He took notice of the two women he had seen during Sister's sermon yesterday. They looked tired and wore no visible makeup. They also didn't acknowledge him in any way. Then Danny came over to him with a full plate. "I'm good," he told Danny.

"This isn't for you. Come on, Sister asked for you."

Danny led the way to Sister's office; once inside he gave the plate of food to Sister and left. "This looks good. Did you get enough breakfast Jonas?"

"I did, thanks," he said, then "why don't you eat with your people?"

"I thought about that at first. But since I saved them from the Rabbit Flu, they...kind of revere me and don't feel comfortable eating around me anymore."

"Oh really? You don't think that's weird?"

"It isn't my job to judge. But it's up to them if they want to think that way."

"And you aren't in any hurry to dispel that?"

"No, I'm not. I can't or else I wouldn't be able to do what God wants me to."

"Let's leave the God stuff for right now, if you don't mind."

"That's fine with me. So, what did you find on your excursion?"

Jonas pulled the map Sister had given him the day before and unfolded it on her desk. "I didn't get too far, but what I found is interesting."

Sister finished eating and threw away her plate. "What's interesting?"

"I circled the places where lights were on and there was movement inside. Now it could be just people, or maybe their pets, I couldn't see that well, especially in some of the taller buildings."

"Good, good."

"But there are definitely people here," Jonas pointed to a red circle on the map, "at this bar called the Spot. You heard of it?"

"I know of it. Never been inside though."

"Someone painted all the windows black at El Supermercado. Don't know why. I couldn't see inside. But there was definitely something going on there. Last place I saw was the police station. There was a dead body outside, and lights on inside. But I didn't get close."

Jonas lied about the last part. He did get close to the police station, close enough to see the dead body was his friend and co-worker Ginger. He replayed the memory, first seeing the body through the night vision binoculars. He didn't want to get closer, but he knew he had to, just a weird feeling. As he approached, he recognized the purple jacket Ginger wore, noticed her dirty blonde hair. He ran to her and turned her body over. "Oh Ginger," he said, and wept. He hid her body as best he could behind some bushes and covered it with her purple coat. He didn't want to tell Sister about this, and didn't feel he had to, so he didn't.

"This is great stuff Jonas and I appreciate it."

"No problem. But there's something else."

"What?"

"At the Spot. I got close enough to look in one of the windows. There were people in there."

"You said that already. And Jonas didn't I tell you not to get too close?"

Cut the shit Sister. You asked me to do this because you knew I'd be thorough. And I was. Do you want to know what I saw?"

"Of course."

"I saw three men and three young kids, maybe teenagers. They all had on the white armbands and white baseball caps-"

"Of Brother Theo's Disciples."

"That's right. You know them."

"Who in this neighborhood doesn't?" Sister said. Then she said aloud, but not to Jonas, "I knew you'd test me Lord, just like you told me you would. But Brother Theo?"

"I didn't see him there though. Maybe some of gang survived and are just using the same markers."

"No, he's alive. I can feel it."

"Whatever you say. Do you want me to-"

Jonas was interrupted by an explosion that felt like an earthquake. Books from Sister's bookshelf fell to the floor along with the crosses that adorned her office wall. Jonas had to steady himself to not fall out of his chair. "What the-?" Jonas said, but was interrupted by Danny running into the office.

"Sister, are you alright?" he asked.

"Danny, I'm fine. But what *was* that?"

"I don't know but the whole street toward the South Highway is covered in smoke. I can't see anything."

"Is everyone indoors?"

"We're bringing them in now."

"Make sure then close all the doors and windows. Don't let the smoke in."

Danny left and Jonas was in awe of Sister's calm. A few moments later another explosion occurred, this time farther off. This one they heard but didn't feel. "What the hell is going on out there?" Jonas asked.

"God said there'd be challenges."

"Are you kidding me? That isn't God doing anything out there, Sister. That out there is something else."

"Jonas, you need to be calm and I need to see to my people. You can come along but if you don't want to wait here."

"I don't want to wait here and you know I don't run from a story."

"Spoken like a true journalist."

| 57 |

Chapter Fifty-Seven

Franklin and Nadia pulled up to the Randy's Sports Emporium; the doors were locked but the windows were busted out so Franklin cleared out the remaining glass with his sleeve and they climbed in. The store's power was still on and the florescent lights were almost blinding, even early in the morning. "What do we need?" Nadia asked.

Franklin took the list he had made and read off, "Tent, propane tanks, camping stove, sleeping bags, ponchos, matches. Those things should be in camping supplies. I'll get them. Here you take the other half of the list."

He ripped the list in half and gave it to Nadia. "Ok, I'll get this side, and we'll meet back here in twenty," Franklin said.

Franklin walked amongst the camping stuff, picked out two hiking backpacks, two sleeping bags and a four-person tent. He felt like he was rich, not looking at the prices of things for the first time in his life. He smelled cigarette smoke in the store, surprised the sprinklers didn't go off, felt like telling Nadia it was a bad habit, then realized he wasn't her dad, or boyfriend. They were stuck together in an incomprehensible situation, yet they were acting like it was a weekend camping trip. Coping.

Franklin found matches; he put five boxes in his cart, then five more, then the whole shelf. He heard Nadia say, "Franklin, hey Franklin, come over here."

He left the cart and jogged quickly over to her. He was breathing heavy when he reached her and put his hands on his thighs. "Hey old man, I'm ok, no need to run," Nadia said.

"I'm not that old."

"Check this out." Nadia aimed a crossbow at Franklin.

"Don't point that at me," Franklin said and moved out of the way.

"Sorry, but this thing is fucking cool," Nadia said, "I'm taking it."

"But you don't know how to use it."

"Says you," and she aimed toward a cardboard cut-out of a hunter in an orange vest about fifty feet away, and smoothly took the head off, knocking the cut-out to the ground. "See?" she said.

"Not bad."

"It's cause I'm a badass," she said and smiled, "Nah, not really. I've used one of these things before, back when I was a kid at summer camp."

"You're still a kid," he said and smiled.

"Screw you Franklin," she returned his smile then said "But there's no guns. Looks like the place was cleaned out."

"Too bad."

"I'll protect you with my crossbow like in that zombie movie."

"What zombie movie?" Franklin said as he inspected the gun case. The glass was broken, and Nadia was right, there were no guns.

"You know that one with that hot red-"

Nadia was interrupted by breaking glass and a loud thud. "What was that?" Franklin whispered to Nadia. She raised her eyebrows and opened her eyes wide, signaling she didn't know.

Franklin, in his loudest voice, said, "Hey, who's there?"

Silence responded. Franklin motioned to Nadia that he was going to go to confront the source of the noise; he had to protect her. He pointed for Nadia to try and flank whatever made the noise but she didn't understand. He whispered, "I'm going to try and see whoever's out there."

"No! Don't go," she said.

"Shhh. You'll be fine. You go around that way, try to get behind it."

"I don't want to. Let me stay by you."

"Fine," Franklin said as he saw tears welling up in Nadia's eyes, "stay behind me."

They proceeded to tiptoe down the aisle Nadia with one hand on the back of Franklin's windbreaker, the other limply holding the crossbow. They heard his footsteps getting closer. Franklin decided to speak first. "We won't hurt you," Franklin called then realized 'what if whoever was out there wanted to hurt him? And Nadia?'

"Don't come any closer," a young man's voice said, "I have a gun."

"So do I," Franklin said, lying.

Nadia said quietly, "Here Franklin, take this," and handed him the crossbow. 'I don't know how to use this, but I guess he doesn't know that either,' he thought.

Franklin heard the footsteps, but still couldn't see who was out there. "Hey out there. My name is Franklin. What's yours?"

"James. Name's James."

"Ok James. It's ok. Be calm. I won't shoot."

"How do I know?"

"You'll have to trust me I guess."

"I don't think so."

Nadia remained right behind him as they backed up into an aisle of hunting clothes and then continued the conversation with James. "What are you doing here James? Are you following us?"

"I saw you two go into the store. I'm still alive. I don't have the Rabbit Flu. I haven't seen anyone in days. I don't want to be left alone."

The tone of James' voice made Franklin feel more at ease. He sounded like a scared kid, just like Nadia. He handed the crossbow to Nadia and whispered "wait here. If anything happens, which I don't think it will, just run. Ok?"

She nodded and Franklin stepped out into the large center aisle that ran down the middle of the store. "Can you see me, James?"

Franklin, hands at his sides, saw his head stick out from behind another aisle. "Why don't you come out James so we can talk."

"Where's the girl?"

She's right over there," Franklin motioned.

"Ok fine. I'll come out. But no funny stuff, alright?"

"Alright, you have my word."

James stepped out into the main aisle and was about twenty feet from Franklin. Franklin could see the gun in his hand. Franklin was surprised at how unassuming James was. He was scared just as Franklin had suspected. Franklin walked toward him slowly with his hand extended. "Hi James, I'm Franklin."

James shook his hand. "Will you put the gun away now James? I'm not going to hurt you."

"Ok," he said and put the gun in his pocket while his finger remained on the trigger.

"Hey Nadia, come meet James."

Nadia stepped into the main aisle and stood slightly behind Franklin. Nadia nodded saying "Hey."

"Hi," James said and blushed.

Franklin asked, "Kid, what were you going to do with that gun?"

"Seriously? Everyone is dead. I've seen some fucked up shit the last couple of days. I own a gun so why wouldn't I have it?"

"Good point. Then why'd you come here?"

"Like I said, I saw you two go in from my apartment window. I've been watching the streets, waiting for somebody to come. Somebody that looked good, like I could trust them. You two were the first I've seen like that. I came down here to meet you. I'm not a bad guy..."

"No worries, James. We aren't either," Franklin said.

"What are you guys doing here?"

"Getting camp-" Nadia said but was interrupted and they were knocked to the ground with a force like an earthquake, the walls shook and tennis rackets and baseball bats and camping gear and fishing poles fell to the ground around them and they instinctively covered their heads. Smoke came in through the broken windows like a strange fog. Franklin rose first and helped Nadia up, then James. "You ok?" Franklin asked Nadia.

"Yeah, I'm ok. What the hell was that?"

"Don't know. You alright James?"

"Think so."

"Good," Franklin said,

"Look at all that smoke. I can't even see the street there's so much smoke," Nadia said.

The three stood looking through the broken windows of the Randy's Sports Emporium in awe. "Damn," James said.

| 58 |

Chapter Fifty-Eight

Rubina was sleeping when the bomb was dropped on the South Highway. She opened her eyes and heard car alarms and dogs barking. Dogs still inside their owner's houses getting restless, hungry, thirsty, desperate. They wanted out, out of their houses, their homes, which had become their prisons. Their barks would become more panicked, more helpless, filling with despair. Rubina thought these thoughts once her eyes opened and rose quickly. She put on a pair of black sweatpants and went into the hallway. Emmalee was standing in the doorway and said, "What the hell was that?"

"Don't know. Earthquake maybe?" Rubina said as they walked down the hallway to the living room, Emmalee right behind her.

Rubina went to the front door and was about to open it when Emmalee said, "Wait. Don't go out there."

"Why not?" Rubina turned and faced her.

"I don't know, just something feels wrong."

"Its fine, I'm su-" Rubina said but was interrupted by the second bomb, this time farther away and thus not as jarring. "I don't think that was an earthquake."

"Should we go check?"

"I'll go check. You stay here," Rubina said and picked up the rifle.

"Why go out there? There's nothing but bad news out there."

"I'm sure it's fine. I at least need to check. I'll be right back."

Rubina went out the front door in her bare feet. She forgot to put on her sandals or shoes or socks even, but her curiosity was more important than covering her feet. The asphalt of the driveway was not too hot and actually felt soothing on the soles of her feet. She held the rifle like she'd seen in the movies; pointed straight ahead into the smoky nothingness.

Smoke clouds billowed in her direction, upward and outward, from the direction of the South Highway. Rubina saw another cloud of smoke to the east, probably what she just heard. 'Are we under attack?' she thought, 'Is this what war is like?'

She saw no one on the streets, but heard the dogs in the neighborhood continue to bark. The car alarms did not cease either, and it was quickly becoming surreal to her. Rubina walked to the center of the road but all she could see was smoke. It was moving toward her slowly, almost methodically. She decided she had seen enough, in her case however she saw nothing at all, and went back toward the door. She saw Emmalee's face peeking through the curtains.

Once inside Rubina locked the door behind her and set the rifle against the door. "You hear those dogs? Their owners must be dead, or why else would they have left them?"

"Awwww, that's so sad. We should let them out."

"Not me. For all you know the first dog we'd let out would be some fighting pit bull, and would probably bite the crap out of us. I don't want to die from some rabid dog bite."

"You're probably right."

"I used to work with an African lady, I think her name was Esther, and she told me that in her country, when they had a civil war, that packs of feral dogs would eat on the people that died in the war."

"That's freaking gross."

"I know, right?"

"What did you see out there?"

"There's a lot of smoke, and the wind is blowing it this way. But I don't know why, I couldn't see very far at all."

In moments they couldn't see the yard or the street, just grey-bone colored smoke. They stood at the window gazing into the mist. "Jesus," Rubina said as she nodded her head.

"This is freaking me out, like we're in some horror movie or something."

"Yeah."

"It's like a bad dream. First everyone dies. Then this..."

"I know," Rubina said and went to get her cigarettes from her purse. She came back to Emmalee. "You want one?"

"I'm not a smoker."

"Neither am I," Rubina smiled, "but you might want one now."

Emmalee took the other cigarette and Rubina lit it for her. Their eyes were transfixed on the window and the smoke that just kept coming, almost in waves.

Rubina chain-smoked another cigarette while they stood there, watching. "Rubina, I'm hungry," Emmalee said, wanting to say something.

"There's food in the kitchen, help yourself."

"Ok," Emmalee said, retreating slowly from the window, "Do you want anything?"

"There's some grapefruit juice in the fridge I think."

"I'll bring you a glass."

"Thanks," Rubina said, not turning around to Emmalee, still enthralled by the smoke clouds.

Emmalee went to the refrigerator and looked inside. A normal refrigerator, full or normal foodstuffs. But fridges usually buzzed, or hummed, and the light was off. "Hey Rubina," Emmalee called.

"Yeah, what?"

"Come here."

"What is it? I'm watching this."

"Come in here. Something's weird."

"Alright," she said and went into the kitchen. "What's up?"

"Fridge's off."

"You sure? It was on last night."

"I'm sure, come see."

Rubina did so. "That's weird," she said and then tried the light switch, which didn't work either. "The power is out."

"You think the smoke has something to do with it?"

"Pretty sure. But what for? I guess it doesn't matter. Will you hand me the grapefruit juice?"

Emmalee did so. "If you're hungry, I'd eat the stuff in the fridge first."

"I'm not that hungry anymore."

| 59 |

Chapter Fifty-Nine

Theo never needed an alarm clock as he always awoke just before dawn. Every day, it didn't matter what he did the night before, he was up with the sun. He ate a simple breakfast of toast and egg whites, did two sets on his bench press, took a shower and got dressed. He wore a plain white t-shirt, blue jeans, black leather duster, and his trademark crisp all-white baseball cap.

Once in his office he looked at the monitor on his desk saw nothing was going on outside his building. Theo was protective of his home, so much so that he rarely brought anybody here, no women, no friends, no family, only his top guys even knew where he lived. If they got arrested they knew better than to talk about this place. If they did they knew their lives would be worth nothing. Theo did not fuck around.

Theo had men inside the police department and even they didn't know where he lived. He had multiple apartments throughout the city but this building was his home. He bought it for ten-thousand dollars cash soon after he left prison and fixed it up himself. The cameras he installed were not noticeable to the naked eye. He was proud of his home, his office, his fortress.

He leaned back in his Italian leather chair and hit up Clint on the walkie-talkie. "Clint, where you at?"

"I'm at El Supermercado. Going over what needs to be done to finish it up here. I'm almost done then I'm on the way to your place."

"Good. I'll be waiting."

Clint didn't mess up this morning and Theo was mildly surprised. Theo knew he could get the men in line, but that wouldn't help him, not in the long run. He couldn't be everywhere at once, he knew that, and if he wasn't around he needed someone else to be. He was hoping that Clint would be able to do it. But it was appearing more and more likely he was not the man for the job. It didn't really matter. He could replace Clint once Shaun was healed up. With a bullet in his arm Shaun wasn't much use for now.

Theo lit a cigarette and exhaled the smoke through his nose. He continued to watch for any activity outside. He still saw nothing and wasn't surprised. People, those still alive, wouldn't be so easy to catch. They still had electricity, hot water, food, and those scared ones, the ones that would make the best workers, weren't leaving their homes until they absolutely had to. The adventurous types, the ones that would soon be leaving the city, they'd be too much trouble for him, too hard to control, so he wasn't as concerned with them. But how many survived? There had to be enough for his purposes, or at least that was what he hoped.

The people at the hospital were stupid, that much he knew, to stay there. Whoever the bitch was that killed Tay, well she might be useful, might make a decent soldier for him, but she was gone and he didn't know where she was. The people already in the jail would be a good start but better to keep them as prisoners for the time being, lower their morale, until he actually needed them. They would all have a job in building his new society.

Theo saw Clint on the monitor before Clint rang the buzzer. He opened the door for Clint just before his finger hit the buzzer which he could see startled Clint. Theo heard the outer door slam and heard Clint's footfalls, loud and sloppy, coming up the stairs. Clint knocked on the door and said, "Boss, it's me, Clint."

"I know. Come in."

Clint entered the office. "Sit down," Theo said as he tapped his fingers on his desk, "Why do you continue to fail me?"

"What do you mean?"

"The shit with the prisoners, Tay being dead. The store not being ready. That's what I mean."

"The store is just about ready, and the prisoners were Tay and Serge's fault. Tay's dead because he was stupid."

"But you're my number two, you're in charge of them. If they fuck up, it's on you, you understand?"

"I know, I'm sorry, it won't happen again."

"Best not."

"The young pups and Serge are at the store now finishing up."

"You sure?"

"I told Serge what you wanted. He said he could handle the pups, and I left them and came right here."

"How was Shaun?"

"He was still sleeping when I left. But I checked, made sure he was still breathing. I left him a note, told him I came to see you."

"After this I want--"

A loud explosion interrupted Theo. Clint fell out of his chair onto the floor. Theo held on to his desk with all his strength to not fall out of his chair. The monitor on Theo's desk which connected to cameras around his building went blank. "What the fuck?" Clint said.

Theo hit the side of the monitor with no positive results only static. Then it went dark, same as the overhead light. There was only one small window in Theo's office that let in minimal sunlight, but at that moment that was all the light they had. He sent Clint outside to check. Once outside Clint yelled back, "Hey boss, you ought to come out here."

Theo went down the stairs and saw the smoke coming from the direction of the South Highway. Another explosion happened as Theo was going to speak, this time farther off. Grey clouds of smoke appeared to the northwest. Theo surveyed the situation, listening. Clint said, "What the fuck was that?"

"See the smoke coming from that direction?" Theo said.

"Yeah, so?"

"Nothing's over there, except the South Highway out of the city."

"Why would they bomb that?"

"Somebody doesn't want us to leave the city, that's what I think. But you know what?" Theo said and grinned, "I hadn't planned on leaving anyway."

Chapter Sixty

Tyreke and the three brothers made their back to El Supermercado. Tyreke thought it odd that they were going to the grocery store, but he didn't ask questions. He just followed them into the store, taking note of the fully obscured windows, almost positive that the windows weren't blacked out before the Rabbit Flu. "Theo had us do this, you know, paint the windows," Markus said to Tyreke.

"Oh," was all he could say, still stoned from the joint they smoked earlier.

"Yeah, Theo's got a plan, use this place for supplies, you know?"

"Serge, hey Serge where you at?" John-Two said.

"Where is that big, dumb motherfucker?" Markus said.

"Don't know, he should be here somewhere. This fucking store is too fucking big."

"You know that's right. He's probably in back," Ptolemy said, and then proceeded to punch a few boxes of cereal as they went down the cereal aisle to the back of the store.

"Quit fucking around P," John-Two said and pushed his brother.

"Fuck off bro," Ptolemy said.

Besides the windows being blacked-out the store looked like it had been hit by a tornado. Boxes and cans bottles broken or crushed adorned the floor, the cash registers were knocked over, emptied of money that had no value now. Crappy elevator music was still playing on the overhead speakers. Tyreke had been in El Supermercado countless times in his life but it felt weird with nobody here. "This is weird, you know, nobody being here and all," he said to Markus.

"Yeah, we tried to open the cash registers, but what's the point? Everything in this store is *ours* now." Markus took a glass jar of strawberry jam from the shelf as they walked by and threw it like a football toward the back of the store. They heard it shatter, and then Markus yelled, "Yo Serge, where you at?" this time getting a response.

"Back here."

The boys went through the large steel doors to the back of the store, past the broken bottle of strawberry jam. Serge was barricading the loading dock, pushing a metal desk across the floor to add to the other pieces of office furniture and cutting tables already in place. Serge stopped what he was doing and leaned on the desk, wiping his brow on the bottom of his shirt. "Where you boys been? I told you to come right back."

"Bitch please, you don't run us," Markus said.

"Keep it up and I'll tell Clint."

"Oh shit! You'll tell that retard? Now I'm scared," Markus said and all the boys laughed, Tyreke included.

"Look man, we were doing shit, and we found us another member," John-Two said, "this is Tyreke."

Tyreke nodded to Serge, who did likewise. Serge said, "Well you guys going to help-"

The ground shook and they stumbled around the back of the store. The boys fell to the floor while Serge steadied himself on the desk. "What the fuck was that?" Markus said while still on the ground.

"Earthquake maybe?" Tyreke said as he got to his feet.

"Man, don't you know anything? There's no earthquakes in this city," Ptolemy said.

"You sure?" Serge said.

"You don't believe my brother?" Markus said, "He's a smart dude he is."

"One of you go check out front."

"Not it," the boys said in unison.

"Quit being such kids," Serge said then, "stay here. I'll go check."

After a few minutes Serge still wasn't back, and the boys decided to follow him. They got to the front of the store, then went out the black-painted glass doors. Serge was standing right outside the front doors, leaning on the brick wall, smoking a wood-tipped cigarillo. It smelled like grape.

"Were you planning on letting us know what was going on, or were you just going to stand out here like a dumb fuck all day?" Markus said.

"Fuck off Markus. Don't you see all that smoke?" Serge motioned toward the billowing smoke coming from the south.

"So?"

"So, unless you want to go find out where that's coming from, shut the fuck up and kick it," Serge said and continued to smoke his cigarillo.

Markus leaned against the wall next to Serge and his brothers did likewise and then so did Tyreke. "You got one of those for me?" he said to Serge motioning to the cigarillo.

"You're too young."

"Fuck that shit. I've been smoking since I was two."

The other boys laughed. "P, bust us out a blunt."

Ptolemy took a marijuana filled cigar and passed it to his brother. He lit it, hit it, and passed it to Tyreke. Tyreke inhaled deeply and coughed.

"Man Tyreke you are a lightweight," John-Two said.

Tyreke kept coughing and the boys laughed. "A few days with us and he'll be just fine," Markus said and whacked Tyreke on the back like one would burp a baby but much, much harder. "Get that bad shit out Tyreke."

Once he stopped coughing it was his turn to hit the blunt again. He nodded no but Markus said, "You got to build up that lung strength."

"No man, I'm cool," Tyreke said.

"Hit the blunt man, I'm not asking," Markus said. His eyes became serious and Tyreke felt a little scared. He was a foot and half taller than Markus but Markus still worried him and the weed wasn't helping.

"Yeah man, don't be a bitch," John-Two said.

"If the kid said he don't want to hit it then he don't want to. More for us," Serge said and took the blunt from Markus.

"Yeah, more for us," Ptolemy said.

After they finished the blunt the boys sat on the ground, with Serge still standing. Markus turned to Tyreke and said, "Hey, man, you know I was just messing with you, right? It takes a lot to smoke with the third street pups, you know what I'm saying?"

"Yeah," Tyreke said and nodded. He noticed the grey smoke cloud coming from the south getting closer and he said, "You guys think we should go inside? That smoke is getting closer."

"Yeah, that's a good idea," Serge said and flicked his cigarillo into the street.

Once inside John-Two asked Serge, "So what do we do now?"

"Help me finish up in the back. It's almost done," Serge said, "Before you guys came outside Clint hit me up on the walkie. He said he's on his way, said to sit tight, so that's what we'll do."

| 61 |

Chapter Sixty-One

Emmalee and Rubina sat in the basement eating prepackaged ham sandwiches and barbeque potato chips that they had acquired from the convenience store the day before. The women ate robotically, taking bites, chewing, swallowing, repeating. Emmalee wasn't fond of silence so she spoke in between bites, "So Rubina what did you want out of life, you know, before this?"

"What kind of question is that?"

"I dunno. Just wanted to get deep I guess."

"Get deep? Screw off."

"I'm serious, tell me."

"Ok," she said and finished chewing before continuing, "My parents have been dead a few years, well before the Flu, in a car crash. My Mimi, she became my legal guardian. After high school I got a job at El Supermercado up the street so I could stay with my Mimi. I got to work with my best friend, it was easy, low stress, no expectations…"

"But you didn't answer my question," Emmalee said as she dabbed the corners of her mouth with the sleeves of her pink sweatshirt.

"What I wanted out of life, damned if I know. I just tried to take life a day at a time. Probably will continue to do the same for the foreseeable future."

"Yeah, well, I was supposed to go to college at State but a few months ago I got busted with a gram of coke and the school found out."

"Damn."

"It wasn't mine, it was my boyfriend's. My parents didn't really care what I did. My dad got a lawyer buddy to defend me and I just had to do some community service and they even paid the fine for me. They both work like crazy hours and I spent a lot of time at the mall. That's where I met my boyfriend. I told him I was eighteen and he was twenty-three. We had been going out a couple months when all this shit happened. Still though I thought maybe I loved him..." Emmalee said teary eyed.

"Hey, it's ok," Rubina said and moved closer and putt her arm around Emmalee.

Emmalee's head sank into Rubina's armpit and Rubina slowly ran her fingers lightly through her dense hair. The moment was soon over and Emmalee wiped her eyes on the sleeve of her pink hooded sweatshirt.

Rubina stood up and stretched her arms until they reached the top of the basement ceiling. She said, "We've both lost people we loved, you know? But in all reality, we should be lucky to be alive."

Emmalee remained seated and said, "I don't feel lucky."

"Me neither," Rubina said, "Fuck it, let's go back upstairs."

Once upstairs they went straight to the front room window. Smoke was still moving slowly down the street but its thickness had begun to dissipate. Still, it made Rubina think of a horror movie. "What do you think happened?" Emmalee asked.

"I have no idea."

"This is just so freaking messed up. First the Rabbit Flu, then the hospital, then that jail, now this…"

"I haven't had such an active week in a while."

"Me neither," Emmalee said as she continued to look out the window, then "Hey Rubina, do you see that? It looks like a person."

Rubina looked out the window and saw a dirty looking man with blood on his chin and shirt. He was stumbling down the middle of the street and looked drunk. "Holy shit! He looks hurt. We should go help him."

Emmalee made her way to the front door but Rubina stopped her and said, "Don't go anywhere. We don't know what he wants or even if we *could* help him. He looks drunk, and I'm not trusting anybody anymore. Let's just watch him, see what he does."

"Are you sure? He looks hurt and maybe he can tell us why the street is all smoky. I'm going to help him," and Emmalee made for the door once more but this time Rubina grabbed her arm forcefully and swung her around, and she fell on the couch.

"What the hell is wrong with you? You're not the boss of me," Emmalee said.

"Don't be stupid. He could be faking, hell he could be part of that gang and trying to trick us. You don't know. I'm trying to stay alive here and I'm not going to let you mess that up."

Emmalee scowled at Rubina and crossed her arms. Rubina went back to watch the man from the window as he continued to stumble down the street. He finally made it to a neighbor's porch on the other side of the street where he collapsed. "Looks like he's down."

Emmalee got up off the couch and said, "Let me see. I told you we should have gone to help him."

"Like you could've done anything for him, you're not a nurse."

"So? Where is your compassion?"

"Whatever. I saved your life, didn't I?"

Emmalee bit her lip and said nothing. Once she did speak, she said, "So are we just going to leave him there or what?"

"I don't know yet. For now, we watch."

"Why are you being such a jerk? You were nice earlier," Emmalee said.

"Just relax. We'll just wait a bit for the smoke to clear and then we'll figure out something."

"Fine."

Emmalee's eyes remained intently focused on the unmoving man. She wanted to go to him, to help him, the feeling as intense and instinctual as any she had ever had, at least since taking care of her boyfriend days earlier. She couldn't sit still, and after a half hour of watching she took two laps of the house, averting any possible eye-contact with Rubina.

An hour passed with no word between them except for small sounds, almost whimpers, coming from Emmalee. Into the second hour Emmalee's restlessness and the dissipation of the smoke to a certain more unobstructed view of their surroundings led Rubina to say "Alright Emmalee, let's go check on him. Get me the rifle and we'll go over there."

Emmalee's eyes lit up and she said, "Where do you keep the band-aids and stuff? Bathroom?"

"Look at you Florence Nightingale. They're in the closet next to the bathroom. Don't get too excited, he might be dead for all we know."

"He's not, I know it."

"Says you."

Chapter Sixty-Two

Jonas followed Sister out into the street where Danny stood. They watched the large plumes of smoke billow from the direction of the South Highway. "Any ideas?" Sister asked the two men.

"Haven't a clue," Jonas said.

"Me neither."

"Alright then let's get inside. No point of standing here staring, we should be helping the others. Where's Anthony?" Sister asked Danny.

"He's out like you wanted him to be. I didn't tell him to go that way so I'm sure he's fine. He should be back soon. Everything else we have it covered Sister."

"Good."

"Who's Anthony?" Jonas asked.

"The guard you met when you came into my church for the first time."

"Oh."

"I'm going to take care of the windows in my bedroom and office. Make sure everyone else is finished and indoors Danny," Sister said.

"Got it," Danny said and was off.

"You want to help me, Jonas?"

"You sure there's not anything else you want me to do?"

"My people are efficient and can handle it. I also want to talk more about our future plans."

Jonas closed the windows in Sister's office while Sister herself went into her bedroom and closed her windows. Once she returned from her bedroom Jonas was sitting in the same spot he was before the bomb. Sister sat in her chair behind her desk and said, "So where were we?"

"We were talking about Brother Theo's Disciples."

"Right. You said they are six strong right?"

"Seven if you include Brother Theo who I didn't see."

"As you said. Alright seven people set on destruction and killing."

"How do you know that's what they're going to do?"

"Why would you assume any other choice for them? They were brutal before the Flu, and I would have no doubt that they'd be brutal after it. The obscuring of the windows at El Supermercado is strange as well. Why take the grocery store unless you were going to hoard food?"

"Maybe they're just trying to survive like you and I are."

"Don't be naïve Jonas, it doesn't suit you. Theo's men were a pox on our society before and I won't let them continue to do so in our new society."

"What are you going to do about it? They're hardcore gangsters, and sorry to say Sister you're not."

"Some are leaders, other's followers. I have a group of loyal followers and they are ready to fight for our cause. I want you to be part of that cause. You've lost everything, I understand that. But so have we all. I invited you into my church because I have faith in you, and I will invite anyone else that wants to be a part of what we're going to do into my church."

"What are you planning to do?"

"Rebuild obviously. With worship of God at the center of everything we do. We already had a world built on fear and hate and look at how far that got us. Now we have a chance to do something better."

"Sounds noble enough. But what are you planning to do about Brother Theo?"

"I had a dream last night. It wrecked my sleep, left me with a cold sweat. I'm forgetting some of it now, but I remember the important parts. There will be more death before there can be a pure and better world. The Rabbit Flu was simply the first major act. I saw that my people will prevail over Theo's but there will be death. I did not see who was to die, but I tell you this honestly knowing that if you help me you may die. I hope and pray that you will not, but it is a possibility. And again, I say I want you to be a part of our future."

"And if I don't want to?"

"I'm not forcing you to stay here Jonas. You would be useful and have a purpose here. But your future is your own, no one else's," Sister said and approached her window, opening the blinds, "The smoke is dissipating. Should be safe to go back outside. Why don't you go into the garden and think it over; it's really quite lovely."

| 63 |

Chapter Sixty-Three

Franklin, James and Nadia carried as much as they could to James' apartment since it was nearest to the store and they wanted to avoid the smoke and dust and the streets, not knowing what caused the explosion and not really wanting to know. James unlocked the door to his apartment and Franklin and Nadia followed him in. 'Why'd I lock the door? Not like anyone was going to break in. Old habits die hard I guess.' Franklin sensed what James was thinking and said, "I locked the door to my apartment before we left too. Can't break that habit."

"Yeah," James said leading them down a thin, hardwood floored hallway into the slovenly living room. "Sorry it's kind of dirty."

"That's ok," Franklin said comparing in his mind the many major differences between his condo and James' apartment.

Nadia casually examined the living room noting the movie posters stapled to the walls, a large TV with stereo with video game controllers on the cluttered wooden coffee table. "Definitely a boys place," she said.

"What's wrong with that?"

"Nothing, just saying."

"I'm sure your place is immaculate."

"I didn't say there was anything wrong with it. I've been in my fair share of boys' apartments," she said, then "Wait, that didn't come out right."

James laughed and Franklin, avoiding his own awkwardness, said "Well I like it, the apartment. Reminds me of my place when I was much younger."

"Have a seat guys, make yourselves at home," James said, "You want anything to drink? I think I have some soda and beer."

"A beer sounds great, thanks," Nadia said.

"Seconded," Franklin said.

James went into his kitchen to get the beers. He opened the refrigerator and noticed the light was out, and it didn't feel cool anymore inside. His stove clock was also off. "Shit. I think the power is out."

"I bet The explosion knocked out the power grid."

"But weren't the lights at Randy's still on?" Nadia asked.

"Store like that probably had a back-up generator or something."

James came back into the living room with the beers and handed them to Franklin and Nadia. "You guys hungry?" James asked.

"Heck yes," Nadia said.

"Me too," Franklin said, "What do we have to eat?"

"I have a bunch of food in the cabinets but if the fridge is off we should think about eating what's in there first."

"I know my way around the kitchen, let me check it out if you don't mind," Franklin said.

"Sounds good to me," James said.

"You have a whole closet full of food, you know that?" Franklin said as he looked through James' pantry, preparing for lunch.

"Well yeah," James said.

"Let me see," Nadia said and went to the pantry, "Wow you got some good stuff in here. You have Twinkies, I love these," she opened the box and took one out.

Franklin said, then "Hey can I ask you something?"

"Yeah," James said.

"This is a lot of food. Like way more than I had, and I had enough food for a couple of months, which we could still go get if we need to but it doesn't look like we will. This food, all non-perishable, what were you preparing for?"

"This."

"What do you mean *this?*"

"I mean the end of the world or something similar. I would say this Rabbit Flu qualifies."

"Ok, that's weird," Nadia said as she ate her Twinkie.

"I'm not weird, just overly cautious, a bit pessimistic maybe, not weird."

"So you say," Nadia said.

"I can understand. I ordered a bunch of food when they were still making deliveries," Franklin said.

"I don't know why, I just started stockpiling little by little, every time I'd go shopping, I'd pick up something else. Then it took over the whole closet. Sometimes I thought it was stupid and that I should just give it all to a soup kitchen or something. But I always came back to the fact that I might need it," James said, "Besides was it weird all those people back in the fifties with their fallout shelters?"

"We had one of those," Franklin said.

"See? Nothing wrong with being ready. Look at those people with their fallout shelters. They had those things built and I'm sure it cost a ton of money, but they wanted to be ready. Like I said I wasn't preparing for this, but I'm glad that I did."

"I guess I see what you're saying," Nadia said.

"Can't fault you for being prepared. You still have some ham and cheese in the fridge, so I was going to do sandwiches and soup. Is that good for both of you?"

"Yep," James said.

"I thought you were going to whip us up something fancy Franklin," Nadia said.

"There's dinner later and with all these options I have some thoughts. I figured for lunch we keep it simple."

"Fine by me."

They ate lunch methodically, not actually enjoying the food they put into their mouths. "If you were going camping you must be leaving the city, right?" James said.

Nadia looked to Franklin who said, "That was our plan. We're heading to Mexico."

"We're going to see the ocean," Nadia said.

"That should be fun," James said.

Franklin looked at Nadia who nodded slightly then he said, "You want to come with us?"

"Really?"

"Why not? We just met; you seem like good people."

"That sounds great. Thanks."

"But what about your stockpile of food?" Nadia said.

"Eh, what good is having all that food without people to share it with?"

"I like that. Glad to have you aboard James," Franklin said as he collected their cleaned plates.

"I got these," James said and took the plates into the kitchen.

He came back into the living room and saw Franklin relaxing in James' recliner. "I'm going to grab a quick nap; too much excitement for these old bones," Franklin said.

Nadia was reading a men's magazine with a sexy model/actress/singer on the cover. "I can't believe you read this magazine. I mean most guys I know do, I just don't get why they do."

"I don't know, the jokes, the interviews, the models aren't bad to look at."

"I guess," she said and tossed it on the coffee table, "Too bad the power's out. We could at least watch a movie or something."

"Yeah that does suck. And it looks like Franklin's out. It'd be nice to take a nap but I'm not tired at all."

"I have an idea," James said and went into his bedroom and returned with a multi-colored bong and a bag of marijuana. "Do you smoke?" he asked Nadia.

"Heck yeah! I'm liking you more already."

"Well good," he handed her the baggie and said, "smell it."

She did and said, "That's some good shit. Mostly I just smoke crappy weed."

"This should help with your nap anyway," James said then, "You think Franklin will care?"

"He's snoring so I don't think he'll notice. And whatever now, what would he do even if he did give a shit, call the cops?"

"Good point," James said and put the bong up to his lips, lit up and inhaled white smoke. He exhaled slowly through his nose then passed the bong to Nadia who did the same. "That's better, thanks," she said.

"Don't mention it."

James and Nadia giggled for a bit and they started talking like normal young people. About music, drinking, other times they were stoned. Eventually the talk turned to God. "I'm not sure if I do or not, what's that make me, atheist?" Nadia said.

"Agnostic I think. Personally, I don't," James said, "I think God's a scam personally. To keep the poor, the peasants, the serfs, the plebs down. Like, 'I know life sucks now, and it ain't getting any better, but after you die, then it's freaking awesome!' Sounds like bullshit to me."

"Yeah," Nadia said.

"I also think people use God and heaven to make themselves feel better about death and dying. It's a lot better thinking your loved one is going to the perfect place instead of thinking of them simply rotting in the ground. More romantic."

"I think there's a heaven. Maybe I hope there is. But I've seen some fucked up shit not even including the Rabbit Flu so I don't know."

"Yeah, what about all the horrible stuff people did to each other before, like wars and genocide and slavery and all that shit? If there was a God, why would he do that? You know?"

"Yeah, no, I don't know. It's fucked up."

"It's funny to me when famous people and people with lots of money say they don't believe in God. Why would you? You don't need God when you're doing blow off of strippers' stomachs, do you?"

"I can attest to that," she said and laughed.

"What doing blow or…"

"Being a stripper. I was. I'm not embarrassed or anything. No one ever did coke off of my stomach though. I made some good money, not that I can do much with it now."

"That's cool," James said and couldn't help imagining her naked.

"What did you do? You know before this."

"Nothing special. Data entry for this big construction company. My dad went to high school with the owner so he got me the job. It was boring as shit but it paid the bills so I did it. I could take the train there so I didn't have to get a car."

"Nice," Nadia said, her eyes barely open.

"It was a job, you know?"

Fucking a," Nadia said, yawning, and went from sitting to lying on the couch, "you mind if I take that nap now?"

"That's a good idea. I think I'll do the same. Wake me up when you guys get up. Do you want a blanket?"

"Sure."

James got a blue and red checkered blanket and when he went back to Nadia she was already sleeping. He placed it on her gently and checked the window looking into the soldier's condo. He saw one pacing around making it clear they were still there. He took the bong and bag of weed with him to his room and fell asleep.

| 64 |

Chapter Sixty-Four

Theo and Clint returned to Theo's office. Theo sat behind the desk and Clint sat facing him just as they had done many times the last few days. "What do we do now boss?"

"You mean right now? Or in the future?"

"I don't know, I guess both, if you want to tell me."

"First hit up Serge on the walkie. Make sure they're cool."

"Ok," Clint said, then into the walkie talkie, "Serge, Serge you there?"

In a few moments the response came through, "I'm here Clint, what's up?"

"Nothing man. You alright over there?"

"Yeah, we're straight. Heard that explosion earlier, you know what that was?"

"Not sure yet. The south highway is gone. How are things with the pups?"

"They're getting high, but not being too rowdy. They found another kid, name of Tyreke."

"He cool?"

"Seems so. The pups seem to like him."

"Everything done at the store?"

"We took care of it, it's ready."

"Good, I'll be there soon."

"Alright. Peace."

Theo sat silently listening and was pleased to see Clint take some resemblance of control. He needed to see more of it to be completely sold on Clint's leadership abilities but it was a start. "What's next boss?"

"Today, once the smoke begins to clear I want you to take Markus and the new kid with you and hit up all the pawn shops. I figure most have probably been cleaned out but you never know. There's what, four in the immediate area?"

"Yeah, there's Lee's and Diamond and Tyronne's and Southside. What do you want be to do there?"

"Look for guns, knives, grenades, any weapons people could use against us."

"I can do that. Why Markus and not his brothers?"

"I could tell in the short time speaking with the pups that he's their leader. He could learn something from you maybe."

"He's a smartass, thinks he's all that."

"Well make sure he knows who he answers to. I want you to feel out the new kid, see if he's on the level, see if he can be trusted. You can do that right?"

"Sure thing, no problem."

"Have Serge and the other pups find a truck and have them pick up some mattresses and some bed frames. Have them bring them back to El Supermercado and set them up. You all will be staying there from now on. Wouldn't want you to have to sleep on the floor now, would we?"

"Um…no."

"It was a rhetorical question. While you're doing that I'm going to take Shaun over to the police station and set him up there. Even with a bad arm he can still guard those prisoners. But they need to eat and I can take care of that. There is one last thing I want you to do."

"What's that?"

"Once you're done at the pawn shops I want you to light them up."

"You sure?"

"Of course, I am. It'll add to the fear created by the bombing. I want to get people out of their homes, into our jail cells. The fastest way we do that is by scaring the shit out of them, and we're going to need labor for the next part."

"Gotcha. You know I can light a fire."

"That's why I want you to do it. Then tomorrow we'll get some school buses and I'll get some cop uniforms from the police station. You all will get to be cops for the day."

"For real?"

"We'll get some bullhorns and we'll tell people the cops are here, and we're going to take them to safe shelters. With the fires you're going to start and the police out there 'to help' they should come running."

"Good plan boss."

"I know it's a good plan, and it'll work if you don't fuck it up. You're not going to fuck it up are you?"

"Hell no."

"Good answer. Hit me up on the walkie when you finish with the fires. Now go."

| 65 |

Chapter Sixty-Five

Tyreke, the pups and Serge all sat in the back of the store. The boys were eating Oreos while Tyreke was munching on chili cheese Fritos. They drank grape soda and laughed until they heard something up at the front of the store. The boys turned to Serge and he took his gun from off the desk in front of him. "It's probably Clint, but you all keep quiet," Serge said and put his index finger to his lips to indicate silence.

Tyreke watched Serge push through the large black doors that separated the employees only section of the store from the customer floor. He heard a voice say loudly, "Where you all at? It's Clint."

Theo heard Serge respond, "Clint? We're back here."

In a moment the two men pushed back through the doors. Clint was a short man, shorter than the pups almost, with a bald head and one large diamond earring in each ear. "What's up kids?" he said and shook hands with Markus. "This the new kid?" he motioned to Tyreke.

"What's your name son? Stand up so I can get a good look at you."

Tyreke rose from his plastic chair while Clint extended his hand, which he shook. Tyreke could see a sparkle between Clint's lips, most likely diamond caps on his teeth. "You're a tall motherfucker aren't you?"

"I guess so," Tyreke said.

"What was that shit with the smoke?" Markus asked.

"South highway is gone," Clint said.

"Shit, for real?"

"You think I'm lying? You saw the smoke."

"What's Theo want to do about it?" Serge asked.

"He's got jobs for us today. You guys ready to work?"

"Hell yeah," Markus said.

"Alright then. Markus, Tyreke, you're with me."

"Why can't we go with Markus?" Ptolemy asked.

"Because I said so, that's why," Clint said, "Serge you take those two and Theo wants you to make this store livable."

"Livable?"

"Yeah man, go to that mattress store on Tenth, you know that one?"

"Yeah."

"Pick up some mattresses, bed frames, pillows, whatever you think we need to stay here."

"We have to stay here? This place sucks," Markus said.

"You want to be a Disciple? Then you do what Theo asks. If you don't you can fuck off."

Markus sulked and his brothers did the same, but he didn't move. "I'm down," he said and his brothers nodded in agreement with their brother as they usually did.

"Good. Now he wants this shit done by dark, so you better get a move on. Tyreke, Markus follow me."

Markus followed behind Clint, and Tyreke was being Markus. They walked past full shelves of toilet paper, paper towels, laundry detergent and cleaners. "What are we doing?" Markus asked Clint.

"We got a big job to do. We're going to set some fires."

"For real? That's cool."

"Tyreke go over to the liquor section and get five bottles of whiskey. Meet us at the car," Clint said.

Tyreke nodded and went to the liquor aisle, looking at all the bottles. He recognized a green bottle of whiskey he had seen before and carried five bottles in his large arms.

Tyreke saw Clint and Markus enter the front seats of a four-door model colored a deep purple, with a spoiler and expensive tires with shiny silver and gold rims. Tyreke got in behind Markus and set the bottles of whiskey on the seat next to him. Tyreke was still worried about where they were going and what they were going to do but he tried not to let it show. Clint started the car with a loud vroom as he pushed his foot down on the gas pedal. Clint adjusted the rearview mirror to observe Tyreke in the backseat. Markus tried the radio, turned it to the hip-hop station, but only static came through. "You got any CDs?" he asked.

"In the console," Clint said.

Markus looked through Clint's CDs, "You got some good shit here Clint. How about this?"

Markus showed Clint a CD and he said, "That's fine."

Markus inserted the CD into the car's stereo and loud bass shook the car immediately. "Hell yeah!" Markus said.

Clint began driving and after the first song was over, he turned the volume down then said, "So Tyreke, you from around here?"

"Yeah, I lived with my mom over by that gas station run by the Arabs."

"Your mom, she alive?"

"I don't know. I don't think so. She took my baby sister to the hospital a few days back. She never came back."

"Shit sucks. My mom's been dead for a long time."

Tyreke nodded and Clint turned the stereo back up. After two turns and eight blocks Clint pulled up in front of a yellow brick apartment building. He turned off the car and said "C'mon."

The boys got out of the car and followed him to a paint chipped dark blue front door. Clint took out his keys, opened the door and led them into the building. There were two staircases inside, one going up the other down. Clint led them downstairs to a basement with ancient washers and dryers on one side and a row of locked storage spaces opposite. He went to the third and unlocked the metal lock. Clint pulled the light string while Markus and Tyreke looked over his shoulders at what was inside.

Unmarked, red, plastic cans with spigots were sitting the floor along with a half dozen large propane tanks while on shelves there were marked white bottles of lighter fluid and boxes of matches. Also on the shelves were numerous sizes of crowbars and rows of duct tape. Hanging on the walls were sledgehammers and pickaxes. "Holy shit man! You are a fire-starter," Markus said.

"Here," Clint said picking up and handing one of the grey cans to Markus, then another to Tyreke, "Carry these out to the curb."

The boys did it in silence but once outside Markus said to Tyreke, "This is the shit I've been waiting for ever since me and my brothers hooked up with Brother Theo. This is going to be fun."

"Yeah, I guess," Tyreke said and set his can on the sidewalk a few feet from Clint's car.

"What's wrong with you?"

"Nothing."

"Tyreke man, you got to enjoy yourself more."

They carried out six red cans, four of the propane tanks, a half dozen bottles of lighter fluid, four rolls of duct tape and two boxes of matches. Clint brought out three of the larger crowbars, two sledgehammers and a pickaxe and proceeded to put them, the duct tape and matches in the back seat. The boys loaded the cans and tanks in the surprisingly spacious trunk. "Where to?" Markus asked once they were back in the car.

Clint turned to face Markus and said "Why do you ask so many questions? Just do as your told and quit bothering me. You're starting to piss me off kid."

"Whatever man," Markus said and crossed his arms.

"Be like Tyreke. He's quiet and listens and doesn't question everything. You want to be a Disciple you better learn how to take orders. I'm telling you a lot nicer than Theo will, and you don't want it to come to that."

Clint started the car and slowly drove to their first stop, Lee's Pawn and Loan. Clint asked Tyreke to take a crowbar and hand him the sledgehammer. The windows of the store were busted out when they arrived and once inside, they saw the place had been trashed. Broken glass cases emptied of jewelry and electronics.

Markus and Tyreke went looking for anything they might want while Clint went behind the counter to a back-office door. He tried the handle but it was locked and lifted the crowbar above his head and smashed the door handle off the door. He pushed the door open and the smell hit him first and then he saw an overweight body slumped on the floor awkwardly like it had fallen out of a chair. "Fucking Lee, the flu got you too huh?" he said to himself and shook his head.

Clint went through the file cabinets looking for anything that might be of use but only found papers. While surveying the room in the corner under a stack of papers and concealed by the body he found a medium-sized safe. He moved the dead body away from the safe with a few grunts. The door was slightly ajar and Clint was happy he didn't have to mess with trying to open it.

Inside was a manila envelope with some court papers which he was all too familiar with but held no importance to him. There was also a diamond and gold encrusted watch which he took out and put on his own wrist. A handgun almost as large as his own was also in the safe next to two boxes of bullets and as well as four stacks of hundred-dollar bills. He took the bills on instinct and stuffed them in his pockets along with the gun. He carried the boxes of bullets and grabbed the sledgehammer before leaving the office.

"You guys find anything worth keeping?"

"Nothing but crap, crappy movies, crappy clothes, crappy shit," Markus said.

"I found this sword," and Tyreke swung it and knocked over a half-empty rack of movies, "I don't know if it'll help but I want to keep it if that's cool," Tyreke said.

"Fine with me, take it out to car," Clint said, "We need to get those cans from the trunk."

They went to car and Clint had the boys carry in two of the red containers while he put the gun, money and bullets in the glove box. Then he brought in one of the propane tanks along with a bottle of whiskey.

"Alright boys. Open the grey cans and pour out some of the gasoline around the store. Not too much though," Clint said and picked up a shirt from off the ground, tearing off a strip. He carried the propane tank to the middle of the store and once the boys were done with the gasoline he sent them outside.

Clint opened the bottle of whiskey and took a shot of it directly from the bottle. He handed it to Tyreke who took a small sip and then gave it to Markus, who did the same. Clint took the bottle back from Markus and inserted the strip of torn clothing. Then he turned the knob on the propane tank and left the store. Once outside he tossed the car keys to Tyreke and said, "Move the car down the block. Markus go with him."

Tyreke moved the car and once done they looked down the block at Clint who was lighting the cloth in the whiskey bottle and then he saw him throw it into the store. Clint quickly ran down to the boys and they stood waiting for the explosion. In a few moments they heard the boom and glass breaking and saw smoke coming from the pawn shop. "Alright boys, good job. One down, three to go."

| 66 |

Chapter Sixty-Six

The dust and smoke had cleared from the yard and a left a mist, akin to a fog. Jonas stepped out the backdoor of Sister's church and saw the fourteen-foot-high fence that enclosed the garden. The lot was bigger than he expected, and a large tree was off to the back corner. Underneath was a metal bench spray painted white, already chipping. He made his way to the bench, past the wire fenced in garden that included ripened tomatoes, green and red peppers, jalapenos, parsley, and eggplants, and these were just the ones Jonas could identify by sight.

A woman was kneeled over working the soil or collecting vegetables, her back was to Jonas so he couldn't be sure. She wore a large straw hat and turned and nodded as he passed, making eye contact with Jonas only for a moment until she went back to what she was doing. Jonas made his way to the bench and sat down. Opposite him and the tree in the back corner of the yard was a young peach tree, and he could see tiny, not yet ripe, peaches hanging from its branches.

'A fresh peach would be great right now,' he thought. He also thought about what Sister had told him. 'She doesn't seem to want to back down. I don't have any plan on what I want to do, but do I want to follow her into a confrontation with a dangerous man like Brother Theo? Do I want to die, more to the point am I ready to die?'

He watched the woman continue to do her work taking no notice of him. 'She's diligent I'll give her that. Just like her leader. I'm not surprised these people follow Sister. In drastic and incomprehensible times when groups of people are involved there will always be those that lead and those that follow. It isn't necessarily the smartest or the brightest – though Sister is a smart cookie – who lead, rather it's those with the capacity for leadership and a steadfast hold on their beliefs. Religion dominates our culture whether I like to admit it to myself or not. It's no wonder that they follow her.'

Jonas looked toward the sky. The sun was overhead obscured by clouds. 'Am I resisting because I thought I would be a leader in this new world? I was, well not a leader in the old world, but I felt like I did something important. If I'm just a lackey of Sister's what's the point? Do I really need to have one? If she's a good enough leader for these people why do I think I'm any more special? I don't know. God, I miss my wife. What would she do? She would tell me to do what I think is right. But what if I don't know? I was so much surer of myself before.'

The woman in the garden rose to her feet, her back still to Jonas. She took off her gardening gloves and shook the dirt off them. Jonas rose from the bench and went toward her. "Hey," he said and she turned toward him.

She didn't respond so he repeated himself. She turned and looked at him with chocolate brown eyes and a weary, worn face. "Yes?"

"I'm Jonas," he said and extended his hand which she limply shook.

"Ellen."

"Nice to meet you."

Ellen opened the door back into the church with Jonas right behind her. Hey Ellen can I ask you something?"

"It's lunchtime. I need to prepare. We can talk over lunch."

Jonas sat in the lunchroom while Ellen and the other woman whose name he did not know prepared lunch. He was alone in the lunchroom for a bit until two other men came in and sat at a table with his back to them. They didn't speak, and Jonas was left still thinking on what he should do with the rest of his life.

Once lunch was ready Ellen brought him a plate of macaroni and cheese along with a bag of salted potato chips and a glass of juice, which from the taste was apple. "Thanks," he said.

"You're welcome."

"Aren't you going to eat with me?" Jonas asked.

"I said I would, I just need to get my food."

"Oh, sorry," Jonas said and watched the other woman go and sit with the two other men.

Ellen returned and sat down across from Jonas. She closed her eyes, clasped her hands and said a silent prayer. When she opened her eyes Jonas was looking at her. He said, "This is good, thanks."

Ellen nodded and put a forkful of macaroni and cheese in her mouth. Once she finished chewing she asked, "So what was it you wanted to talk to me about?"

"I was wondering what it was that brought you here?"

"What do you mean?"

"I mean what brought you to this church?"

"Oh. Well...it was Sister."

"How so?"

"I don't know if you know this but Sister started this church at the Y. I was there at the beginning. At first, we only had a few members. We were up to twenty-five before the flu..." Ellen said and looked off into a nondescript corner of the lunchroom.

"And then what?"

"Right, Sister would hold service in a small chapel on Sunday afternoon, three o'clock. I was staying there on the nights I could. They only let you stay three days in a row and then you'd have to find somewhere else, and then in a couple days you could come back."

"You were living at the Y?"

"You could say that. I didn't have many choices. I lost my job a couple months before I met Sister. I tried to find another job, but I couldn't. Stuff got bad, and I wound up at the Y."

"That's too bad. But then why join Sister's church?"

"I grew up Catholic. Later on, I went to a Presbyterian church. I did that just cause it made someone else happy. First my parents, then my ex-husband. I never found much use for religion though. But when I met Sister all that changed. She said 'put your faith in God and put your faith in me.' She didn't tell me a bunch of crap like Jesus will save me or anything like that. What she said made sense. I put my faith in God, and in her, and I felt better, like I belonged. I survived the Rabbit Flu like so many didn't. That's all cause of her."

"I get what you're saying," Jonas said.

"A lot of our members died from the flu. But those that really believed, me and Danny, we lived. We're alive today because of her. That's why I keep up the garden and do whatever I can. I owe her my life. Now if you don't mind, I need to get cleaned up and get to working on dinner."

"Already? We just had lunch."

"It helps to be prepared."

"Ok. Thanks."

"Don't thank me. Thank Sister."

"I will."

Jonas followed her inside, still unsure of his next move. Her faith was interesting to him, but it didn't exactly change his mind.

He was hoping she'd say something more profound, not sure what, but something. He wanted to talk to Sister again and made his way to her office.

As Jonas went inside, he saw a man sitting in the cafeteria, smoking and flicking his cigarette ash into a cheap aluminum ashtray. Jonas decided to sit and talk to him, as maybe he would have something more profound to say. Jonas pulled out the metal folding chair across from the man and sat down. "I'm Jonas," he said.

"Marcos."

"Nice to meet you, Marcos."

"Hmmph," Marcos said and took a drag off his cigarette.

"I was wondering, how did you come to be at Sister's church?"

"You really want to know, or you just making small talk?"

"I really want to know."

"Alright, I'll tell you," Marcos said and took another cigarette out and used his current one to light it.

"My wife and I were at the hospital, like a lot of people. We didn't have any guns, we were just trying to get her help. The rumors of a vaccine were all that was on our minds. My wife was already showing the signs of the Rabbit Flu; we prayed for a vaccine. Everyone there did. But the National Guard with their guns kept us from getting into the hospital. Then someone started shooting and I swear I saw the soldiers shoot first."

"From what I heard no one knew who started the shooting."

"From where I stood it was them. We were packed in like sardines and could barely move. Once the shooting started I lost her, I lost my wife. We were holding hands so tightly I thought I might rip her arm off, but still we got separated. She was sick and by the time I found her she had been...trampled. I felt her body; it was lumpy and there were footprints, dirty footprints, all over her clothes. She wasn't breathing."

"I'm sorry. I lost my wife too."

"So, you know how it feels then?"

Jonas nodded and looked away.

"I found a spot to hide and watched the National Guard keep shooting at people."

"They said they were using rubber bullets."

"I don't know about that, but the blood certainly looked real to me," Marcos finished his cigarette and lit another. He offered one to Jonas who declined.

"After they had gone, I headed home. On the way I saw Danny and he invited me inside. He asked if I had anything worth going home for, and I said no. Then I met Sister. She weirded me out at first, but was she said, she sounded genuine. I stuck around. A day or so later that guy Anthony got here. He came in wearing his uniform and I wanted to kill him then and there. He's bigger than me, but I swear with my bear hands I could ring his neck."

"Whoa," Jonas said and after thinking for a minute continued, "But there was no vaccine anyway, so you couldn't have saved her life."

"Maybe so, but she didn't deserve to die like that. Being trampled, that's no way to die."

"Absolutely. So do you get along with Anthony now?"

"Haven't said two words to him. Won't look him in the face, he doesn't deserve it."

"But you're going to stay?"

"Yeah, I mean what else do I have to do? Sister and Danny and the rest of the people here are good, so why not?"

Jonas thought about this for a bit as Marcos finished another cigarette. This time he didn't light another, instead, he rose from the table and said, "I got to take a piss. Good talking to you."

"You too," Jonas said and went to see Sister.

| 67 |

Chapter Sixty-Seven

Empty green beer bottles began to overfill the coffee table in the apartment where Jackson and Crudo were. They ate cold cuts, sliced cheese and pretzels washing them down with beer. "Man, you remember back in the day, that football game versus Hidden Valley?" Crudo said.

Crudo and Jackson were from two small country towns about twenty miles apart. Their towns were so small that they went to the same high school, played football, were the big men on campus. But they weren't good enough to play in college so when Jackson signed up for the National Guard Crudo did the same. This was their third year in the Guard.

"I remember getting rocked when I tossed you the ball and you ran in for the score. Then they carried you off the field. Dick."

"Yeah, yeah you're just jealous," Crudo said.

"I remember that party afterword in the barn, now that was some fun."

"Oh yeah, you were hooking up with, what was her name? Maggie what's her face?"

"Jennings. Maggie Jennings. She was smoking hot, wasn't she? Who'd you hook up with that night?"

"Don't remember…"

"The hell you do. It was Ashley Schmidt. Man, she had some craters and like no tits."

"Whatever, I was drunk."

"Yeah, yeah that's what you always say."

"Cause it was true. I've got a pretty good buzz on now too. Cheers bro," Crudo said and clinked glasses with Jackson.

They heard an explosion, this one much quieter than the bombings earlier. Both men went to the window and saw smoke coming from a small building a few blocks away. Crudo grabbed the sniper rifle and looked through the sight while Jackson looked down at the fire through his binoculars.

"You see those guys? Why are they doing that?"

"Don't know."

"You want me to shoot 'em?"

"If they're not trying to leave the city let them alone. Maybe they're just crazy."

"Looked like they planned to do that, but it's not affecting us so…"

"That is still fucked up."

"I think that's just the way of the world now. Let's finish our beers."

They sat staring at the walls, swirling the beer in their bottles, smoking cigarettes, drinking more. "You think it's weird we're in someone's apartment that we'll never meet?" Jackson asked.

"I guess. I don't know, I hadn't really thought about it."

"Like take this lamp," Jackson picked up the boring green lamp with cream colored lamp shade, "Somebody saw this and thought, 'you know what? This will look good on this end table,' and now here it is, in my hand."

"You getting philosophical on me? You always do that when you're drunk."

"So? I don't know man, it's just weird to me. Like this is some strange dream and tomorrow we're going to wake up at the base or at home and none of this would've been real. You know what I'm saying?"

"Yeah, I hear you," Crudo said as he rose from the couch, "you want another beer?"

"Do you even have to ask?"

"Good," Crudo said and went to the fridge and once there continued, "Man I'm hungry. What else do they have to eat in this place?" Crudo searched through the freezer, found some frozen pizzas and said, "Think the stove still works?"

"Hell if I know, try it and see."

Crudo turned the new age stainless steel stove on and opened it. He smelled the gas and heard the flame kick on. "Sweet! It still works, how many pizzas? Two or three?"

"Make them all, if we don't eat them who cares?"

"Good call."

Twenty-five minutes later they were eating pepperoni and sausage pizzas, washing them down with more beers. "This is some good shit."

"You said it," Crudo said with a mouthful of pizza.

"You know," Jackson said, "not to get all philosophical on your ass again, but I've been thinking, what the hell are we going to do now?"

"Keep drinking."

"That's for sure," Jackson said and raised his beer to clink it with Crudo's, "I mean tomorrow."

"I don't want to stay here."

"Me neither."

"I'm worried about my mom, but I bet the Flu…but maybe not. We should go home. There's nothing keeping us here."

"I hope my parents are alright too. Maybe the Lieutenant Colonel was right. Maybe the rural citizens didn't get sick. If we can get back there, we can protect them," Jackson said.

"Sounds as good a plan as any. I'm more surprised that you don't still want to get back to central command."

"I've thought about that too. But they're opposite directions. We have to choose. I tried the radio earlier and still nothing. No response."

"They don't give a shit about us."

"I don't know about all that. But after the hospital and the highway and Radio and Hermes…"

"Those two guys, God bless 'em. But that was some bullshit. For our homies," Crudo said and poured some of his beer on the floor.

Jackson did likewise and said "So what do you want to do?"

"I say we go home. This city ain't for me. This was the second time I've been here. I remember once as a kid we came up here. I remember the elephants from the zoo and driving through a bad neighborhood where my mom rolled up the windows and locked the doors, told me to stare straight ahead. That's it. So the sooner we leave here the better."

"Alright then. Tomorrow morning, we get the hell out of dodge. But tonight? We drink to our dead brothers."

"I can do that. Cheers," he said and the men clinked beers again.

| 68 |

Chapter Sixty-Eight

Rubina and Emmalee approached the man cautiously, almost tip-toeing up to the porch where he lay, motionless. Dried blood and dirt enveloped his clothes and face, hiding his blonde goatee and slightly receding hairline. "Don't get too close," Rubina said to Emmalee but she wasn't listening and ran up to him, putting her face up to his mouth. "He's breathing, he's not dead!" Emmalee said.

"Shake him, see if he wakes up," Rubina said holding the rifle, her eyes surveying the street looking for any movement, any possible trap. She felt powerful and scared at the same time.

Emmalee cooed and rubbed his shoulder, which did not wake him up. After a bit of this Rubina, finished checking the surroundings, said "Hey! Hey! Wake up!"

The man awoke with a "He-Hello?" followed by a shaking of his head and then a "What?"

"You alright?"

Startled by her being so close the man then rubbed his eyes and focused on her face. Emmalee smiled at him, and he half-smiled back. Then he focused on Rubina and her rifle, pointed right at him. "Don't shoot! I don't have the flu," he said.

"She won't hurt you," Emmalee said using hydrogen peroxide and cotton balls to clean his face.

"Says you," Rubina said.

"C'mon Rubina, take it easy," Emmalee said, "I'm Emmalee, by the way."

At first, he winced when Emmalee touched his face with the damp cotton balls but still, he allowed her to do it. "Thanks," he said to her and she noticed his blue-green eyes. He looked to Rubina and said, "You want to stop pointing that gun at me?"

"Nope." She didn't like holding the rifle but knew it gave her power over this man. Right now, she was in control and she continued, "First I want some questions answered. Who are you? What are you doing here?"

"Name's Tod. I don't remember how I got here. I remember I was on my way to get a coffee when there was some kind of explosion…"

"I know, we heard it too," Emmalee said applying a band-aid to a cut on his cheek.

"What do you know about the police station?" Rubina asked.

"I know where it is, I used to drive by it on the way to work. But that's it."

"Hmm…"

"You mind if I smoke?"

"Go ahead."

Tod reached in his pocket and pulled out a battered cigarette pack, and proceeded to smoke. "What was your plan, coming and waking me up?"

"Not sure. Trying to do the right thing I guess," Rubina said.

"I'd appreciate if you put that rifle down. I answered your questions, I don't mean you any harm."

"Fine," Rubina said and let her arm holding the rifle fall to her side.

She still didn't trust him, just something about the guy, and she didn't want to bring him back to her grandmother's house. She said, "We shouldn't be out in the open like this. Let's go inside."

"Here?" Tod said, "This isn't my house."

"It'll do. I doubt anyone's home."

The door was open and Tod leaned on Emmalee as they went inside. Rubina had been in this house as a child as the owner was a friend of her Mimi. It still smelled like orange blossoms, just as it did when Rubina was a child.

Tod sat on the couch and finished his cigarette, putting it out in a crystal ashtray on the coffee table. Emmalee sat next to him and asked, "Do you need anything?"

"You have any aspirin?"

"I brought a bottle just in case," Emmalee said and took the bottle out of her pocket, and handed it to Tod, "You need some water? I can get you some."

"Nah."

Rubina sat in an antique olive chair, one that shone in the light and was extremely rigid. She crossed her legs and the rifle sat across her lap. "What your story?" Rubina asked.

"You want the whole story?"

"Yeah, why not? I think we have time."

Tod took a deep breath and began, "My wife was sick and I didn't know what to do. Our baby girl died right away. They couldn't even bury her; she's still at the hospital morgue. After that I went home to be with my wife. She couldn't even leave the house. I didn't know what else to do. I heard from a neighbor that South General had a vaccine so I got my gun and joined the people at the hospital. What was I supposed to do? My wife was dying..."

"Damn," Emmalee said.

"You have a gun?" Rubina asked.

"Not anymore. Ran out of bullets and left it at the hospital."

"Sorry but I don't believe that. Empty your pockets and pull up your shirt."

"Seriously? Why would I lie?"

"Yeah, why would he lie Rubina?" Emmalee said.

"Why wouldn't you? is a better question. Just do it; it's not asking too much."

"Fine," and he did so then once Rubina was satisfied he sat back down, "Like I said I'm not a bad guy."

"We've had our own problems so far, so I'm just being cautious."

"I guess I should be lucky that you two came along," Tod said and smiled.

Emmalee returned his smile but Rubina did not. She said to him, "Go on with your story."

"Right. My wife, she was dying and I went to the hospital. The National Guard was there already. The situation was tense, I can't really describe it. Fear and anger and sadness. I wasn't there long before someone started shooting, I couldn't tell what side, but the soldiers weren't fucking around. They just started shooting back and everybody ran. It was insane."

"How'd you get away?"

"I hid in an office building, on the second floor. I watched from a window. I waited until the soldiers left. What I saw then I wish I hadn't. So many dead bodies; some with bullet holes, a lot of people were trampled, some just dead from the Flu. Dead soldiers, dead kids, dead nurses and doctors. Once the soldiers were gone I saw a couple people crawl out from their hiding spots and go into the hospital so I followed them in. We tore that hospital apart looking for the vaccine. But we didn't find it."

"We were at the hospital! We must've just missed you. Weird..." Emmalee said.

"After that I couldn't get my car out of the parking lot the roads around the hospital became, so I walked home. My wife was dead by the time I got back."

"That sucks. I'm sorry," Emmalee said.

"Thanks. I didn't know what to do. I slept on the couch then decided I'd go make a coffee at my favorite coffee shop. I was craving a coffee real bad. I was on my way there and then the explosion happened. I don't remember how I got on the porch."

"We saw you. You were stumbling down the street and you passed out on the porch," Rubina said.

"Well thanks for having a heart," Tod said.

"We're good people too. And we escaped from some bad mofos. They had us locked up in jail," Emmalee said, "but Rubina stabbed one in the neck and we escaped."

"Damn. I can understand why you're leery of me."

Rubina said, "You don't know what I've gone through. I can only believe you because I trust you, which sorry to say I don't. It's not you; anyone who comes along from here on out I'm going to be on guard about. Just the nature of living now I guess."

"Fair enough. At least you're not pointing your gun at me."

Rubina returned a slight smirk.

"Rubina he's not going to hurt us, can't you see that? Let's go back to your grandma's house and get some food. I bet Tod is hungry."

"Fine," Rubina said, not wanting to deal with any more of Emmalee's whining, which was becoming a reoccurring theme when dealing with this man. Rubina then led them back across the street to her grandmother's house.

"We still have some of those sandwiches left," Emmalee said and went to get one for Tod.

"Thanks," he said when Emmalee handed it to him.

After he finished eating Tod stood up and said, "Thanks for the food and for patching me up. I appreciate your kindness here, I really do, but I think I'll be heading on my way."

"Where are you going?" Emmalee asked.

"Not sure yet. I just don't want to stay here."

"You'll be missed," Rubina said.

"You better watch that attitude. Someone else might not be so cordial," Tod said.

"I don't care what anybody else thinks, especially you."

"That's been made obvious. Anyway, thanks for the food and the conversation," Tod said and went toward the door.

"Wait, can I go with you?" Emmalee asked.

"Emmalee?" Rubina said.

"Sure, if you want."

"Seriously Emmalee?" Rubina said.

"Yeah, why not? You've got no plan and you've been a bitch to Tod for no reason."

"I saved your ass, you know that? You would still be in that jail cell if it wasn't for me."

"I'll say it again then. Thank you!"

"Don't yell at me!"

Emmalee lowered her voice and said, "I'm leaving with Tod. He feels safer. See you later."

Emmalee walked past Tod who nodded at Rubina making eye contact for only a moment and then he followed Emmalee out the front door. As the door began to close behind them Rubina said, "You feel safer? After a couple hours? Good luck assholes."

Rubina locked the front door behind them then pushed the couch in front of it just in case. 'That stupid ungrateful brat,' Rubina thought as they left, 'After what I did for her? You know what? Screw them. I have to look after myself.' She watched them from the window and saw them go into the house across the street.

'What are they doing in there? I hope they don't stay there. They better not fuck with me.' She paced her grandmother's house, chain smoking.

| 69 |

Chapter Sixty-Nine

Theo put on his two-gun holster over his white T-shirt and took his black duster off to the coat rack in the corner of his office. He felt for the guns in the pockets of the coat, removed them and checked the safety on each weapon. Then he slipped them into the holsters, and put on first his white bandana and covered that with a pristine white baseball cap slightly askew.

Theo left his office and went down the stairs back into the street. He walked the two blocks to where he had parked his cousin's SUV with his right jacket sleeve covering his face from the slowly moving smoke clouds.

He wished he hadn't broken the window on it earlier but there was nothing he could do about it now. Theo had to take the bandana off his head and tie it around his face like he was a robber. He hadn't had to wear his bandana like this in a good long while but when he did he always felt like he was in Western movie.

He could see barely well enough to drive but he didn't figure to run into any drivers so he drove slowly. As he drove he inspected as much of the streets as he could, looking for any signs of movement. He drove past El Supermercado and saw Clint's car in the parking lot but no one outside. He thought about placing a guard out front but that might draw more attention than he wanted. He decided he would think it over.

Cars sat empty, glass littered the sidewalk, and quiet abounded. But no people, no movement. He heard the muffled whining and crying of locked in pets as the silence with no power, no people was startling almost. The smoke from the explosion hadn't reached here.

Theo pulled in front of the Spot and turned the car off. Nobody had messed with the glass pane windows and doors of the Spot. Everyone knew it was Theo's and even during the rioting and looting nobody tried to harm it. The neighborhood respected him or feared him, he didn't care which. He smiled at the thought.

The windows made it brighter in the Spot than he would've figured but when he opened the door the table candles were lit, creating a dim glow. "Hey! Who's there?" Shaun said, gun drawn on the door.

"Relax cousin it's just me," Theo said as he closed the glass door behind him.

"I've been jumpy, sorry."

"No problem. It's not too dark in here. Would be worse if I didn't put these windows in here last year."

"No doubt," Shaun said from his seat at the bar.

"How's the arm?"

"Still hurts like a bitch but at least my hand is working again."

"That's good. I'm sure in a few days, maybe a week you'll be fine. Now what're you drinking?"

"Whiskey. Chasing it with some grape soda. It's still cold but not for much longer. Power's been out since the boom."

"You heard that earlier?"

"I heard it, but damned if I knew what it was," Shaun said shaking his head, "The power is out. Light comes in good here, but I lit these candles anyway."

"The South Highway blew up, big time. Knocked out the power at my place too. I figure that's what did it."

"Damn man."

"Yeah. Pour me a shot."

Shaun did and they clinked shot glasses before they downed them. "Damn that's refreshing," Theo said as he put his shot glass down on the bar upside down and waved off the offer of the grape soda chaser.

"So cuz what are you doing here?" Shaun asked, "Making sure I'm alright?"

"I got a job for you."

"Cool, I've been bored as fuck sitting around here."

"How much you drink today?"

"Four, maybe five."

"That ain't too bad. For this job you don't need to be stone cold sober anyway."

"What do I got to do?"

"Right now, we're going over to El Supermercado, see how things look, pick up some food for the people at the jail. You know about Tay right?"

"Yeah, Clint told me. That shit is fucked up."

"This time I'm bringing those people food, and if they try any shit they're dead," Theo lit a cigarette, "So the plan is you're going to guard the jail. Shouldn't be too hard and it'll give you something to do while you're arm heals up."

"Cool."

"You ready? Let's go."

They left the Spot and drove to El Supermercado. Theo spoke with Clint on the walkie-talkie, "You on your way to the pawn shops?"

"We just left boss."

"Good I'll on my way over there now. It should take you more time than Serge so I'll let him know when I'm leaving and to get his ass back there. You guys find any keys or anything to lock the doors?"

"We didn't look, store was open already."

Theo's sigh could be heard even through the hiss of the walkie-talkie static. "You want me to go back?" Clint asked.

"No. It's fine. Just hit me up when you're done with the fires."

"Will do."

Theo and Shaun pulled up in front of El Supermercado and Theo first noticed the painted front windows. "You can't see shit in there," Shaun said.

"That was the plan. Let's go inside."

Theo was pleased with the obscured windows and the stacks of carts, boxes and crates in front of them. They made their way to the back of the store and went through the large double doors into the employee area. "All this shit is going to go bad," Shaun said as they looked over the coolers of meat, cheese, milk, and frozen food.

"Better we use it now. Get a box and start packing that lunch-meat and cheese."

Shaun did so as Theo checked the loading docks and back door and saw they were barricaded well. He found the manager's office and went looking through the desk for the keys. He found paper-clips and timesheets, backup disks and pens but no keys. 'I'll have to check the front desk on the way out. Keys weren't likely necessary but they wouldn't hurt,' he thought.

"You got the food?" Theo asked Shaun when he emerged from the manager's office.

"Yeah man, packed it up."

"Can you carry it?"

"Yeah."

"Let's go. Grab a case of soda and some loaves of bread. I'm going to check the front desk for a key."

"Alright."

Shaun went off looking for the things Theo asked for and Theo went to the desk. Once there Theo looked in drawers and found lottery tickets, rolls of quarters and nickels and dimes and pennies, and finally found a ring of keys. He saw Shaun awkwardly trying to carry the box of food and case of soda. "Here cuz let me help you," Theo said and took the case of soda from his cousin.

"Thanks, I thought I could carry it all."

"We have to help each other out in times like these, you know what I'm saying?"

"Did you find the keys you were looking for?"

"Yeah. Let's go."

Theo locked the door to the store after trying some of the keys on the key chain. He tried some more and found that three keys worked to lock and unlock the front doors. He left one on the key ring and put the key ring in his pocket. The other two keys he left under a one of the legs of a bench that was outside the store. He used the walkie-talkie to tell Clint and Serge where they were and they left for the police station.

Once they arrived at the police station, they approached it cautiously just as they had a couple days earlier. Inside the headless body was still there, and neither of them went into the part of the jail where Theo's brother was still dead. "Looks empty," Shaun said.

"I would agree. Go get the food from the car."

Shaun left and Theo went to the cells. He looked in the first one and saw Tay's body face down with the knife still in his neck. 'You stupid motherfucker. What'd I always tell you? Never underestimate anybody. You got killed by girls. Stupid...' he thought.

Theo went to the cell across the hall, where the people were and looked in the small window and saw them. They saw him too. "Please, please, don't leave us here," one of them said.

"I'm not going to. I brought food. If you know what happened in the other cell then I want you to know there won't be a repeat performance. If any of you move toward the door, or try any shit, I promise you I will kill you and it won't be nice. Nod if you understand me."

They nodded. "Good, now you," Theo motioned to a young boy of about twelve, "boy, come toward the door."

The boy didn't want to move. The woman next to him gave him a slight nudge but he didn't want to, and small tears began to well up in his eyes and stream down his cheeks. "Don't worry kid I won't hurt you, but I won't ask again."

"C'mon Charlie go," the woman who had nudged him before said.

The boy approached the cell door tentatively while Shaun came up with the box of food and case of soda. "Theo where do you want this?" Shaun asked.

"Bring it over here," Theo said then to the boy, "I'm unlocking this door. Come out here kid, and the rest of you keep your asses glued to that wall."

The boy stepped out of the cell and Shaun handed him the case of soda first. The boy's arms weren't strong enough and the case of soda dragged them to the floor. "C'mon kid, push that in if you have to," Theo said.

The boy did so and then returned for the box of food. "Here," Shaun said and handed it to him.

Theo closed and locked the cell door behind him. "Hey, why aren't you letting us go? We won't bother you we promise," the woman said.

"I'm not worried about that. Besides I have important plans for you. Eat up."

Theo and Shaun left the cells and went back to the front of the police station. "I want you to sit here, not right in front of the door but off to the side a little bit. Take this walkie-talkie. Clint and Serge have one as do I. If you need us use channel four."

"Cool."

"Shoot anyone who tries to get in here if we don't hit you up on the walkie first. Something else you can is find me some police uniforms, seven or eight of them. I have a plan where we'll need them. You need anything else before I get out of here?"

"Nah I think I'm good."

"Ok then. I'll see you when I see you."

| **70** |

Chapter Seventy

Tod and Emmalee walked back across the street to the house they had broken into earlier. Tod locked the door behind them and once he turned around Emmalee began kissing him with a feral intensity. He kissed back and they made their way to the bedroom.

It felt different than normal sex for both of them, maybe it was that they just met, maybe it was the fact that they were probably some of the only people on the planet fucking at that moment, maybe it was the old person's bed they were in and it smelled like it. In any case it was intense and both wound up sweaty and tired once they were done.

After they finished Emmalee found a cigarette in Tod's jacket and lit up. "I didn't know you smoked," he said.

"I don't usually, but I do after sex. Just a habit I learned from TV and movies," Emmalee said, trying to seem older and more confident, "It is relaxing."

"Well, you've convinced me. I'll have one."

As they smoked and basked in the afterglow of their sex Emmalee turned on her side and asked, "So, you have any plan on what you want to do?"

"No idea. I just had to get out of there. I was getting some bad vibes off that Rubina."

"I hear you. She was cool before we met you. She did stab somebody."

"What?"

"For real, she did. Killed him too I'm pretty sure."

"How'd you meet her?"

"I saw her first at the hospital. I was there with my boyfriend; he was dying. He's dead now," she paused and Tod rubbed her shoulder. She brushed him off and said, "I'm ok cause now I have you."

She smiled at him and then got up, naked, and went looking for an ashtray. She came back with a fancy crystal ashtray originally filled with lemon candy that fit very well in the house they were in. She continued, "Anyway these gangbangers came in and took us. Rubina ran, but they caught her. They took us to the police station and put us in a cell with some other people."

"So then what happened?" he asked.

"So Rubina gets this plan. I had a hunting knife my boyfriend gave me and I had it hidden on my arm. Those gangsters didn't find it. I gave it to her and she used it to stab one of the gangsters when he brought us food. The other gangster chased us and killed this one old lady that tried to escape with us. It was fucking crazy but we got away. Then we wound up at that house across the street. It was Rubina's grandmothers."

She paused before continuing again, playing the escape scene over in her head. "Something changed in her after that shit at the police station. You saw it; it's why you wanted to leave. But she's a lot tougher than me and probably you too. We should get out of here and away from her, just to be safe."

"Where do you want to go?"

"I don't know. I don't want to stay around here, not with those gangsters around."

"Ok, let's get to walking. I'm sure we can find some nicer place to call our own."

"That's you plan?" Emmalee asked.

"We should probably get dressed first."

"Quit playing around."

"I'm serious. Walking around naked is a bad idea."

"Stop it," Emmalee said and nestled herself into Tod's armpit, "You have to have some thought as to what you want to do now."

"Not really. I'm a 'take it as it comes' type of guy. I'm not a good planner, that's why I got married. I also had an assistant, and she did everything for me once I got my first divorce. The job is currently open if you're interested."

"What a chauvinistic jerk you are, but I can't be mad at you. Not after you screwed me like that. My last boyfriend never made me feel like that. And I'm pretty sure he was older than you."

"Is that you're deal? You like older guys?"

"Yeah, so what?"

"Nothing, I'm just glad I met you."

"Me too," she said and kissed him.

"You know it's getting dark. Probably better to stay here until morning. Besides there's no hurry. I think we could do it again, if you want."

"How can I resist when you put it like that?"

Chapter Seventy-One

Three more pawn shops, three more fires, and by the end Tyreke, Clint and Markus had gotten quite efficient at blowing up pawn shops. However, they did not find many usable items. The back room at the final shop did yield a few sticks of dynamite and a couple Vietnam-era grenades, but no guns or even knives.

Tyreke was surprised that Clint allowed him to drive his car from the third pawn shop to the fourth but he was excited about driving anyway. One of his mother's cousins had let him drive once, last year, an old olive colored Buick that had seen better days. Tyreke drove it a couple blocks to the store and back because his mother's cousin was drunk or high and needed cigarettes. Still, he liked being behind the wheel and had hoped to have a car of his own one day.

The sun began to go down as they drove back to El Supermercado and the road took them through some residential neighborhoods. "These places look nice," Markus said, "better than where we stay."

"Where rich people live," Clint said and took the walkie-talkie out of his pocket, "Serge you there?"

It took a few moments until a crackled response came through. "Yeah, I'm here Clint, what's up?"

"You take care of the mattresses and what not?"

"We're setting them up in the back corner of the store now. You see Lee's on fire? What was up with that?"

"That was us. It's what Theo wanted."

"Nice job then. Looked good and burnt."

"We're on our way," Clint said into the walkie-talkie and put it back in his pocket.

"Take a left here Tyreke," Clint said as he surveyed the road, then "Hey slow down a sec."

"What?" Tyreke said.

"Back up. That looks like Tay's jeep. Don't suppose many people have a yellow jeep like Tay's around here. Go around the block and drive real slow."

Tyreke did as Clint ordered and once they were just around the corner from the jeep Clint said, "Stop and kill the engine. I bet those bitches that killed Tay are around here. Markus, you packing?"

"You know it," and he lifted up his shirt and pulled out his gun.

"Tyreke?"

"No, I don't have one."

Clint took the gun he found at the first pawn shop and handed it to Tyreke. "You ever used one of these before?"

Tyreke remembered back to Cedric and the gun earlier, the gun that was still in the apartment with his dead friend. He answered, "Yeah."

"Good, take this," Clint said and took out his own gun, "Let's go check. Get out real slow and don't slam the doors."

Clint led the way and they approached the house the jeep was parked in front of. Clint led them to the front door which was unlocked. "Keep quiet," Clint told them.

He opened the door with quiet care and what little sunlight was left allowed them to see into the house. As soon as he opened the door a white cat ran out past them out into the street and it startled Clint. "What are you scared of, it's just a cat," Markus said.

"Shut up."

They checked the bedrooms, bathroom, basement but found nothing. "Where they at?" Markus asked once they finished looking through the house.

"I don't know, maybe they ditched the car. But I know Theo will be real happy if we find them. Maybe they're at another house around here. Let's check."

They tried two other houses on the same side of the street as the jeep; both front doors were unlocked and no one alive was in the house. They did find the dead body of a naked older woman in the bathtub of one of the homes which almost forced Tyreke to throw up. But he held it in and they continued their search onto the next house. The taste of bile was creeping up his throat and he wanted a piece of gum but didn't have any.

Clint approached the door and tried to turn the handle but it was locked. He put his ear up to the door and could hear murmuring sounding like voices. "Be fucking quiet," he said and looked right at Markus who nodded.

Clint readied himself and stepped back turning to the boys to make sure their guns were drawn. He lifted his leg and kicked the flimsy door in. "Where you bitches at?" he said in his deepest and loudest voice.

***

Rubina sat on her couch chain smoking for what felt like hours but in actuality not much time had passed since Emmalee and Tod had left. After her fifth cigarette she rose from the couch and went to the window to see if Tod and Emmalee were doing anything she saw the sun setting. Since it was so quiet she heard what she thought were moans and grunting coming from across the street. 'That stupid whore. He'll fuck her, but I doubt he'll protect her. He looked like a pussy. 'They're not my problem anymore,' she thought.

Rubina then went to kitchen and took out one of the lukewarm sandwiches. The bread was becoming mushy but still she ate it, not really tasting it. She drank it down with tap water from her favorite faded Minnie Mouse plastic cup. 'Probably time to find and set up some candles,' she thought.

Rubina was searching the kitchen, not finding any candles when she heard a distinct noise like a door slamming and a loud, muffled yell. 'God, those two, what are they doing now?' she thought and walked to the window. She saw the door across the street was kicked open and people were going inside. "Fuck fuck fuck!" she said as she dropped her cup of water and ran to her bedroom to get the rifle.

'They saw the jeep,' she thought, 'glad I parked it across the street.' She went back to the window and saw the door still open. Then she heard Emmalee scream.

***

Tyreke and Markus opened the door to the bedroom with their guns drawn. "Put your fucking hands up," Markus ordered them, "Yo, Clint we found them!"

Both Tod and Emmalee were still naked and Tod raised his arms while Emmalee pulled the blankets up with her hands to cover her breasts. "You too bitch," Markus said as Clint entered the room.

Emmalee did as she was told and her breasts were displayed for all to see. "Nice titties," Clint said upon entering.

"Fuck you," Emmalee said.

Markus said to Clint, "Can I get a piece of that or what?"

"Usually, I'd go first but she's a bit young for me. Since you've been a pain in my ass Tyreke gets to go first if he wants to."

"I'm ok," Tyreke was scared for the girl and her striking green eyes that pleaded for help. He had to look away and focused on the tips of his white tennis shoes.

"He said he's cool, so can I?" Markus asked.

"Hey, hey guys, let's just take it easy for a second," Tod said.

"Shut the fuck up bitch! You ain't got nothing to say unless you want to get shot," Clint said and pointed his gun at Tod.

"Ok, ok," Tod said motioning his arms in a calming fashion.

Alright Markus, if you want to, I don't care," Clint said.

"No!" Emmalee screamed.

"You," Clint motioned to Tod, "get your clothes and come out here. You do anything stupid I *will* kill you. Now let's give them some privacy."

Tod picked up his clothes from off the floor and avoided eye contact with Emmalee who grabbed the covers and wrapped herself in them. Clint followed Tod into the living room with gun pressed into Tod's back where Tyreke was sitting in a plastic covered chair.

In the bedroom Markus set his gun down on the dresser nearest the door and began pulling the covers away from Emmalee who used her hands to cover herself. Clint closed the door behind them but still heard Markus say, "Man this bitch is wet."

"Tyreke go to the car and get the duct tape," Clint said and Tyreke did so.

Clint then ordered the naked Tod to get dressed. Emmalee's screamed and it made Tod wince. "You know my boy is giving it to your girl right now, right?" Clint said and laughed.

Tod didn't respond as he pulled his shirt on and buckled his belt. By the time Tyreke had returned Markus was coming out of the bedroom with the haphazardly clothed and weeping Emmalee. "I gave it to her good and she was into it that freak," Markus said to Clint as Tyreke re-entered the house with the duct tape.

"You and your three minute stamina," Clint said.

"What? You making fun of me?" Markus said.

"If you have to ask son…" Clint said then, "Tyreke tape up their hands."

Tyreke wrapped the tape tight around Tod's hands first and then the shaking Emmalee's. Once done he handed the roll to Clint who tore off two small pieces of tape and used them to cover Tod's mouth first and then Emmalee's. As he was about to tape Emmalee's mouth shut he realized that he was looking for two women, not one, and slapped his forehead. "Shit," he said "I was in such a fucking hurry. Where's your friend, the white girl with the tattoos?"

"No," Emmalee said through quiet sobs.

"What'd you say?"

"I don't know where she is."

Clint raised his gun and put it to Emmalee's forehead. "I don't believe you. Tell me or you're dead."

Emmalee began crying and Tod said, "Wait, wait. I know where she is. Just don't kill us."

"Aren't you sweet? You didn't even lift a finger to help her earlier, and now you're going to give up her friend? So where is she?"

"You won't kill us, right?"

"If you tell me, I won't kill you. At least not right now. You got three seconds to decide."

Clint began to count as Emmalee pleaded wither eyes. At two, Tod spoke up, "She's in that house right across the street, I swear. She should still be there."

Chapter Seventy-Two

Jonas returned to Sister's office, walking past Danny and the guard named Anthony who were sitting at a table talking over something intently. The others of Sister's congregation were sitting at another table playing a card game. Jonas made no eye contact with any of them as he went straight to her office. "Sister?" he knocked.

"Come in," she said then, "Jonas, how was your time in our garden?"

"It's nice out there if that's what you mean."

"You've had some time to think?"

"I have."

"And what have you determined?"

"That I don't have much of a purpose at this point in my life. And while I may not be completely on board with all your plans and ideas I think you have a good heart and will do the right thing. If you want my help, I'm willing."

"That's good to hear Jonas."

"There was something I was wondering about though," Jonas said.

"What's that?"

"I spoke with Ellen earlier."

"She's been with me for a while."

"That's what she said. You said earlier you saved all the people here. But she said only Danny and her were with you before the Rabbit Flu. What gives?"

"By having this church I was able to save those that needed it, like Anthony and the others. Anthony, believe it or not, was a soldier who lost track of his unit when the shootout happened at the hospital. I saw him from that window there walking the streets and told him he should come inside. He did and I told him about the same things I've told you. He has chosen to stay."

"But he's not wearing the soldier uniform anymore."

"That was his choice. He also volunteered to guard the church."

"What about the others then?"

"They wandered in after the flu began to really take hold. I'm sure more will come, I know it. We will grow as God intended," Sister said, then "Was Anthony downstairs when you came in?"

"He was talking to Danny."

"Good, will you go get them? We have plans to make."

Jonas brought Danny and Anthony back into Sister's office. Jonas and Anthony sat in the chairs facing Sister's desk while Danny stood. "What did you find out Anthony?"

"I checked in on El Supermercado. There were four teenagers and one big dude. They were just sitting out front, but that's when the bomb or whatever that was hit. I waited for a while and then another guy came up. A bit later they split up and left the store. I followed one of them on the bike you gave me but they didn't see me. I followed them to a couple of pawn shops. They burned them down but I don't know why."

"Interesting, go on."

"After two of them I went back by the store and saw the others bringing in mattresses and bed frames into El Supermercado so I'm pretty sure they're staying there. I saw Brother Theo too; he was carrying out a box of food and there was someone in the passenger seat of the green SUV he was driving. He took off pretty fast so I couldn't follow him. I watched for a bit longer but I didn't see the three who were burning down the pawnshops come back, so I came back here."

"Well done, Anthony. Thank you," Sister said.

"You really want to mess with these guys?" Jonas asked Sister.

"It's not a question of want. They need to be taken care of if our new society is to work. They will undermine progress and we can't allow that to happen."

"Me and Anthony were talking and I think we should hit them at El Supermercado," Danny said, "We know that's where most of them are. Theo might be back again and we can take him out too."

"With what? I know Anthony here has a gun but you know Theo's guys are going to have some guns too," Jonas said.

"We're not without resources ourselves Jonas. Take a look."

Sister stood and directed them to the corner of the office were Danny cleaned off a long, unassuming looking desk covered with papers. Once done he took a key and opened the top of the desk to reveal a weapons cache that surprised Jonas. Danny took a rifle from the desk and handed it to Jonas. "See newsman? Now don't hurt yourself."

Jonas held the large rifle in his hands and peered into the desk to see three more rifles and an assortment of handguns, boxes of bullets, and extra rifle clips. "Where'd you get these?" Jonas asked.

"Once the looting started Danny went out and collected these. It's truly amazing the number of guns in just our small section of the city. He's made sure that we could always defend this place if needed."

"Good job, I guess."

"Thanks, I guess," Danny said, "We're thinking it's best to get them at the store when they'll all be there. Stake them out to-morrow morning and once we know they're in there go get 'em."

"You want to kill them?" Jonas asked.

"Not if we don't have to," Danny said, "But I'm thinking they're not going to just join up with us or leave the city willingly."

"Theo and his men need to be dealt with. The boys you should take more caution with," Sister said, "we might be able to salvage them."

"Right. We will."

"Wait, you can't just go killing people that don't agree with you, that's crazy," Jonas said.

"There are no plans to kill them. But as I told you earlier, in my dream, there was blood and death. It may happen. If it does my people have God on their side."

"You know that's bullshit," Jonas said.

"Hey man, shut up. You're only here because Sister said you can handle yourself so act like it," Danny said.

"I don't have a problem with wanting to restart society, or at least create some type of community. Peacefully. But purposely going to kill people, even if they are as bad as Brother Theo, there's something wrong with that too."

"God has the plan, we are only servants of his will," Sister said.

"Will you cut that religious bullshit?"

"I won't tell you again to back off," Danny said, standing face to face with Jonas.

"Calm down, both of you. Danny, get out of Jonas' face," Sister said.

Danny backed up with a huff and Jonas said, "Fine, whatever. I want no part of this. I'm leaving."

"Jonas don't be rash. Here is where you belong. Besides its safer here than out there," Sister said.

"I'm not scared. I just can't follow you along this path. I thought I could but I was wrong. I wish you luck."

"Good riddance," Danny said.

Anthony, who had up until this point been silently listening while the others spoke, said, "You're not going to tell Brother Theo or his guys what we have planned, are you?"

"I wouldn't worry about that. I have no desire to get in the middle of your little war."

"Jonas, it's getting dark out," Sister said, "You can stay here tonight if you want."

"Thanks for the offer but I'm good. I can take care of myself...I just hope for your sake God takes care of you. See you around."

Jonas opened the door and left Sister's office and in a few more steps left her church altogether. He came upon the garbage can where he had left his gun days earlier. He reached in and felt for it. The gun was still there, and he took it and put it in his coat pocket. 'Hopefully I won't need this, but if I do...' he thought as he walked in the direction of his condo.

Chapter Seventy-Three

Rubina heard Emmalee scream and grabbed her backpack; throwing clothes, make-up case, phone, wallet and portable music player with headphones into it along with a flashlight and the extra clips she had found in the jeep for the rifle. She was in a hurry and not thinking but it only took her moments to pack her bag. She ran back to the door and saw figures moving inside the house across the street then heard Emmalee scream again. She picked up the automatic rifle and slung her bag across her shoulder and made for the backdoor.

She opened it and stepped out as quietly as she could and made her way around the corner of the house so she could still see the house across the street. No one was coming out so she moved quickly to behind the house next door. She peeked out again before moving behind the next house over. Rubina knew she should have run as fast and as far as she could but she remembered the last time she ran at the hospital. They caught her then and she wasn't planning on getting caught again. She took her time, watched the house across the street, and waited.

She got five houses away where she still had a good view. Finally, they came out of the house, Tod and Emmalee first, their hands bound, followed by three men with guns. The men made Tod and Emmalee sit on the curb while one stood behind them, his gun drawn.

Then the other two made their way to her grandmother's house. 'Those assholes giving me up,' Rubina thought, 'serves them right getting caught…well Tod at least. That guy was a jerk, I knew it by looking at him. Emmalee, she's just a kid, she didn't deserve whatever happened in that house. I tried to help her. She picked the wrong protector. It's not my fault.'

***

Clint said to Markus, "Keep an eye on these two. If they run, shoot 'em. If you see their friend come running out the house shoot her."

"You better not run or he says I get to shoot you," Markus told Tod and Emmalee, slapping the back of Tod's head for effect.

"Tyreke come with me, we're going to find their stupid friend. And she's going to pay for killing Tay."

Tyreke nodded and followed Clint. They approached the door the same way as they had the others, carefully trying the door handle and seeing that it was locked Clint tried to kick the door in. But this time it didn't work and he said, "Fuck, that hurt! There's got to be something behind it."

Clint looked tried to look through the windows, but couldn't see into the dark house. "Let's go around back," he said.

They went to the back door and it was open. "Look around, you see her? She might've run off," Clint said.

They surveyed as far as they could see but it was dusk and visibility was low. "Let's go inside."

They checked the house and saw the couch barricading the front door but no girl. Clint called, "It's ok girlie. We won't hurt you. We just want to talk is all."

Tyreke opened one of the bedroom doors and saw a body on the bed. He turned it over and found an old woman, dead. She had a look on her face of contentedness, and it reminded him of his best friend, sleeping, just before Tyreke blew his brains out. He pushed the image from his head and turned out the light and left the room. "Clint," he called.

"You find her?"

"No, but I found an old dead lady."

"That doesn't help us much does it? Keep looking."

They checked under beds, in closets, even the basement but didn't find her. Tyreke looked at the pictures on the hallway wall and saw one of girl that looked like the one Clint described. "Hey Clint, check this out. Is this her?"

"This looks like the girl we picked up at the hospital, but she ain't here. Fuck," Clint said, "But I got an idea. At least we can send this little bitch a message. Go get the gasoline."

***

Rubina watched as her grandmother's house burned. She was kneeling behind a black, iron fence, tears welling up in eyes, but she didn't allow them to fall down her cheeks by wiping them on the sleeve of her shirt. The only home she had ever really known, gone. She heard them yell that they would get her, that this was just a warning, and the things they would do to her once they found her. 'Fat fucking chance you fools find me,' she thought but wanted to scream it at them.

Rubina heard the car's doors slam and they drove off. She thought about trying to rummage through the house, finding pictures of her parents, her Mimi, and saving the heirlooms like Mimi's

John F. Kennedy plate set. But she didn't. She just watched as her home burned.

She thought about where she could go, where she would be safe. 'Work? Mae's house? It's already too dark to go too far. They can't check every house, right?' she reasoned with herself. She began walking through alleys and backyards, keeping as quiet as she could, listening for sounds of cars, watching for headlights. She saw none and once she was about two miles away from her grandmother's house, she tried the back door of a one-story house that had still budding lilacs in the front yard and a porch with a swing. It just felt safe and she went to the door.

The door was unlocked and she went inside. The air inside was stale and she could tell the windows hadn't been opened in a while, but she didn't smell the horribleness that accompanied dead bodies. She took tiny steps while feeling for anything that might trip her in the dark. She went in the first door she found and it was the bathroom.

Rubina used the toilet and then went in the door across the hall. It smelled of perfume and body spray, definitely a girl's bedroom and not unlike how her room smelled. The familiarity was calming, like being a beach all by herself, hearing only the waves. She felt a dresser, picked up a brush, smelled it, then set it back down. The scent was a familiar one from her younger years and figured the girl that lived in this bedroom must have been a teenager.

She felt for the bed and found it without tripping on anything. She ran her arms across it, hoping not to touch a body, rather she felt a stuffed animal, squeezed it, and set it back down on the bed. Rubina sat on the bed feeling the walls for a window. She found one under ample drapes, and once she moved those the full moon gave her a slight amount of visibility. Rubina saw the drapes were a deep red with the bedspread matching.

Rubina tentatively looked out the window and saw the street, dark and quiet. 'No way they can find me now, right?' she thought as she laid down on the bed, her head sinking into the soft down pillow, 'But what am I going to do now?' This question had lay at her core during the entire Rabbit Flu situation, as she imagined it had on the minds of the other, living people out there.

'Why is it so important to decide what to do?' she thought. When there aren't many choices, it seemed a lot easier of a question to deal with, if not altogether forget. But now? With an infinite number of choices as to how to live out the rest of her life, the question became all encompassing.

Sleep began to rear its head as her eyes got heavy, and she couldn't concentrate on anything, but her mind wouldn't quiet enough to allow her to sleep. 'I know what I should do. I should help those people still stuck in the police station, which is probably where they took Tod and Emmalee. I don't owe those pricks anything, I know that, but those other people are still there. But what happened to Ginger and probably Emmalee...' She couldn't say or even think the word. 'I need to help them. It's what Mimi and Mae and my parents would want me to do. What's the point of going on if I leave those people to die or worse? What kind of person would I be?'

As her thoughts began to overwhelm her, she heard something move in the house. "Who's there?" Rubina said as she went to grab the rifle, "I'll shoot! I have a big fucking gun and I'll shoot I swear!"

The door opened ever so slightly and she saw eyes near the bottom of it, then heard the soft meow. "Shit, kitty, I was going to kill you."

The cat sauntered to the bed and Rubina extended her hand. The cat sniffed her hand and she said, "It's ok kitty, I won't hurt you."

The cat seemingly understood her and jumped up on the bed next to Rubina. The cat curled up next to her as Rubina lay back down. She flipped the pillow to the cool side under her head and took a deep breath. "Fine. If those gangster assholes want to fuck with me I'll show them I'm not to be fucked with. Not anymore. If they think they can come after me I'll go after them. They don't know where I am but I know where they are.'

Rubina smiled and pet the cat who was purring softly. Her mind continued to race and she had problems quieting it, just when she thought she was about to fall asleep another thought popped into her head, but sleep finally came to her that night.

Chapter Seventy-Four

When James awoke it was almost dark. He rubbed his eyes and looked instinctively toward his alarm clock but it was off. "I need a watch," he mumbled to himself and rose from bed.

Nadia was still asleep on the couch and Franklin was looking out the telescope at the soldier's condo. "See anything?" James asked.

"There's two of them. They've been drinking beers nonstop since I started watching."

"There were four before. I wonder where the other two are."

"I don't know. Hey, James, why don't you step out into the hallway with me for a minute. I want to talk to you and I don't want to wake Nadia up."

James followed Franklin into the hallway and closed the door gently. "What's up Franklin?"

"I wanted to talk to you about what we're going to do about those soldiers."

"What do you mean?"

"If the news reports were right and by what you said those soldiers have no problem killing regular people like us. I don't think we can get out of the city without either waiting them out, leaving before they wake up, or confronting them which I don't want to do."

"Me neither."

"I'm thinking if there are only two of them and they're drunk tonight they probably won't be up early. We can go around the hole in the highway if we leave at dawn. Or, like I said, we can wait for them to leave."

"But we don't know if they will leave; I see the issue. We can stay here to keep an eye on them and know we'll have enough food to last for a long while, but I think you're right. Are you sure we shouldn't just leave now once they pass out for the night?"

"I thought about that. If we leave at night, we're going to need flashlights to get around the highway and that's going to draw attention."

"Right. Then it's settled. We'll leave in the morning."

"Alright let's go tell Nadia."

"Wait a sec I wanted to ask you something," James said, "What's your guys' deal?"

"What do you mean?"

"Are you together, or what?"

"Umm…no, not really. Why, are you thinking of making a move?"

"No, not at all. I was just wondering. Then…how'd you two get together?"

"I found her in her car in the parking lot of my building."

"Huh?"

"I think she was trying to kill herself."

"Really? That sucks."

"I think she's alright now. In the short time I've known her I've learned she can be a bit emotional, so go easy on her, ok?"

"Sure, I understand. Let's go."

As they entered the apartment Nadia was waking up, stretching her arms and rising from the couch. Her shirt came up past her navel and James looked out of the corner of his eye. She adjusted her shirt and asked, "What were you guys doing in the hallway?"

"Just talking. We didn't want to disturb you," Franklin said.

"You weren't talking about me, were you?"

"No, we were talking about those soldiers."

"What about them?"

James returned to the window, looked through the telescope and said, "It looks like they're still getting drunk."

"Not a bad idea," Nadia said and smiled.

"The plan is to leave early in the morning. If they're drinking tonight we figure they won't be up early so we can slip past them and go around."

"Nice work guys. Didn't you promise us some fancy dinner Franklin?" Nadia asked.

"I did, didn't I?" Franklin said and made his way to the pantry.

"Hey I think it might be a better idea for you to cook in the apartment across the hall, just to be on the safe side," James said.

"Good idea," Franklin said and took a handful of cans, a bag of half frozen chicken, some utensils and some spices and asked James to get the door for him. "This one good?" Franklin said and motioned to the door right across the hall.

"Nah let's try the one here," James said and led the way to the apartment of the cute girl that lived on his floor.

From wrong mail he had received he deduced that her name was Erin, and he pictured her in his mind. Her dirty blonde hair always tied back, her long legs when she'd wear a skirt, her fit body and large butt in workout clothes on her way to the gym. 'I should've asked her out,' he thought, 'Shit I should've at least checked in on her once the Rabbit Flu was in full effect. What an asshole I am.' James tried the doorknob but it was locked. He put his shoulder into the door twice and the lock broke. "Crap locks," he said to Franklin, who followed him inside.

Franklin set the things in his arms down on the counter. "I'll check the rooms, just in case," James said. He opened the door to the bathroom; it was set up just like his but with strands of blonde hair all over the place, canisters of hair spray and lotion and curlers and a hair dryer. But no person.

He closed the bathroom door and tried the one to the bedroom. He knocked softly and said, "Hello?" but received no response. He knocked again but still nothing. He tried the handle but it was locked and James figured she must've put a lock on it and thought her smart, but this door he wasn't going to break down. It just didn't feel right knocking down her bedroom door. It wasn't that exactly, more it was the fact that if she was in there dead...he just didn't want to remember her that way.

Then James heard the frying pan sizzling and went back to Franklin. "You can go back over to your apartment if you want. Dinner should be ready in about twenty-five, maybe thirty minutes."

James left and returned to Nadia. She was looking at his movie collection, but he could tell she was doing it out of boredom. "You want to smoke some pot?" he asked but she declined.

"Maybe after dinner?"

"Cool. I hope you don't mind if I do. I can't eat unless I smoke first."

"I've known a few people like that. It's fine with me."

After James smoked he asked Nadia, "So what's up with Franklin?"

"What do you mean?"

"I mean how'd you guys get together?"

"We're not *together*, if that's what you're asking."

"No, that's not what I meant."

"Oh...ok. My boyfriend, he got the flu and he died..."

"I'm sorry."

"Thanks," Nadia said and paused for a few moments, surveying the room, focusing on nothing, before continuing, "So I was going to leave his place, and that's where Franklin lived too, I guess, but I never saw him there. He took me to his place, and we made plans to leave the city. That's why we were shopping for camping stuff."

"That's cool," James said, "Hey let me ask you something? What's with the tattoos? You don't have as many as a lot of people I see, but I just don't get it."

"I have more than you can see," she said.

"Haha," he said, letting him imagination try and figure out where her other tattoos were hidden, "But for real, what's the deal with them?"

"I don't know. They look cool. Each one I have means something to me and some are more important than others."

"Ok, how about that small one at the nape of your neck, the one with the skull and crossbones with a big pink bow on it?"

"You wouldn't have seen that one either if I wasn't wearing my hair up, which I almost never do 'cause it looks like crap."

"No, it doesn't," he said and she rolled her eyes, "So what's the meaning of that one?"

"Don't you know you never ask a girl about her tattoos? It's rude."

"Well excuse me," James said laughing.

Nadia laughed as well and motioned for James to hand her the bong so she could smoke it. She did and coughed afterward.

"For real, you're not going to tell me?"

"Not now. Maybe once I get to know you better. I'm not going to give all of my secrets away to some guy I just met. But if you're lucky…" Nadia said and smiled.

"You're such a tease," he said and laughed again.

Just then Franklin came back with three plates of pesto chicken along with garlic bread and a side salad. "Hope you like Italian dressing, all the others I could find looked way past expiration date."

"I'm not a big salad eater as it is anyway," James said.

Franklin left and returned with a bottle of red wine and three glasses. "I figure we're not savages yet, right?" Franklin said and handed the bottle to James who poured the wine.

"The food smells awesome Franklin, thanks," Nadia said.

"Yeah thanks," James said with a fork full of pasta on the way to his mouth.

They ate by the moonlight and when they were done James and Nadia shared a joint. "This is just what I needed," James said, "good food, good people and some good smoke."

"True that," Nadia said.

"You sure you don't want to smoke this Franklin?" James asked as Nadia passed him the joint.

"Nah, I'm good."

"You ever smoke pot before?" Nadia asked.

"I did. Back in my younger days. But it's probably been a good ten or fifteen years since."

"All the more reason to smoke up," James said laughing.

"It's ok. You kids have fun," Franklin said and considered smoking just to impress Nadia, but he just as quickly realized how if anything were to happen at least one of them should be sober. That's why he only had the one glass of wine with dinner. Then he went to the window to check on the soldiers. "I think they're out. They were moving before dinner but I don't see them moving now. We should all get some sleep. We'll plan on leaving at dawn."

| 75 |

Chapter Seventy-Five

Jonas walked quietly, almost stealthily, taking back alleys to his condo building. He saw no one on his trek home. 'Sister and her people are just as bad as Theo's,' he thought as he walked, 'and I am not getting in the middle of their power struggle. They're like two sides of a quarter, both fighting for control. Their people, they're the nickels and dimes that make up the quarter. Then what am I, and the rest of the people out there that don't want to play their games? Maybe we're the pennies, worthless but enough together to actually make some real money. What a stupid analogy. It doesn't really matter. All I know is that they're not worth it. Let them play war without me.'

He walked up the many flights of stairs to his floor, tired and out of breath by the time he arrived. The hallways were pitch black and he had to walk slowly while gripping the walls until he reached his condo. He opened the door to his condo deliberately, not wanting to disturb his wife. He knew she was dead but still he respected her presence. He just didn't want to go into their bedroom if he could help it.

A stale, stuffy smell inhabited his condo while he made the way to a drawer in his kitchen which held a flashlight. He turned the flashlight on and panned across his condo. He felt like a burglar for a moment, and then when the light hit his bedroom door he stopped. 'Why? What is wrong with this world? Why'd this happen?' he thought and tears began welling up in his eyes.

Jonas began to feel unsteady and kneeled on the floor. He set the flashlight down next to him and the light coming from it made shadows around his condo. He put his hands to his face and wept.

After a few moments Jonas rubbed the tears out of his eyes and picked the flashlight back up. He rose from the floor and went to open the living room windows. Once done he stepped out onto his balcony, looking down at the city below. He poured himself a drink, unfortunately with no ice, and gazed at the city. No lights and the immense quiet made it all seem surreal. He did take notice of a fire about a mile away amid a block of one- and two-story homes. The flames were still burning bright in the darkness, meaning the fire was recent. 'I would be reporting that on the news tonight,' he thought and shook his head.

He began thinking back to something Sister had said earlier, about him being a 'true journalist.' He realized it hadn't been true in many years, not once he got the big desk job. Anchor. It was a big deal for him, especially in a city of this size. It was the sign he had made it. But now, now he couldn't even remember the last time he had been out on a story, reporting, investigating, interviewing. He didn't even write his own scripts anymore even though he swore when he took the job that he was going to. That lasted three months.

He didn't miss the news though. Having to sit through the mindless sports reporter Chris talking about meaningless sports. Or Harry the weatherman. Harry wasn't a bad guy but weathermen were akin to economists Jonas always thought. 'When things are going well they take all the credit. Then when things go bad like it's raining or snowing or the economy is in the toilet they throw their hands up and say, 'it's the weather/economy.' What a bunch of frauds,' he thought but that led him back to being down on himself.

'What a shitty journalist I am,' he thought as he watched the fire, 'Wait! I got it! That's what I'm supposed to do! I'm an observer. Not a participant. I observe and report.' Jonas began thinking about writing a news script for all that had happened. Sister, Brother Theo, the explosion, the fire. 'I could put it on myself. I did the last one all on my own. Ah shit, the power's out. That won't stop me. I'll record it, I know I have a Dictaphone around here somewhere,' he thought and went back inside to look for it.

It took him a while but he found the Dictaphone he was looking for along with some blank tapes. The batteries were still inside and not corroded, which surprised him as he couldn't remember the last time he had used it. Jonas began speaking into it, chronicling his finding of Sister's church, his night mission to scout out Brother Theo's locations, the explosion or bombing from earlier that day, the fire that was currently burning not far away. The excitement in his voice was hard to contain, and he re-recorded his initial message with a more subdued, professional tone.

Once finished he felt exhausted. 'This is what I should have been doing from the beginning. I know it's stupid, and it's not like anyone's going to listen, but at least I have something to do. I have a purpose again!' He wanted to high five somebody but there was nobody else.

Feeling better Jonas took linens and a pillow from a hall closet and set them up on the couch. 'Tomorrow. Tomorrow will be a big news day. I know Sister's people are going to attack El Super-mercado. I'm getting there early, find a good building to watch and report from.' Jonas lay on the couch with a light sheet on top of him, feeling the cool breeze coming in from the open windows and slept a contented sleep.

THREE DAYS AFTER THE END OF THE WORLD

Part IV: Confrontation and Resolution

Chapter Seventy-Six

Franklin woke up first that morning; the sun had yet to show itself but its brightness was already being felt. He stretched after sleeping in the recliner and cracked his back. He tapped Nadia on the shoulder and she woke up sleepily. "Is it time already?"

"Yep, I'm going to go wake James is up."

Franklin knocked on James' door, first quietly then increasing the loudness of his knock. James opened the door looking as sleepy as Nadia had. "It's time to go," Franklin said.

"Gotcha. Let me just get my stuff together."

The shower still worked so they all did that and then ate a small breakfast. The sun was beginning to show itself and Franklin hurried them along. The three of them, with their backpacks and other supplies looked like they were ready to hike up a mountain. "I feel like such a dork," Nadia said.

"You don't look like the hiking type to me," James said.

"It's true, for sure. But I am the adventurous type so I bet this trip should provide some of that."

"I'm sure it will. You guys ready to go? Got everything? Crossbow Nadia?"

"I'm never going anywhere without it. It's just too cool," she said as she aimed it at robin perched on a nearby tree.

"I'm ready, just have to go get something from my room," James said.

James returned to his bedroom and felt downhearted to be leaving his place for what was most likely the last time. His unmade bed, his posters, his bong; he didn't really want to leave any of these things. But it was time to go. He took his handgun from out of his nightstand and put it in his left windbreaker pocket and put his keys in the right pocket and left his bedroom, closing the door behind him. "Let's go," he said.

"You remember your gun?" Franklin asked.

"Yep."

"Alright then let's get out of here."

The plan was to head southeast around the now non-existent South Highway, through the extensive forest that ran alongside it. The map they had showed the vast forest preserve and from their own experiences they knew it was dense and good for cover. Actual trails unfortunately were not on their city map and for those they would have to use the compass.

They began their walk all engulfed in silent thought; Nadia looked around at the surrounding buildings, James fidgeted with the compass, and Franklin meticulously inspected the map. They hadn't made it four blocks when they heard a car coming. "Hey, hey, slow up," Franklin said, "You hear that?"

"Sounds like a car," James said, "Follow me. Behind this dumpster."

They ducked behind the dark green garbage dumpster which was located in a nondescript alley between two tall buildings as they discreetly watched for the car. Then they saw it; the car painted metallic purple with a spoiler and rims that sparkled in the rising sun. The windows and windshield were tinted so black they couldn't see inside. The car looked ridiculous to Franklin, hot to Nadia and overdone to James.

"Ok guys, let's go down this alley, and be quiet," James said, "we should pop out near the highway."

They tip-toed down the alley and James motioned for Franklin and Nadia to let him go first. He leaned against the building, poked his head out the alley and saw a gun pointed at his forehead.

***

Theo was standing on the stoop of his building, smoking slowly and exhaling through his nose. He thought back to the night before when, after leaving Shaun at the police station, he had decided to walk the three or so miles back to his home. He could drive; he could've taken Shaun's car but didn't feel the need. Cars weren't a necessity to Theo; he had access to them if he wanted one but it made him feel more powerful, more in control, to have another do the driving for him.

Past one of the pawn shops that Clint had destroyed was the first stop on his walk; the fire was out but the place was still smoldering and the smell of burnt tinged his nostrils. Theo then went past El Supermercado; saw the obscured windows and almost empty parking lot with Clint's car parked in the handicap spot. He felt no need to stop inside and didn't. He took in the city, his city, as he continued his trip home. The cool air felt good against his skin; after two miles he removed his duster and carried it in his large hands.

Theo thought of his plans; he wasn't necessarily out to hurt anybody but would if the situation called for it like it had at the police station. The police, the government, society had made him out to be a bad guy but he felt he was more a victim of circumstances. He wouldn't play the role of victim in their game was what made them fear him.

But make no mistake; Theo wanted to rule, to be king. These people, the ones still alive, would be his subjects. Once his plans were completed, once his power and the city's resources consolidated, he would rule with an iron fist but also be known for his benevolence. That is what he wanted his legacy to be. He would also need to find a queen, a strong woman, to rule with him.

He heard Clint's car before he saw it and it snapped him out of his daydreaming. Theo dropped the cigarette to the ground and crushed it under his boot. Clint pulled in front of Theo's building and Theo got into his car. "What's up boss?"

"Everything taken care of?"

"You know it. And I got a surprise for you."

"Better be a good one."

"It is. We found one of those bitches that killed Tay. She was with some guy and now they're both back at the jail, locked up tight. They told us where the other bitch that killed Tay was but she was gone. We burned her fucking house to the ground though. We'll get her, I know it."

"That's good Clint. You did good."

Theo's faith in Clint was growing. He had watched the pawn shop fires from his roof and that plan looked like it worked. Today the plan was to use the school buses and police uniforms to round up more people, more workers. 'If today goes as well as yesterday this shit will work out,' he thought. Now it was time for Theo wanted to take a more hands-on approach. "Let's go by the store. I want to talk to our guys," Theo said.

"Sure thing boss."

As they drove down the empty streets Theo saw them. Three people. "Clint, you see them?"

Clint turned his head around to look and said, "No, you see something?"

"Yeah, yeah, some people," Theo said and pointed, "They went down that alley. Take a right up here and we'll wait for them on the other side."

They parked the car and got out, being careful and quiet as they did so. Theo took out his two guns and Clint his one and Theo whispered, "Get on that wall," Theo motioned for Clint to stand just around the corner from the alley, "and don't look around the corner. Just wait. They'll come out."

Both men leaned against the stone building, with Clint closer to the alley opening and Theo a few feet behind him; both had their guns drawn. It didn't take long until a young man's head came out from behind the alley, and Clint met it with his gun.

Chapter Seventy-Seven

Jonas rose early and made his way to El Supermercado. He knew he would be taking a risk, risking his own life possibly, to accurately document the first battle after the end of the world. But he felt, he knew, it would be worth it. It had to be. 'Other cities had to have people like these, right? A hardcore gangster who still had a gang at his disposal; a transvestite religious zealot with the need to take out the gangster; and the rest of us, people like me, waiting for our new leaders,' he thought.

Jonas arrived at El Supermercado but got no closer than a drab office building across the parking lot from the store. He entered through the revolving doors and walked up three flights of stairs to the third floor. He found an office that he thought would face El Supermercado marked as Denilson Home Health Services and went inside. A waiting room with red ochre carpeting and a secretary's desk with a bowl full of peppermints and a small sign that read "sign in please" and a clipboard with a list of names and dates were the things he noticed first about this office.

He strode past bland offices with no windows until he came to the office at the end of the hall. The office had a painting of two white dogs on a beach; opposite this was a framed poster of a man hiking a mountain encouraging "Determination." A cheap, worn nameplate read "Denise O'Neil." Jonas picked up a framed picture on the desk and examined the faces; two auburn-haired children two young to determine their gender, a sunburned man with hair that matched the children, his Hawaiian shirt open, exposing an unhealthy belly, and a rather large blonde woman in a blue swimsuit that was two sizes too small, at least. Jonas assumed the blonde was Denise. 'They look so happy…it's too bad,' Jonas thought and placed the picture, face down, on the desk.

An ancient, yellowing computer and disorganized papers littered the rest of her desk but Jonas paid them only a glance. He moved to the window which was covered in closed blinds. He poked his finger into the blinds to open them so he could see El Supermercado. 'What a spot. I can see everything from here. This is going to be perfect.'

Jonas took out his Dictaphone, checked the batteries, recorded a test message, and set it down on the desk. Next, he used his binoculars to get a close-up view of El Supermercado. The windows were painted black so he couldn't see inside. There was no one in front of the store so he set the binoculars on the desk as well.

His stomach soon realized he had forgotten breakfast in his hurry to find a good spot to report on the shootout. Jonas opened the desk drawers but only found a can of Italian Wedding soup which he wasn't going to eat cold. Jonas left the office and rummaged through other desks in the office and returned with a half-eaten pack of powdered donuts, a bag of pretzels and a warm can of lemon and lime soda.

Back in the office he checked the window again. A few random cars parked haphazardly and turned over carts not in their designated areas littered the parking lot but he still saw no people. He sat in the surprisingly comfortable office chair and ate his food, barely able to contain his excitement on getting to be reporter again. Sister's people would be coming soon.

| 78 |

Chapter Seventy-Eight

The sunlight shown through the now curtain-free window and Rubina awoke with a yawn and a stretch. She looked around the bedroom and confirmed she was in a teenager's room. Pictures of the latest heartthrobs cut from magazines and taped to the walls; writing on the ceiling in a variety of colors, quotes, poems, messages just to say 'hi,' designs and drawings. Rubina herself was never able to write on her walls, but she really, really wanted to when she was thirteen. Mimi wouldn't have it. 'Oh Mimi, I miss you. I hope you're in heaven,' she thought even though she didn't believe in it. But if there was a heaven, she was sure Mimi was there.

Rubina looked toward the automatic rifle as she rose from bed, the carpet comforting her bare feet. The door was open a crack and she noticed the cat was no longer in the room with her. "Here kitty, kitty," she said as she stepped into the hallway. The cat did not appear.

She used the flamingo inspired bathroom with its pink walls, flamingo-laden shower curtain, and flamingo soap dispenser. 'I don't get flamingos. They're pink, I get it, but I'm a girl and I think they're so weird,' she thought, then, 'I really need to brush my teeth but I left my toothbrush at the house. Shit. I am not using someone else's toothbrush.' Rubina rummaged through the bathroom but didn't find any unused toothbrushes, so she put some toothpaste on her finger and used that to brush her teeth.

Once done in the bathroom she checked the other bedroom at the end of the hall. The door was closed but unlocked and she opened it slowly. Rubina found there was a queen-size waterbed when she touched it and immediately jumped on the bed, letting the waterbed ripple and wave her body.

She lay in the waterbed and observed two massive Oscar fish, both a dirty brown and dayglo orange color, swimming in a fifty-gallon tank. The fish tank's motor and light was out but still the orange of the fish shone brightly. She saw a cylindrical bottle labeled 'fish food' and sprinkled some food in the tank which the fish ate voraciously. As she fed the fish she noticed a full length mirror was on the wall. She looked at herself in the mirror, critiquing her pale skin, smallish breasts, short legs, tangled hair that desperately need a brushing, then moving closer and doing the same with her face. She plucked a blond hair on her chin which with her fingers and rubbed the beginning of a pimple on her chin. With a shake of her head she left the bedroom and returned to the kitchen to see her available breakfast options.

'I can't believe I'm in some stranger's house, eating untoasted Pop Tarts, thinking about assaulting a jail. Fuck, a week ago I was happy in my little life,' she thought, 'Working a no stress job, hanging out with my best friend, taking care of my grandma, no real responsibilities, just living. Now almost everyone is dead. Every person I ever loved, ever cared about, shit ever *knew*, dead and gone. It's just me now...'

'And I killed a guy. With these hands. I mean, he was going to rape me or worse, but still I killed him. Not those other two women.

Me. Why don't I feel worse about killing that guy? Shouldn't I feel remorse? Or at least feel bad about it? But I don't. Not one bit. Billions of better people died than that asshole. Now I have this rifle, this tool for killing, and I might have to do it again. What the fuck has happened to my life?'

'What a fucking week. I could just stay here, never leave, eat Pop Tarts and canned tuna fish the rest of my life, and I bet those bad guys would never find me. But I don't want to hide, don't want to be weak, feel insignificant anymore. Those dipshits burned my house down. I owe them a bit of payback. I remember on the cross-country team, a coach saying something like, 'Winners step up when their time comes. You never know when it might be your time, but you need to be prepared, be ready.' I'm ready. Those people are locked in jail and for what? For some sadistic gangsters to do with what they please? And burn my fucking house down to boot? Hell no.' "Hell no!" she yelled.

Rubina got her bag together and said goodbye to the house where she had slept the night before. She took the extra clips of ammunition for the rifle and practiced replacing them once they would become empty. She practiced until she felt she could reload the rifle as fast as she could. She looked at her watch. The time read 7:00am. 'Time to be a badass,' she thought.

Chapter Seventy-Nine

"Don't fucking move," Clint whispered with a smile to James, who answered his words with a slow nod.

"C'mon, slowly," Clint said not taking his gun off of James' forehead as Theo walked around to face them.

"Haha, I knew I saw you people," Theo said and then to Nadia, "drop that crossbow sweetheart."

Nadia placed the crossbow on the ground delicately while Clint pushed James toward Franklin and Nadia. The three stood facing Theo and Clint who both had guns aimed at them. James wanted to pull out his gun and kill these two but he didn't figure he could hit both of them without Nadia or Franklin getting shot, so he didn't. Franklin said, "Hey guys, we don't want any trouble."

"It's not really up to you is it? It's up to this man right here," Clint said.

"Clint, take it easy. I don't think these three are going to be a problem. Are you going to be a problem?"

They shook their heads. "Take off those backpacks, you won't be needing them. You guys have any other weapons besides that crossbow? Where'd you get that? I bet you don't even know how to use it."

"Fuck you," Nadia said.

Theo laughed. He had forgotten how ornery really pretty girls could be. "It would be stupid to be out here unarmed, right? Clint, search them."

Clint patted Franklin and Nadia down first and found nothing but he found James' gun tucked in his jacket pocket. "What the fuck is this kid?" Clint said and hit James in the stomach with the butt of the gun.

James dropped to the ground holding his stomach. "Hey! What'd you do that for?" Nadia said as she kneeled down next to James, putting her arm around him.

"You ok?" she asked James.

He nodded and grimaced. "He's fine. Help him up," Theo said.

Nadia did and the groups stood facing each other once more. Clint still had his gun aimed at them but Theo had let his fall to his side.

"Hey, you look familiar, are you on TV or something?" Franklin said.

"You don't know who this is? This is Brother Theo and he *owns* this city," Clint said.

"You're the cop killer?" Franklin said.

"I never killed any cops, at least nothing they could prove. I guess it doesn't matter now anyway. So yeah, I've killed cops. I've killed enough other people too who stood in my way so you should be careful what you say to me," Theo said as he approached Franklin, walked behind him, sizing him up.

"You three are coming with us."

"No," Nadia said defiantly.

"I wasn't asking," Theo said as he stood behind them and began herding them toward Clint's car. Clint led them and was about to open the passenger door when Franklin turned and tackled Theo to the ground. "Run!" he yelled at James and Nadia, who hesitated for a second, then ran in opposite directions.

"Fuck!" Clint said and went to help Theo, but Theo said, as he punched Franklin in the ribs, "Go get them!"

Franklin and Theo wrestled on the ground, knocking Theo's gun from his hands. Franklin was on top of Theo and punched him in the face, cutting his lip and loosening one of lip studs. "You dumb motherfucker," he mumbled as he tasted his own blood.

Theo reached into his coat and pulled his other gun from its holster. Franklin choked him as Theo tried hitting Franklin with one arm and with the other was trying to pull his other gun from his holster. As Theo fought to breathe, he was able to reach his other gun and put it up against Franklin's ribs and pulled the trigger. Franklin fell back on the ground while Theo got up slowly. Theo then stood over Franklin as he writhed in pain, holding his side. He kicked Franklin in the side where he was shot. Franklin let out a howl. "I told you I wasn't going to hurt you. I wasn't lying," Theo said as he touched his now tender lip with his finger then sucked the blood off of it.

"But you had to fuck it up, didn't you old man? Well too bad, it's over for you," Theo said as he aimed the gun at Franklin's forehead and fired.

Theo kicked Franklin's dead body with force and spit on him. Then he went to find Clint. Clint was pulling Nadia back toward Theo by her hair as she stumbled along. "I got the bitch. The other guy went down the alley that way I think."

"I think I know how to get him back here," Theo said and took Nadia by the arm, holding her with a force that would most likely leave a mark.

"Hey kid," Theo said, it being so quiet he didn't need to yell, "I got your girlfriend here, and if you don't want her to end up like the old man here, you better come out."

'Fuck, shit, fuck!' James thought as he hid behind an industrial-sized garbage dumpster. 'I could leave her. I barely know her, I mean I just met her yesterday. No one would even know I left her. Left her to die…God I wish I still had my gun…'

"Kid you're running out of time," Theo said, "get out here now or else I'll kill her."

'What am I doing?' James thought as he came out from behind the dumpster, "Alright, I'm coming out, don't shoot."

Theo and Clint watched as James emerged. Clint's gun was aimed right at him. "Good boy," Theo said as he let Nadia go and she moved quickly toward Franklin's body, which was only a few feet away.

"Oh Franklin, Franklin, what the hell did you do?" she said.

"Clint, you have tape right?" Theo said and Clint nodded.

"Well go get it."

Clint went to his car as James approached. He went to console Nadia when Theo said, "Not so fast kid. Come over here."

Theo had his one gun aimed at James loosely, using it like a pointer. He saw his other gun a few feet from Franklin's body. He walked over to it slowly, almost as if he was daring James to try and pick it up. James looked at the gun but knew he had no chance to get it so he instead went to Nadia as Theo picked his other gun up. Theo returned both guns to their holsters and grabbed James by his neck and took him off of Nadia. "C'mon," Theo said as he pushed James toward Clint.

Clint returned with the duct tape and wrapped James' hands first, then Nadia's. Clint put his hands on Nadia's breasts once she was bound and she tried to wriggle away but couldn't. "Fuck you asshole! Don't fucking touch me!" she said as she tried to bite at him, her teeth clicking as she did.

"Clint, really, show some class toward our new prisoners."

"What boss, can't I have her? She's hot as fuck."

"Not now you can't. We have a schedule and this has already put us behind. Put the kid in the front seat. I'll sit with the girl in back."

"Oh, so you want her boss? That's fine with me."

"Don't be crude," Theo said and before they got into Clint's car he looked at James and Nadia, "Your friend was stupid. I hope you two aren't as stupid."

Nadia and James nodded their heads, not making eye contact with Theo or each other. "Good. You'll both be fine as long as you don't fuck with us like your dead friend over there."

"You want to take them to the jail boss?" Clint asked.

"Let's go to the store. No reason to mess up the day's schedule on account of them. There must be a cooler or something and we can hold them there. Later on you can take them to the cells."

Once in the car Theo sat behind Clint to prevent Nadia from possibly trying to kick Clint's seat and get them in an accident. "What's your name?" Theo said to Nadia.

"Fuck off."

"That's no kind of name. What about you?" Theo asked James, tapping him on the shoulder with James' gun.

"Same as hers."

"You both are ornery, like a couple of puppies. I've had my fair share of puppies, and you know how you get them to listen and obey?"

Neither responded. "You have to beat them. Not bad, mind you, but enough so they know who's boss. I'm sure you two will know who the boss is soon enough."

| **80** |

Chapter Eighty

Jonas looked at his watch; it was a thirty-eighth birthday gift from his wife. With a tiny diamond at the twelve spot and a jet-black background, it made him happy just to look at it. It was amazing that she was always able to get things for him that he actually liked. Most couples, when they buy things for each other, smile and don't like what they've been given but accept it anyway because they love each other. Jonas' wife was different. Whether it'd be suits, shirts, ties, paintings, curios, whatever gift she had bought him he always genuinely liked it and by liked it meaning he would buy it for himself. 'God, I miss her,' he thought.

Jonas spoke into the Dictaphone while looking through the blinds at El Supermercado. "The time is 7:05am. A metallic purple car is parking in front of the store, four passengers appear to be inside. Two men exit the car, both on the driver's side and walk to the other side of the car. They each open the passenger side doors and get out two people whose hands are bound with what looks like duct tape. One woman and one man are bound and are being led into the store."

'I wonder where Sister's men are?' Jonas thought, 'They said early in the morning. Maybe they rethought their plan. I don't know if that makes me happy that they want to avoid the violence or sad that I'll have nothing newsworthy to report.'

He knew Sister and Theo both were wrong to try and control the city; that was the old way and he had hoped that the new way would be more peaceful but he knew that at its heart, humanity was violent. He had seen it all over the world in different cultures and languages. It was just how people were. Jonas didn't want these people to die and it wasn't their fault they were manipulated by power hungry egomaniacs.

Fifteen minutes past with no action until "Wait, wait. I see four armed men approaching, walking slowly down Grand Avenue. One is holding some kind of assault rifle, the other three are holding handguns, all aimed at El Supermercado. They are now nearing the parking lot of the store. No one from Theo's Disciples is guarding the front door. The group of four with handguns are now ducking behind the metallic purple car while the one with the assault rifle nears the door to El Supermercado. He tries to open the door, but it appears to be locked and he returns to his men."

Jonas recognized Danny and Anthony immediately and the other men he vaguely remembered seeing at Sister's church. He continued speaking into the Dictaphone, "Now the one with the assault rifle, the leader, named Anthony, unknown last name, is ordering the other men to set up behind the other cars in the parking lot. Each man is kneeling behind one of the cars. They seem to be waiting for something…"

***

Tyreke laid in his bed, awake, on one of mattresses they had set up in the cereal aisle of the store. Five beds were set up along the aisle with Serge in the bed closest to the front of the store, Tyreke in the farthest bed, and the three pups in between them. He didn't want to be the first one to get up, so he lay in bed and let his mind wander.

After seeing those people trapped in the jail, hearing Markus rape that girl, watching the perverse pleasure Clint got out of burning down those pawnshops and the missing girl's house, he began to question his decision to stay. 'Is safety worth this? I don't know, I don't know…but I do know I deserve this. I killed my best friend. I didn't protect my family. I feel safe I guess, better than being alone. They'll protect me now because I'm one of them. A member of Brother Theo's Disciples. Great. Cedric should be here, not me. He wanted this. I don't but now I'm stuck with it.'

Tyreke awoke fully when he heard Clint's voice giving orders loudly. He sat up and the others did so as well. Serge got out of bed and went to see Clint and Tyreke could hear what they said.

"I told you to have them up early," Clint said.

"It is early man. The sun is barely up," Serge said then, "Who're they?"

"We found them on our way here."

"Nice, this chick is hot," Serge said as he licked his lips.

"Gross," Nadia said.

"Serge," Theo said, "help Clint take these two back into the cooler."

"Ok boss."

"Clint, make sure they're locked in there and they don't have any weapons. Search them again. We don't need a repeat of what happened to Tay."

"Will do, c'mon."

They went down a different aisle than the one that the beds were in but Tyreke could hear their footsteps on the concrete. He saw Markus, John-two and Ptolemy sitting up in their beds, whispering. He rose and went to them. "What are you guys talking about?"

"I was just telling them how I tore up that bitch yesterday and how hot she was," Markus said, "Wasn't she a piece of ass Tyreke?"

"She was cute."

"And did you hear Serge talk about that new bitch they picked up? Another hot one. I hope I get a chance with her."

"If you're lucky, you liar," Ptolemy said.

"I'm not, Tyreke said so. Maybe if you two ever got lucky you'd know what I'm talking about," Markus said.

"Whatever Markus," John-two said, "You only got with that slut Catrina because she gave it up to everybody."

"So what? You didn't fuck her."

"Cause she probably had like ten-million diseases," John-two said and he and Ptolemy laughed.

"Shut up fuckers," Markus said and tackled John-two.

The boys wrestled until Tyreke said, "Hey, cut it out, Theo's coming this way."

The boys went silent as Theo approached. "Boys, you ready to put in some more work today?" Theo said as he lit a cigarette.

"You know it," Markus said, speaking for all of them.

"Good. Get ready because we have work to do. I heard you boys did well yesterday. Keep it up," Theo said and walked past them toward the back of the store.

"Man, that dude is badass," Markus said, "I want to be just like him."

Tyreke thought just the opposite.

| 81 |

Chapter Eighty-One

The door to the cooler closed with a whooshing sound leaving James and Nadia alone in the dim and damp cooler. "You could've turned on the lights assholes!" James said as he pounded on the thick cooler door. They didn't have to be so rough with you," James said to Nadia who was hunched down on the ground with her head in her knees, slowly rocking.

Nadia didn't respond and simply sobbed quietly. "Hey, hey, it's going to be ok," James said as he kneeled next to Nadia and put her arm around her.

"We'll get out of this I promise. I wish I had my gun…"

Nadia looked at him and with tear-soaked eyes said, "Franklin's dead. He's dead…"

"I know," James said as he went to stroke her hair but she shrugged him off.

James went from kneeling to sitting on the cool ground and stared at his hands. 'What could I have done? I didn't know Franklin was going to do that. And now? What now? I saw the way those guys looked at Nadia, and what kind of man am I that I can't protect her? Shit I can't even protect myself. I should've shot those assholes when I had the chance. But I didn't have a chance. That guy with the gun to my head, he's a killer. I just know how to shoot. Just to let off some steam. Hell, I never killed anything before. They're going to come back for us and what am I going to do, throw gallons of milk at them? Shit…'

Nadia changed positions and sat on the ground next to James and wiped her tears on the hem of her shirt. She leaned on his shoulder and they sat in silence for a time. James didn't want to speak first so he waited for her to do so.

"Hey James?"

"Yeah?"

"It's not good right now. I was so happy this morning, before…"

"Me too."

"What are we going to do?"

James said nothing; he just shook his head and stared at his hands again. "Don't get weird on me. Please don't do that. I can't take it," she said.

"I'm not," James said and looked at her. Even with the runny make-up and teary eyes she was still beautiful. "What do you want me to say Nadia? That I can fix this? That I can bring Franklin back and kill those assholes out there and make everything better? I can't. It's not possible. We're fucked. That's it."

"No, c'mon James, don't."

"Honestly? I think we should savor these last moments until they do with us whatever they're planning to do. 'Cause once that cooler door opens again, like I said, we're fucked."

Nadia began crying again. "I'm sorry Nadia, I am. I fucked up. I should've shot those guys. Then we wouldn't be here. It's on me. I know it."

"Don't say that. It's not your fault."

"Doesn't matter now, does it?" James said and rose from the floor.

The cooler they were in was behind the dairy section of the store. The milk wasn't even expired yet, and the light that came through was from the fluorescent lights that hung above the store itself. James took a strawberry milk and drank half of it, then offered to get something for Nadia.

"I don't like milk," she said.

"Do you want some sour cream then?"

Nadia laughed meekly. "Good to see you smiling again."

"Yeah," she said and got up off the floor and went to James.

She hugged him for a solid minute, speaking inaudibly into his chest between sobs. He held her with one arm and with the other stroked her hair. This time she didn't stop him. Once they separated James said, "Can I ask you something?"

"Ok."

"Why'd you do it? Franklin said he found you in your car. He thought you were trying to kill yourself. Why?"

"I don't know. God, what an answer. How stupid I sound. My boyfriend was dead, I mean he died while I was taking care of him…"

"I'm sorry."

"Thanks," Nadia said, "I don't know, I just didn't see a point anymore. Everyone I ever knew was dead. I'm not a strong person, I at least know that."

"Don't say that, it's not true," James said.

"You hardly know me. But I think I know myself. I never had any big dreams or plans. For fuck's sake I was a stripper in a piece-of-shit dive club. My boyfriend was in business and he was trying to help me and I loved him. Once he was gone I just didn't know what to do. I should've died, not him."

"But you didn't die."

"You're right, I didn't die and Franklin found me and it felt like a jolt to my system. I was ready for whatever came, or at least I thought I was. But now Franklin's dead too and you think we're screwed. So, I'm back where I started."

"I'm sorry, I was wrong. Sometimes I get down and I say stuff I shouldn't. I know how it feels to get depressed. I used to see a psychologist for it."

"Really?"

"Yeah. This red-headed lady with tiny glasses. The day after the TV went off and I felt like I was the only person alive I called her, even though I knew she was dead. I must've left her like ten voice-mails, freaking the fuck out. I'm embarrassed even to tell you."

"It's ok. Thanks," Nadia said, then "So you want to know about my tattoo?"

"Now?"

"Well, if you don't want to…"

"No, I do. Tell me. The bow and skull and crossbones one?"

"Yeah. My dad, the last time I saw him, I was maybe twelve or thirteen, he was yelling at my mom. Yelling at me. He's drunk and breaking dishes and being a total asshole, and I'm yelling at him to get out, yelling at my mom to kick his ass out, and in the middle of our yelling match he calls me poison. Said I poisoned my mother into hating him, poisoned his life by being born."

"Jesus…"

"After that he left. I never saw him again. A couple weeks later I went with some friends to get tattoos. We weren't old enough but they didn't care, and I figured if I was poison at least I'd be a sweet one, you know, with a pink bow."

"Whoa. I'm sorry."

"It's not your fault."

"Yeah, I know, but still…" James said, then after a few moments, "Nadia, we'll figure a way out of this, I know it."

"I hope so," she said.

| 82 |

Chapter Eighty-Two

Theo's Disciples gathered at the back of El Supermercado. Clint, Serge, Markus, Ptolemy, John-two and Tyreke stood facing Theo. "Today we have big plans. We're going to need people, workers, to do what needs to be done to consolidate our control of the city. Clint has done a good job finding some and we have them at the jail already. After this meeting, Clint, I want you to take our two new friends in the cooler over to the jail."

"Can do boss."

"Good. Bring Shaun back from the jail with enough police uniforms for everybody. I told him to find some."

"Ok," Clint said.

"One more thing," Theo said, "give me that gun you took off that kid in the cooler."

"Alright," Clint said and handed the gun to Theo.

"Now get a move on," Theo said and Clint left the backroom of the store.

"Are you all packing?"

Serge, Markus and Tyreke all nodded, but Ptolemy and John-two shook their heads no. "Here," Theo said and handed the gun to John-two.

"Do I get one too?" Ptolemy asked.

"We'll get you one, don't worry. For now, you two can share," Theo said, "Serge you take the boys and find us three school buses. We're going to use those to collect people. Make sure they have some kind of loudspeaker. If not find some bullhorns. We need to be loud, tell everyone the cops are here to save them. Then we'll take them to-"

***

"This is Jonas Johnston, reporting on the attack planned by Sister's Army against Brother Theo's Disciples, who are currently inside El Supermercado. There are four armed men are outside the store, stationed behind parked cars for cover. Wait, wait, one of the men, named Danny, has just thrown something threw the blacked-out window of the store..."

Jonas had the Dictaphone in one hand and was looking through his binoculars with the other. The glass shattered and moments later he heard the explosion and saw the fire and smoke seep out of the broken window. He continued, "A grenade has hit inside the store and one of the armed men, Anthony, is making his way to the front door. Another man is crouched and moving quickly toward the blown-out window..."

***

"What the fuck was that?" Crudo said from his horizontal position on the floor.

Jackson, from his position on the sofa, looked at Crudo and said, "Hell if I know."

They both got up, slowly, and went to the window. "Fuck am I hung over," Crudo said.

"Me too," Jackson said and rubbed his eyes with his hands.

"Look down there, there's smoke coming from that store."

"Damn," Jackson said and went to get the binoculars while Crudo went for his sniper rifle.

Jackson returned to the window first with the binoculars and examined the scene below. "There are some dudes with guns attacking that store."

"What the hell for?" Crudo said as he looked through the scope on the sniper rifle.

"Damned if I know."

"You want me to shoot them?"

"No unnecessary killing right?"

"Yeah, but it's so *fun*," Crudo said and laughed.

"Hey wait a second, doesn't that look like Anthony down there?"

"Where?"

"Right under the window, see?"

"Fucking a it is. That's crazy. Should we help him?"

"Doesn't look like he needs it, at least not yet."

"I can always pick them off from up here."

"Screw that, let's get suited up and get down there."

"Now you're talking. Can I get some aspirin first?"

"Grab me like four."

***

Theo's Disciples ran through the double doors separating the back of the store from the front with their guns in hand. "Serge, take Tyreke and find out what the hell that was," Theo said, "Markus, take your brothers and get behind the desk upfront. Shoot anyone that comes in."

Theo then took the walkie-talkie out of his pocket and spoke into it, "Shaun, Shaun."

"Yeah cuz," Shaun replied after a few moments.

"Get over here now! Someone's fucking with us. Bring your gun and don't drive up to the store. Park in the back and walk around. Hit me up once you get here. I want to know what the hell is going on out there."

"Got it. On my way."

"Hurry the fuck up!"

Tyreke's gun felt heavy in his hand as he followed Serge. He could see the sun shining through the broken window and smoke seeping out of it. Clint was on the ground, grasping for his now non-existent left leg. "Holy shit, Clint!" Serge said, "Tyreke go get him!"

Tyreke went to Clint and helped him up with a struggle. "They got me good man…" Clint said as they stumbled behind register number six. Serge was hiding behind register seven and said, "You alright?"

"Fucking grenade…"

"Who's out there?" Serge yelled as rapid gunfire entered the store.

Once the gunfire ceased Serge peaked his head out and saw someone climbing in through the window. He began firing and hit the intruder in the arm. Markus stood behind the customer service desk and fired five shots at the man coming in through the window, hitting him twice. The intruder crumbled in a heap on the floor, wailing in pain.

Markus remained standing, high-fiving his crouched brothers, as Tyreke watch another one of Sister's men enter the store through the regular entrance and shoot Markus twice, once in the chest and the other in the cheek. Tyreke watched as Markus fell and ducked even further behind the register. Clint was shaking and grasped for Tyreke's hand as Serge moved to register five, closer to the entrance. "I don't want to die," Clint said as he gripped Tyreke's hand.

Tyreke looked directly into Clint's pleading, dying eyes but could not say anything as Clint seized and then slumped into the corner of the register, his eyes now closed. Tyreke could hear the static of the walkie-talkie in Clint's pocket and he reached for it. He heard Theo's voice, "Clint, Clint, you there? What's going up there?"

Tyreke hit the talk button and said, "Clint's dead. They're shooting at us! Help us!" and then dropped the walkie-talkie. He took his gun and fired it wildly over his head toward the window, hitting nothing.

Chapter Eighty-Three

Rubina stood behind a yellow, aluminum-sided, house across the street from the police station. She held the automatic rifle in her hands, ready to shoot anyone that came near her. She stared at the police station, remembering the last time she was here, running away from those bad men, escaping. She saw the rows of forest green bushes that lined the paved walkway to the front door and knew she would have to go back in there. Nothing moved and there was no breeze as she surveyed the street and grounds around the police station.

As she did something caught her eye, something purple, hidden in the bushes. 'Ginger the newswoman,' she thought, 'they just left her body behind some bushes? My God…'

'This is so stupid,' she told herself, 'What am I doing here? I'm going to die if I go in there. I know it. What for? So many people died already, why do I want to join them? I don't owe anybody anything after what I've been through. I can just turn around and leave, find some other place to live and forget about all this bullshit.'

Her thoughts were interrupted by gunfire; not at her, but farther off. 'What the hell is going on in this city? First the flu, then the explosion, now all that gunfire,' she thought, 'Fuck it. I'm going in there. If I'm not willing to die for other people what I am willing to die for? If I die, I die. But at least I know what I'm doing is the right thing to do.'

As Rubina stepped out from behind the yellow house she saw the glass doors of the police station open and a man with a gun in his hand. He began running toward a green SUV parked in front of the police station with one of his arms dangling at his side. Rubina moved quickly back behind the house and watched him drive off, tires screeching. 'What the hell was that? Are they setting me up?' she wondered, 'No, they can't know I'm here, can they? Wait, I heard those shots, then the guy left. I bet they're under attack, wherever the rest of them are. I figured they all weren't at the police station, but that doesn't mean there aren't still gangsters inside. I have an idea on how to get them to come out.'

She carefully proceeded to the bushes at the end of the walkway, kneeling behind one row. Rubina took the rifle in both her hands, with the butt nestled in the crux of her arm, her other hand holding the muzzle. She aimed at the glass entrance doors and fired then ducked behind the bushes. The glass shattered and she hid, waiting to see if anyone would come through the doors while looking for movement inside. She saw none and after two minutes of waiting she cautiously made her way to the entrance. She saw the purple coat covering Ginger's dead body a few feet away from her, a set of pantyhose covered legs with no shoes, glad that the dead newswoman's face was covered.

Rubina felt like a soldier as she had her rifle aimed at the door as she approached. In a movie she had seen a hitman through something when they couldn't see what was around the corner, so she picked up a large rock from the ground and threw it into the open police station. It crashed with little fanfare and no reaction from inside. She stepped inside carefully and remembered again her time here two days earlier. The dead cop's body was gone but she could tell the body had been dragged away, the blood smearing the floor in a direction opposite the cells.

Inside the police station the sound of the far-off gunfire was muffled. Rubina approached the cell where she had been and looked in through the tiny glass window. 'Holy shit they didn't even take care of his body. Fucking assholes,' she thought as the man she had killed was still lying, face down, with the knife in his neck. The knife she had used to stab him…to kill him.

She quickly looked away and turned toward the other cell. She peered through the tiny window into the cell seeing Emmalee, Tod and the other people all seated, leaning against the walls. "Rubina? Rubina is that you?" Emmalee said as she rose from the floor, "Get us out of here!"

"Yeah, it's me. I saw one of the guys leave, is there anybody else here that you know of?"

"I don't think so. One guy was guarding us. Are you going to let us out?"

"Yeah, yeah, where's the key?"

"I don't know."

Rubina searched a nearby desk, looking for cell keys when she noticed them hanging on a tack board. She found the right one and opened their cell. Emmalee ran out and almost tackled Rubina, hugging her tightly. "It's ok, it's ok," she cooed.

Emmalee released her and the rest of the people from the cell followed her out. Tod exited last and mumbled, "Thanks," before walking past her, avoiding eye contact with Rubina, toward the jail exit.

"God you're such an asshole. I ought to shoot you now for all the fucking trouble you've caused me."

"Whatever," Tod said without turning around.

Rubina walked quickly and spun him around. "Listen jerkoff, I know it was you who told them where I was. They burned my grandmother's house down, you fuck. Why don't you show me some fucking gratitude?"

"What do you want me to say? They had guns. They were going to kill us. And look, you got away. I said thank you, what more do you want?"

At that moment she really did want to shoot him. Really, really badly. Not kill him, but make him hurt. Instead, she said, "Get the hell out of here. If I see you again, I swear to fucking God I'm going to hurt you. Bad."

Tod didn't respond; he simply turned around and left the police station. Emmalee came up behind Rubina and put her hand on Rubina's shoulder. "I'm sorry Rubina, I should've stuck with you. And you're right, he did tell them where you were, but they had a gun to my head, and one of them…" Emmalee said and began to cry.

"I heard you scream…" Rubina couldn't finish the sentence.

Rubina walked Emmalee outside with her arm around her. The woman and boy followed. Once they were outside Rubina and Emmalee turned to face them. She figured they weren't related as they didn't look alike at all to Rubina. "Thank you for getting us out of there," the woman said to Rubina as Emmalee's tears began to cease.

"No problem."

"I'm Betsy. This is Charlie," the woman extended her hand which Rubina shook while the boy of thirteen didn't look at her.

"Hi Charlie," Rubina said.

The far-off gunfire had been intermittent when Rubina had opened the cell door but now had grown in intensity, especially being outside again. Betsy said, "Don't you hear that shooting? What's happening out there?"

"I don't know where it's coming from, but that's why the guard left I figure. I wouldn't go towards it if I were you," Rubina said.

"We won't. I'm going to take Charlie with me to my house. Is that ok?" Betsy asked.

"Fine by me. Just be careful out there."

Betsy and Charlie left the police station, walking the opposite way from the sound of gunfire. "Where are you going to go Rubina?" Emmalee asked, "and can I come with you?"

"You can if you want. But I'm going that way," she said, pointing in the direction of the gunfire.

| 84 |

Chapter Eighty-Four

Bullets continued to riddle El Supermercado, shattering all the glass windows that had been painted black. Tyreke had no more bullets in his gun and really wanted to through his gun at the intruders, just wanted to be rid of it, but he didn't. He put his hands over his ears and tried to shut out the carnage but to no avail. He could hear Markus' brothers wailing but did not see them over the customer service counter.

***

Jonas watched from his office view and spoke into the Dictaphone, "All the windows of El Supermercado have been blown out and I now have a better view of what is happening inside the store. After the smoke cleared from the grenade thrown into the store I saw one man inside clutching his leg. The other man who went in through the window was shot upon entering the store. Sister's man Anthony entered the store through the entrance doors to the left of the front and began firing into the store however I cannot see if he hit anyone inside."

Jonas was sweating, his heart rate going a mile a minute. Being able to watch but not participate was where it was at for him. He continued his report as he saw two men dressed in military garb approach the parking lot from the far end. "Now two more armed men are approaching from the opposite side of the parking lot. Sister's attackers do not see them, nor by what I know are they part of Sister's group."

In his head Jonas thought of Anthony, his being a soldier and all and figured it was possible he knew them and had told them to be here. Why they weren't at Sister's church or part of the original attack he couldn't figure out. But after what had happened to the world the past few weeks nothing surprised him anymore.

***

Crudo and Jackson appeared on the street and began looking for their fellow soldier Anthony but did not see him. They did see two men leaned against cars in the parking lot firing into the store. "Why are they doing that?" Crudo asked.

"Damned if I know, but I think they're on Anthony's side, right?"

"Looked like it from up there," Crudo said, "Let's see if we can get their attention."

Crudo fired three shots into the air and waved at the two men. They did not wave back, instead one chose to fire at them. They didn't know the man, named Marcos, who fired at them had lost his wife in the deathly scene outside the hospital days earlier; that Marcos had been planning to kill Anthony from the first time he had seen him, and that the current attack coupled with seeing Crudo and Jackson in military uniforms made him snap.

Crudo and Jackson quickly ran and hid behind a brick red conversion van while they heard bullets hit the other side of the van. "That wasn't very friendly," Jackson said.

"No shit. You think those guys are really with Anthony?"

"I don't know now, but they screwed up and got on our bad side."

"Yeah, fuck'em," Crudo said as he moved to the front side of the van while Jackson stayed at the rear.

Crudo fired enough shots from his automatic rifle that the car Marcos was hiding behind exploded in a ball of fire. "Got him," he said and gave the thumbs up sign to Jackson.

Meanwhile Jackson continued to shoot at Danny who had moved to the car closest to the storefront but didn't shoot back. Crudo came up next to him and said, "Be careful shooting into the store. We don't want to hit Anthony."

"You're right. That guy isn't firing back, at least for now. Let's get closer."

The soldiers moved to a closer car when bullets came at them from another direction. "What the fuck? Now who's shooting at us?"

Crudo peeked out from behind the car and saw another man, Shaun, with a gun shooting at them from next to the store. "Where'd he come from?"

"Don't know, just take him out."

"No problem."

Shaun had no cover and couldn't use his one arm but continued toward them. Once he stopped Crudo stood and shot him square in the chest, and in a moment Marcos' dead body tumbled forward. "Two for two bitch," Crudo said and went back beside Jackson.

***

"He's coming in!" Ptolemy warned from behind the customer service counter in a loud, prepubescent yell. Neither he nor John-two could fire at Anthony, their fear and their brother's dead body next to them having paralyzed the boys from taking any action. Anthony cautiously went to check on his friend, and when he bent down to check for the man's pulse Serge came up behind him with his gun to the back of Anthony's head. "What the fuck was this about man?"

"Sister's plans."

"Who the fuck is Sister?" Serge said then pulled the trigger and Anthony's body fell on top of the other dead body.

The shooting ceased and Serge said, "Tyreke, go tell Theo we got 'em. Boys you can come out now."

Tyreke hesitated and the boys ran from behind the counter, past Serge, out of the store. "Where are you going?" Serge asked but they didn't respond.

"Tyreke, go tell him!"

Tyreke ran to the back of the store, through the double doors, and said, "Theo? Serge said we got them."

Theo was seated, both his guns sitting on the desk in front of him. "Are you sure?"

"That's what he said," Tyreke said, "but Markus and Clint are dead, and so are their guys."

"And what for I wonder? Who wants us dead *now*, after all that's happened?" Theo said to which Tyreke did not reply.

Theo picked up his guns and as they were about to pass through the double doors the gunfire began again.

***

Crudo looked out from behind the car and saw two boys running away from the store. "Where are those kids going?" Crudo asked.

"Who cares?" Jackson said.

"You want to shoot them?"

"Leave them be, they're just kids."

"Alright but if they come back and shoot us I'm going to be real pissed at you."

"Noted."

"There's still at least one guy left, maybe more. Thoughts?"

"We still haven't found Anthony so let's go inside."

"I was hoping you'd say that."

The soldiers moved from parked car to parked car, looking for movement inside the store and seeing none. From behind them they saw Danny who had been shooting at them earlier running away, back toward Sister's church. Crudo raised his rifle and aimed it at Danny's back. "What do you want to do Jackson?"

"He's running away, and by the looks of it he didn't want to shoot at us; that seemed to be his buddy that you took care of already."

"Ok," Crudo said, "I guess."

"Don't sound so disheartened, you did well."

"Yeah, yeah."

The soldiers moved into a position with a clear view straight into the store and saw Serge standing near the window, looking out. He yelled, "You motherfuckers fucked with Brother Theo's Disciples, and look what happened to you. That's what you get. No one fucks with us!"

"Can I shoot him? He seems like a bad guy."

"I'd agree. Go ahead."

| 85 |

Chapter Eighty-Five

Theo saw Serge get shot and watched him fall on top of the two other bodies already lying there on the cool tile at the entrance to El Supermercado. He didn't see who had shot Serge so he retreated back through the double doors. Tyreke followed. They heard James and Nadia banging on the cooler door, screaming to be let free. Theo approached the cooler door and said, "If you two don't shut the hell up I'll give you something to scream about."

Nadia and James went silent and Theo turned to Tyreke, "Tyreke, do you still have your gun?"

He shook his head no. "I ran out of bullets and left it up there."

"That's no good, and I don't have another one for you. It doesn't matter, you don't need a gun for what comes next."

"You're not going to kill me, are you?"

"Don't be stupid. You're the only guy I have left. Shaun didn't answer his walkie so I figure they got him too. If you do what I say we'll get out of this alive, ok?"

Tyreke nodded, but thought to himself, 'I don't believe him. I can tell he's lying and that he doesn't care what happens to me. But what can I do? I can't run away, I don't have a gun, he'd kick my ass if tried to fight him. Crap.'

"You hear that?" Theo said.

"What?"

"I can hear their footsteps. Two of them. They're close."

"We should hide then, right?"

"Not a chance. Sorry to do this to you," Theo said and grabbed Tyreke, putting one of his guns in Tyreke's back.

"I thought you said you wouldn't kill me?"

"I won't, but they might," Theo said as he pushed Tyreke through the double doors.

***

Jackson and Crudo made their way into the store through the entrance, not the glassless windows. They saw the man Crudo had just shot on top of two other bodies. They got close and saw one of the bodies was that of their friend Anthony. "Damn man," Crudo said, "what was he doing here?"

Jackson bent down next to Anthony's body and closed his open, staring, dead, eyes. "Rest in peace brother," Jackson said.

"Hey Crudo, you hear that?"

"Sounds like someone is trapped," Jackson said as they heard the pounding and yelling coming from the back of the store.

Then all of a sudden it just stopped. No shooting, no loud thump, just silence. "There's someone back there. You ready?" Crudo asked as he changed the clip on his rifle.

Jackson got up from next to Anthony and nodded. "Alright you go around that way," Jackson said, pointing to the farthest aisle and I'll go down the other side. We'll meet up in the back."

"Sounds like a plan."

The soldiers made their way as quietly as possible to the back of the store. Crudo was on one side of the double doors while Jackson was on the other; both men got on one knee and were about to go through the doors when someone came through them and crashed on the floor.

"Don't shoot! Don't shoot me please!" Tyreke pleaded as tears rolled down his cheeks.

Both Crudo and Jackson were startled by Tyreke and they aimed their guns directly at him, but they didn't shoot. Jackson could see in his eyes he was scared shitless and that whoever they wanted was still behind the doors. Jackson met Tyreke's eyes and put his finger to his lips, indicating silence and motioned for Tyreke to move behind him. Then he fired his gun into the air, apparently wasting four shots.

"We got your boy you fucking coward," Crudo yelled, "Now why don't you come out here and die like a man."

Theo did not respond, he just aimed one gun to the left of the door and the other to the right and waited. Jackson and Crudo remained kneeling on either side of the double doors and Jackson motioned that Crudo would aim low with his assault rifle and Jackson would aim high with his handgun. Jackson mouthed the words, "One. Two. Three!" and they pushed open the doors.

Theo shot both his guns, aiming as if the soldiers had been standing, while Crudo shot at his legs and Jackson at his chest. Theo fell onto his back, still shooting his guns, bullets now hitting the ceiling. Theo's bulletproof vest kept him alive, but he couldn't walk and could barely breathe.

Jackson and Crudo ceased shooting and approached Theo's body. They kicked his guns out of his hands while Theo mumbled, "It wasn't supposed to be like this. I had a perfect plan. It was already in motion and you ruined it. Why?"

"That's what we do. Ruin the plans of assholes like you," Crudo said and put his rifle up to Theo's forehead and pulled the trigger.

The double doors slowly swung back and forth until they closed completely. Jackson said as they stood over Theo's dead body, "Hey kid, he's dead now. You can come in here, we won't hurt you."

Tyreke was still on the ground just outside the double doors, and he rose and pushed through them meekly. "It's ok man, it's going to be ok," Jackson said, putting his arm on Tyreke's shoulder, "What's your name?"

"Tyreke."

"I'm Jackson, this is Crudo."

Crudo cleared his throat and spit on the ground, near Theo's dead body. "Don't worry about him, he's crude, why we call him Crudo."

Tyreke smiled. "Who is this guy?" Jackson asked, motioning to Theo's dead body.

"Don't you know?"

"Sure don't. We're from out of town."

"Oh. Well, that's Brother Theo. He's been in charge of this neighborhood ever since I moved here."

"What do you mean, in charge?"

"He runs shit here. No one steps to him. After the Rabbit Flu some kids I kind of knew got me to join his gang, Brother Theo's Disciples. I was too scared to say no. But I didn't want to do anything they did, I swear. I just went along because I didn't want to get hurt."

Chapter Eighty-Six

Rubina and Emmalee traveled toward the gunfire, Emmalee walking almost directly behind Rubina. "What happened in that house?" Rubina asked.

"I don't want to talk about it."

"Sure, fine, I understand. But I knew that Tod guy was bad news."

"He's an asshole. Definitely not a man, more like a slug."

Rubina shrugged. "Do we have to go that way?" Emmalee asked.

"Why not? I have this rifle, it will protect us, and maybe some more people need my help."

"I guess but it doesn't seem safe."

"Neither did breaking you out of that jail but I did that, didn't I?"

"Yeah…"

"It'll be fine. Don't worry. Once we get closer just stay behind me."

Once they were about a block away from the store they saw two kids running toward them, fast. "Hey, hey! What are you kids doing?" Rubina said, her rifle aimed at them, "Stop. Don't move."

The boys, Ptolemy and John-two, stopped and put their hands on their thighs, breathing heavy. Emmalee hid behind Rubina as she recognized their faces. "Rubina," she whispered, "It's them, or at least one of them, that, you know…"

"Do you know her?" she asked the boys.

They shook their heads. "One of you does! Don't you remember me you little assholes?" Emmalee said and tried to punch Ptolemy, but Rubina held her back.

Ptolemy dodged out of the way while John-two realized that this was the girl Markus had raped the day before. "It wasn't us, I swear. It was our brother Markus. We're triplets. Honest," Ptolemy said.

"No lie," Ptolemy said, "It was him, not us. He's dead now. You can see for yourself in El Supermercado. We swear."

'El Supermercado?,' Rubina thought, 'so that's were whatever is happening is going down. Why my store? People just can't leave my stuff alone, can they?'

How do we know you're telling the truth?" Rubina said, "To do that to a woman is the lowest form of scum."

"We wouldn't do that, promise," John-two said, "Somebody killed our brother, he's dead. Please just let us get out of here. Here, take this gun, we don't want it, it wasn't even ours. Theo gave it to us."

Ptolemy took the gun from his pocket, barely wanting to touch it, and handed it to Rubina. Rubina handed the gun to Emmalee and said, "What do you think Emmalee?"

Emmalee paced around the boys, examining them, trying to confirm if they were the one. She looked them both in the eyes, the one who had done it might have looked just like these two, but his eyes weren't the same. The boys' eyes were filled with fear and sadness, not rage and evil like the other. "I think they're telling the truth. I just have a feeling."

"We are, we are. Please don't kill us. We won't hurt anybody. Promise. Just let us go," Ptolemy said, tears welling up in his eyes.

"Fine. Get out of here, and I don't want to see either of you, ever again. You stay out of this neighborhood, got it?"

The boys nodded sheepishly. "Now move!"

The boys began running again. "You sure it wasn't them?" Rubina asked.

"Positive. But they did look just like him. You think its possible triplets could've survived the Rabbit Flu?"

"Anything's possible I guess," Rubina said.

| 87 |

Chapter Eighty-Seven

After the shooting of Brother Theo they heard no more gun-fire. James looked to Nadia and said, "Should we pound on the door again? Maybe that Theo guy bit it and whoever else is out there will let us out."

James wasn't sure and after Theo's warning earlier and his murder of Franklin he didn't want to piss the guy off. But they heard muffled talking and figure eventually someone, whether it was Theo or someone else, would let them out. He said to Nadia, "Let's do it," and they banged on the cooler door while yelling to be let out.

The cooler door opened and they stood face to face with Crudo and Jackson. James took Nadia by the arm, backed up and whispered into her ear, "It's them. They killed those innocent people."

"A thank you would be just fine," Crudo said.

"Thanks," Nadia said.

"You guys can come out of there," Jackson said.

James hesitated and held Nadia back, clutching her arm. "We won't hurt you," Crudo said.

"Yeah, right," James said.

"What'd you say?"

"I saw you. I saw you shoot those innocent people on the highway before it blew up. And what about the hospital and all the people you probably killed there. You're murderers."

"Screw you buddy. We just saved you and now you're talking shit?"

"Relax Crudo," Jackson said then to James, "We were following our orders. Our friends died when the highway got bombed and our friends died at the hospital. But we're not out to hurt anybody."

"Yeah at least no one that doesn't already have it coming," Crudo said.

"That's reassuring."

"I give you my word," Jackson said and extended his hand toward James.

"I guess we don't have a whole lot of choice, do we?" James said, not shaking Jackson's hand.

"You do. You can go where you want and we won't stop you," Jackson said, leaving his hand extended.

"Ok, fine," James said and finally shook Jackson's hand.

"They call me Jackson, this is Crudo, and our young friend over there is Tyreke."

"I'm James."

"Nadia."

"It's good to meet you, James and Nadia."

"You too," Nadia said.

"So can you explain to me who these people are and why this happened?"

"We were going to leave the city this morning and this guy," Nadia said, motioning to Theo, "and his buddy killed our friend Franklin and took us here. They locked us in the cooler, and now here we are."

"Did you know our friend Anthony?"

"No."

Even from the backroom they heard glass cracking under some-one's feet. "Now what?" Crudo said.

| 88 |

Chapter Eighty-Eight

Rubina approached from the same side of the store that Shaun had earlier and they saw his SUV, empty. As they got closer to El Supermercado they saw Shaun's body face down on the cement dark red blood around him. "He's the guy from the jail, right?"

"Yeah, it's him," Emmalee said, taking a wide berth around the body.

Rubina picked up Shaun's gun, which was a few feet from the body, and put it in her backpack. The gunfire had ceased when they turned the corner and faced the front of the store. They surveyed the parking lot and saw the dead bodies with pools of blood underneath them reflecting the bright sun. "Jesus, Rubina, do you see that one? He must've been shot like a hundred times."

"Leave it alone."

"I wasn't going to go check it out. This distance is just fine."

As the women approached the broken storefront windows they heard more shooting, this time coming from inside the store. Instinctively Rubina dropped to one knee and grabbed the sleeve of Emmalee's pink hooded sweatshirt and pulled her down next to her.

Rubina peeked over the broken window but couldn't see the back of the store, but she could see the bodies in front.

"You're not going in there, are you?" Emmalee whispered.

"No way. We'll wait and see who comes out."

They waited with Rubina periodically checking to see if anyone was coming. They tried to stay as quiet as possible however the massive amounts of shattered glass under their feet made it harder and tiny sounds of crackling glass could be heard. "Stop moving so much," Rubina said to Emmalee.

"You too, there's just too much glass."

Rubina looked inside the store once more and saw five people walking toward her, two in military uniforms carrying guns. "Emmalee, they're coming. What should we do?"

"Do they look bad?"

"I don't know. Two are dressed like soldiers and they have a girl with them."

"I don't want to look."

Their conversation was interrupted by Crudo saying loudly, "We know you're out there. We're armed and have taken out Brother Theo, so if you're with him you better run."

The women didn't move. "We've had enough death and violence for today," Jackson said, "we won't hurt you unless you try to hurt us. Honest."

"It's ok, we're the good guys," Nadia added.

Rubina and Emmalee heard their footsteps getting closer, their feet crackling the broken glass. Rubina looked at Emmalee, her eyes insinuating that she wanted to stand up and face them. Emmalee nodded in agreement and they stood up.

Rubina leaned on her rifle as they stood up. Emmalee grasped Rubina's hand. Tyreke, James, Nadia, Crudo and Jackson stopped, facing them. Emmalee tugged at Rubina's sleeve, turned her head and whispered, "that boy. He was there. He didn't do it, but he was there."

Rubina took her rifle in both her hands and held it in a guarded position though not aiming it at them. Crudo and Jackson quickly aimed both their guns at her. "I thought we told you we weren't going to hurt you. And then you pull some shit like this. What's up with that?"

"My friend here says your guy there watched her get rap- I mean assaulted. I can't stand for that," Rubina said, still not actually aiming her rifle at anyone, "and I've been through too much shit the last week to just lie down anymore. Not anymore."

Jackson lowered his gun to his side and instructed Crudo to do the same, which he did reluctantly. "Let's all just calm down. This is Tyreke, and he told us he was basically a prisoner of those psychos. Isn't that right Tyreke?"

"Yeah," Tyreke said, "I didn't want them to kill me too. I'm sorry I didn't help you. I'm so sorry."

"What do you think Emmalee? That apology enough for you?"

"I guess. But you're still a coward."

"I know," Tyreke said, his tear-filled eyes glued to the floor.

"Can we get on with it then? No more shooting today?" Jackson said.

Rubina nodded. "Crudo?" Jackson said.

"Yeah, yeah, I hear you."

"Ok then. We're going to come out of the store. No one is still out there, are they?"

"No one we've seen. Two boys ran past us earlier, but that's it."

Tyreke said to Jackson, "Ptolemy and John-two. They're brother is dead behind that counter over there. He's the one that did that to the girl…"

"I want to see," Emmalee said.

"You sure?" Rubina asked her.

"Positive."

Emmalee and Rubina entered the store with Emmalee walking past the group to the customer service desk. Rubina introduced herself to the group. "You must think you're pretty badass with that rifle, don't you?" Crudo asked her.

"You don't know the half of it," she said and smiled at him.

"Stupid fucker! I'm glad you're fucking dead! You deserve it you piece of shit!" Emmalee screamed at Markus' dead body, kicking it with such force that she slipped and fell on the floor.

Rubina went over to her and helped her up. She didn't say anything, just put her arm around Emmalee and led her and the rest out of the store, into the bright, sunshine-laden day.

ENDINGS & BEGINNINGS

Epilogue

| 89 |

Chapter Eighty-Nine

"The gunfire finally came to end and seven people, three women and four men, emerged from El Supermercado. Brother Theo did not emerge. The only other survivors observed by this reporter were two boys, most likely a part of Brother Theo's gang, and Danny, a member of Sister's gang. There are still dead bodies in the parking lot and inside the store, however this reporter will be waiting until later to confirm the exact number of the dead. Today we have witnessed a standoff between two powerful egos and those that followed them, and saw another, unknown group, emerge victorious.

Let us hope this is the end of the violence that has plagued this city and the world the past weeks. The Rabbit Flu has decimated humanity's numbers, and it appeared that those left were going to destroy each other until there was nothing left. But a group appears to have emerged victorious and let us hope that their decisions are better than the ones that are no longer with us. Maybe there is hope for this world, after all. This has been Jonas Johnston reporting."

Jonas set down the Dictaphone and sat in the office chair, exhausted. 'I could have gone to them. Followed them where they went, reported on their travels while within the group. They looked nice enough. But most likely control, control over others, would eventually win out in that group like it did with Theo and Sister. My place is here, in this city, my city, my home, and I will ensure that the events that take place here are documented, recorded, re-membered for more than just posterity's sake, but for my sake…and someone needs to keep an eye on Sister.'

***

Sister arrived at the El Supermercado at dusk with Danny beside her. He had told her what had happened, told her about the dead, but still she wanted to see for herself. She stopped at every dead body in the parking lot, knelt beside each, and turned the bodies on their back. She put their hands over their chest and whispered an inaudible prayer while one hand she placed over theirs, with her other hand she rubbed her rosary beads. Danny stood silent behind her.

Sister did this to each body outside, then told Danny she wanted to go inside. Alone. "Are you sure?" he asked.

"Why wouldn't I be?"

"I don't know. Maybe someone's still in there. I should go with you."

"That won't be necessary. Wait outside."

Sister entered the empty store and saw the pile of bodies right inside the entrance. She set each body as she had done outside, saving a special prayer as well as her first tears for Anthony. She found Markus' body and couldn't help feel sad for this young boy, unaware of his previous atrocities.

The store felt especially large and cavernous with the coming darkness outside and the weird glow of the remaining generator powered fluorescent lights. She wanted to scream just to hear the echo but she didn't.

Sister made her way down the frozen food aisle, past the soon to be melted ice cream, sherbets, frozen pizzas and frozen chicken, frozen peas and whip cream. She arrived at the double doors that separated the main floor from the back and saw bullets holes in the doors. She said, "Hello? Anyone there?" but received no response.

She slowed pushed through the doors and saw the body lying on its back. The silver face piercings reflected in the dim light, the body covered in blood and holes, the black leather duster, the forehead partially missing, she knew this was her enemy. She nudged the body confirming he was dead. "So, you're the famous Brother Theo, are you?"

Sister knelt down next to Theo. "You had your time and what did you do with it? Inspire fear and violence and hatred throughout this city. But no more. You don't get to rule anymore. It's my city now. And I promise you and with God as my witness I will do better than you. Though I will pray for your soul," she said and crossed his arms across his chest like the others, put her hand over his hands, and prayed a silent prayer.